Gray is my Heart

Elise Noble

Published by Undercover Publishing Limited

Copyright © 2016 Elise Noble

ISBN: 978-1-910954-26-3

Edited by Amanda Ann Larson

Cover design by Elise Noble

www.undercover-publishing.com

www.elise-noble.com

Dedication. Commitment. Obsession.
Or maybe I'm just crazy.

CHAPTER 1

I SIPPED MY glass of alcohol-free fruit punch, trying to make my face convey excitement I didn't feel as I glanced at my watch. How soon could I leave without appearing rude?

My friend Monica's baby shower had promised to be a ridiculously over-the-top affair, and it didn't disappoint. And when I said my friend Monica, I actually meant my husband's work colleague's wife Monica, a vacuous blonde with a love of gossip and a tendency to laugh far too loudly at anything and everything.

Monica's equally insipid friend Mindy organised the shower, and she'd decreed that since Monica couldn't drink any alcohol, none of the guests were allowed to either. Hurrah. Mindy had giggled like crazy when she announced that, head bobbing but hair firmly held in place by enough hairspray to be a fire hazard.

As was usual for that sort of affair, Mindy had reserved the conservatory attached to the country club's restaurant. Birthdays, christenings, bar mitzvahs —it saw them all. Although as Mindy lacked a little in the taste department, she'd filled it with so many balloons and streamers it reminded me of a high school dance.

The mid-January temperatures hovered around

freezing, but despite the last stubborn drifts of snow from last week's storm clinging to the edges of the golf course outside, the conservatory must have been ninety degrees. The outfits in there all cost at least four figures and would probably only be worn once, so nobody wanted to ruin the effect by covering up with a thick sweater.

I sighed as I nibbled on a sushi roll, bored out of my mind. The rebel inside of me wished I had the guts to stand up for myself. Oh, how I longed to say, "You know what, Monica, I can't think of anything I'd rather do less than spend another afternoon with people I barely know, eating low calorie canapés and taking four hundred photos every time you unwrap yet another pair of baby booties."

But of course I never would. Monica's baby shower was just another chapter in the story of my life. Chapter after chapter, all the same, until the story ended. My epilogue would be a tombstone, a perfectly uniform white slab with nothing to make it stand out in a row of thousands.

Here lies Georgia Ann Rutherford-Beaumont,
Wife and daughter,
Did exactly what everyone expected her to.

I'd much rather be curled up on the sofa with a good book and a glass of proper alcoholic red wine by my side. I loved to read a good thriller, to secretly wish I was one of the characters caught up in a web of espionage or faced with the challenge of solving a seemingly impossible mystery. That was the only excitement in my life—the adventures in my head.

Staying at home wasn't an option though, because that wouldn't make a good impression on my husband's colleague, would it? I sighed quietly and glanced at my watch. Another half hour before I could reasonably make my escape.

My mind drifted. How had my life come to this? I'd grown up as the daughter of State Senator Robert Rutherford, and for as long as I could remember, I'd been expected to toe the line, never doing anything without considering how it might reflect on my father and his chances of reelection.

My mother, my role model, spent her life supporting her husband, trotting along by his side like a perfectly turned out show pony. Try as I might, I couldn't recall her having a hobby of her own, or friends, or any kind of interest she didn't share with my father. And now I'd grown up and turned into her.

To make matters worse, my husband, Douglas Beaumont, never Doug, never Dougie, was becoming my father.

The good senator, having just been elected to what would be his final term, announced his retirement last month and would therefore be leaving a vacant seat at the next election. A seat Douglas was determined to fill. My father, delighted his son-in-law wanted to continue in the family business, was behind him all the way. Which meant I was expected to be as well.

So in public, I plastered on whatever facial expression the situation required—joy, sadness, excitement, seriousness, I could do them all. Really. Douglas insisted I practice my expressions in the mirror just like he did to be sure I didn't slip up at some vital moment.

At the table another gift was unwrapped.

"Ooh, diapers!" squealed Monica. "And look,

they've got little teddy bears on them."

Cloth diapers, of course. One had to at least pretend to care about the environment, even if one got one's nanny to use disposables as soon as nobody was watching. I carefully arranged my face into expression number seventeen, "excitement with a hint of responsibility."

Was this really what the rest of my life would be like? I feared I knew the answer. What other alternative did I have? At twenty-nine years old, I'd never done a proper day's work in my life.

Sure, I'd gone to college and got my degree, a major in accountancy, a fittingly dull subject. But when it came to actually getting a job, both my father and then later my husband insisted I didn't need to work. According to Douglas, supporting him *was* my full-time job, and he generously provided me with a monthly allowance so I could buy "whatever it is women buy." He did let me out one day a week to volunteer at the animal shelter, but he moaned about the smell every time I got home.

All that meant I got lonely. But what was new?

The buzz of conversation about kids made me think back to my own childhood. A little girl, sitting in a professionally decorated bedroom, surrounded by the latest toys, accessories and outfits. But no friends.

"Mom, nobody likes me."

"Nonsense, Georgia. You've been invited to Lucinda's party this weekend."

"Lucinda's mean."

"Don't be silly. She wouldn't have invited you if she didn't want you to go. Now, wash your hands for dinner."

Ten-year-old me was always the good girl, so I did go and wash my hands, even though I wasn't hungry. Lucinda never passed up on an opportunity to be nasty, and her party wouldn't be any different. Yesterday, she'd stolen my homework out of my bag, then I got told off by the teacher while Lucinda and her cronies stood around sniggering. And I heard them talking about me in the bathroom at lunchtime while I sat in a stall, too scared to leave.

"What did you do with Georgia's homework?" I recognised the lisp of Lucinda's best friend.

"Threw it in the trash. It was garbage anyway."

A chorus of giggles. How many were out there? Three? Four? Then, "Is she coming on Saturday?"

"Mom made me invite her. My daddy wants Georgia's daddy to invite him into some club."

"Eew! And I bet she'll bring that creepy bodyguard."

"And wear one of those stupid frilly dresses."

"Mom says I have to be nice to her, but I stole chilli pepper to put on her food. You guys have to help me."

They moved away while I sat shaking with my underwear around my ankles, vowing not to eat anything at Lucinda's, not even a slice of birthday cake.

Things hadn't changed a whole lot now, although the lack of food at parties was due to most of my acquaintances being anorexic. I still only got invited places because of who my father and husband were. People only talked to me because they wanted something.

Oh sure, conversations would start off innocently enough, but sooner or later, usually sooner, they'd turn to Douglas or the senator. Did I think Douglas might be interested in a new business opportunity? Was my father free three weekends from now to open a school fair? Did the senator's office have any vacancies for interns? Because a second cousin twice removed was just dying to work in politics.

Of course, I didn't know the answers to any of those questions. Over the years I'd learned how to let people down gently, and once they realised I was of no use to them, they drifted away.

I didn't have an identity of my own.

My thoughts were interrupted by Mindy. "Georgia, darling, would you like more faux champagne?"

No, I wouldn't. I'd drunk one glass, and I still had the bitter aftertaste in my mouth. It would be rude to decline, though. "I'd love some. How kind of you to offer."

Discreetly, I looked around for a plant pot to pour it into, but the potted palms were on the other side of the room. Getting to them would require me to brave the gauntlet of the tennis club, and I'd rather die of alcohol poisoning.

Would I ever have the guts to live my own life? Rapidly approaching thirty, I couldn't see any prospect of change on the horizon. Perhaps this was my destiny, to live out my days as a Stepford wife.

I sighed as I pretended to sip. I really should try harder not to be ungrateful. There were most likely women out there who'd kill for my life.

As well as money from my father and Douglas, I'd got full control of my trust fund at twenty-eight, and that was not insignificant. My days spent shopping and supervising the household staff were hardly taxing, and considering the big birthday I had coming up in a few weeks, I didn't think I looked half bad.

Monthly salon visits meant my blonde hair was perfectly highlighted, I could put on make-up like a pro, and regular yoga and half an hour a day on the StairMaster kept my butt looking perky. My clothes were always fashionable, if somewhat dull, chosen to accentuate my behind and boobs. Not my knees—I hated those so short skirts were out, but as Douglas informed me, anything above the knee made me look like a lady of the night so I wasn't allowed to wear them anyway.

The downside was that every other day I had some function or other to attend, where I had to be nice and polite to a bunch of people I didn't like, all while trying to remember their names and other pertinent facts so people would smile at Douglas and remark what a lovely wife he had.

Monica let out a squeal of glee, bringing my attention back to the room. She'd just unwrapped Mindy's gift, which was so big it had had to be carried in from her SUV by two of the waiters.

"A stroller! I can't believe you got me a stroller!"

She leapt up and hugged Mindy, who grinned as wide as her Botox would allow.

At some point in the future, I'd be expected to have a child or two of my own. My father, impatient for a grandchild, had already given Douglas a long lecture on the importance of family to an election campaign. He needed to show voters he could empathise with them on family-related policies, and what better way to do that than to have his own child?

I wasn't so sure about that idea. I still had nightmares about my own childhood, the whirlwind of rallies and meet-and-greets where I'd been passed around strangers like some sort of novelty. I wouldn't wish that on any child of mine.

Speaking of Douglas, tonight was date night. Every week he made sure he took me out for dinner, just the two of us. Like I said, I should make more of an effort to appreciate him because he did try to make me happy, in his own way. He just wasn't terribly good at it.

We'd be going to Claude's, which was where we went in the third week of every month. Why? Because it was the third most expensive restaurant in Richmond. Douglas hated five week months, because it meant he had to stoop as low as La Gallerie, a restaurant-slash-art gallery, which was only the fifth priciest place in town.

Several months ago, I suggested we could make a small variation to our repertoire and visit a different restaurant, but Douglas stared at me, aghast, as if I'd just grown horns and a pointy tail.

"Darling," he said, "we always go to Claude's. You love the salmon coulibiac there."

"Maybe we could try something new?"

"Let's not do anything rash."

And so that was that.

After dinner, we'd have sex, which was another area where my life was lacking. Sex. That was all it was. Not making love or fucking or anything that could be construed as having emotional involvement. Douglas didn't use the Kama Sutra. His approach came straight out of a biology textbook. Insert part A into aperture B.

And I would lie there, making appropriate noises while Douglas pounded into me until he came and I didn't. Always in bed. Always in the missionary position. Never taking more than half an hour. I swear Douglas allocated sex a time slot in his schedule just like everything else, and he also thought foreplay was something to do with golf.

Then while I lay there, trying to recall the last time I'd felt my belly flutter or my pulse race, he'd disappear off to play on the stock market or write campaign speeches or whatever else it was he felt an urgent need to do at eleven o'clock at night.

At first it used to bother me. I'd done that to death with my therapist as well. He'd helped me recognise that I valued responsibility, respectability and safety above excitement and thrills, and that was what I'd chosen when I married Douglas.

Sure, there were times when I wished he'd cuddle me or even just look at me with love in his eyes, but those were outweighed by the life he provided for me. Over the years my heart froze over. Love wasn't a factor in the life I picked.

Monica unwrapped another gift.

More applause sounded.

Oh, right, I brought that one. A tiny T-shirt with the slogan "My mommy loves me." Yellow because I hadn't a clue whether the bump was going to be a boy or a girl. Judging by the abundance of pink all over the table, Monica was having a girl. I must've missed that announcement. I arranged my face into expression number twenty-four, "gratitude," as Monica offered me faux-thanks.

At long last, Monica opened the final gift, and I let out an internal cheer. A blue bunny? Either somebody else hadn't got the message or Monica was having twins.

I put on expression number fourteen, "disappointment."

"Monica, thank you so much for inviting me. It's been a wonderfully enjoyable lunch. I really do need to get home, though." I started to stand, and the waiter hovering behind me leapt forward to pull my chair back.

Monica's face fell in faux-disappointment. "Oh, Georgia, such a shame you have to go. We're just about to play baby-themed charades."

Oh gee, in that case... It would be a lucky escape.

"If only I could stay. Douglas is expecting me back, though."

Mindy leaned towards me as I put on my jacket. "As you're leaving, I should probably mention that we're also using today to help mothers less fortunate than ourselves. We're each going to donate a hundred dollars to the Baby Basket."

"What's the Baby Basket?"

"It's a charity that helps poor people to buy basic necessities for their babies." She wrinkled her nose, as if talking about poor people might somehow associate her with them.

"Oh, sure, I'll just grab my chequebook."

It was Douglas's money anyway, and he always liked giving to charity. He liked it even more when he could do it while handing over one of those big, oversized cheques, preferably with a photographer or two in attendance.

I rummaged in my purse, finding my chequebook and the ridiculously expensive fountain pen my father had given me last Christmas. Pretentiousness above practicality every time, that was my dad.

In my haste to get the cheque written, I flicked off the cap, and the damn thing flew under the table. I cursed as I bent to retrieve it, only in my head of course, as a lady should never say such things out loud. Not when anybody could hear, at least.

As I stooped, the splatter of something warm landed on the back of me and gelatinous lumps slid down my neck. That damned waiter! He must have dropped something on me. As if today hadn't been bad enough already, with my mother's company at breakfast then Monica's party, and I still had the joy of dinner to look forward to.

Well, at the very least the country club would be paying my dry cleaning bill. I only hoped that whatever it was came out. Not that I particularly loved the outfit, but having to go to the effort of choosing a new one to wear this evening left me feeling peeved.

The first screams came as I turned to make my feelings known to the hapless clown, biting back the words I really wanted to say.

It took a second for me to register the waiter was no longer standing behind me. A further second to see him lying on the ground. Time slowed as I took in his head, or rather what wasn't now his head, but instead a mass of bone and blood and grey mush. The pale edge of a chipped tooth stuck out like a small white flag of surrender.

All around, screams continued, high pitched, getting louder.

The last thing I remembered, before everything went black, was realising my voice was among them.

CHAPTER 2

THE WORLD CAME slowly back into focus as somebody half carried, half dragged me across the floor. I cringed when I realised I had a gaping run in my pantyhose, from knee to ankle, and I'd lost one of my pumps. Odd that I should feel so upset about that, given the circumstances, but it was yet another layer of my dignity that had been peeled away.

I was dumped onto a couch, one of the beige ones next to a matching coffee table where the club served up drinks and a selection of petit fours if you didn't feel like ordering a proper meal.

What just happened? My thoughts were hazy, a black fog across my mind, so thick it was suffocating. Sucking in each breath took effort as the air weighed heavy in my lungs.

In. Pause. Out.

In. Pause. Out.

I tried to sit up straighter in the chair—Mother told me never to slouch—but I didn't slide freely across the leather. My ass stuck like a piece of gum on a ballet pump.

I gingerly reached a hand up and touched my back. The hand-woven silk came from a collective in Afghanistan, sold by the wife of one of my father's friends as part of a project to empower women. Once it had been soft as clouds, and now something gloopy covered it. But what? My fingers were splodged with something maroon, almost black. I sniffed, and as the metallic tang wafted under my nostrils, it all came rushing back. My pen cap. The screaming. The waiter. Oh-hell-oh-hell-oh-hell! It was his blood. I was covered in his blood. My other hand brushed against the back of my neck, and it came away wet. I stared down, marvelling at the redness, a brighter shade this time, interspersed with lumpy little cauliflowers that clung to my fingers. Another second passed as I processed that.

Bile rose in my throat, and I clutched at my stomach, leaving a crimson handprint on the cream wool. It was no good—I couldn't hold it in. I threw up right on the coffee table, the smell of vomit mingling with the odour of a dead man.

I clawed at my jacket, at my cashmere sweater, at my hair. "Get it off! Get it off! Get it off!"

A woman in a badly-fitted suit rushed over to me. "Calm down, ma'am, please." She spoke with a Hispanic accent, so fast I barely understood what she was saying.

"No, I won't calm down! His fucking brain is on me!" I batted her hand away and tore at my jacket. It ripped as I yanked it away from my body and flung it as hard as I could across the room.

"Please, it will be all right. Please, ma'am."

"Just get away from me!"

I struggled out of the sweater, forgetting to undo the buttons at the neck. For a moment, it got stuck halfway over my head, and I gulped for air, feeling dizzy as it smothered my nose. I tugged harder, writhing from side to side until the seam gave and I was free of it. It was left inside out, but the blood had soaked all the way through, and the stain spread out like a gruesome Rorschach test.

I could almost hear my psychiatrist, his reedy voice needling at my brain. "So, Georgia, tell me what you see here."

"Death, you imbecile! I see death! Isn't it obvious!" I yelled in my head. Or maybe I shouted out loud, because all the people in the room who weren't already watching me swivelled their heads in my direction.

I'd become an exhibit in a sick circus.

My fingers were slick with blood, and I lost my grip on the tiny zipper as I tried to undo my skirt. Tears streamed down my face and my nose ran, all mixing with the gore that covered me.

I'd got the damn zipper halfway down when a man rushed in and smothered me with a blanket. He pinned my arms to my sides, and I fought to get them free as he hung on tight.

"Let me go! I need to get out of these clothes," I shrieked.

I couldn't have the material touching me anymore.

"Calm down, ma'am."

He was stronger than me, and I couldn't escape from his grip. "Get off me!"

He didn't, and I heard his yelp of pain as my one remaining high heel made contact with his shin.

Then my feet left the floor, and he carried me away from the gawking onlookers, out of the restaurant, through the bar, past the squash courts. I went limp as three-day-old arugula, my energy gone as I resigned myself to going wherever I was being taken.

The man's steps sped up, his heels clicking on the

tiled floor until he pushed through a door. Next thing I knew, I was sitting on the floor, still wrapped in the blanket, then a raincloud burst over me. Torrents of water fell, washing all the blood and flesh and brain off me. When the blanket released its hold, I scrambled to my feet, kicking it to the side of the shower stall. I didn't want its filth anywhere near me. The rest of my clothes followed it. I spied a shelf full of complimentary toiletries and poured the contents of a tiny bottle of shower gel into my hand. Then another, then another, scrubbing at myself until my skin turned as pink as the water once ran.

The water swirling down the drain took on a new fascination as I tried to block the waiter's misshapen head from my mind. *Don't think about it, Georgia.* Instead, I stood under the scalding stream, concentrating on the burn until the Hispanic lady called me again.

"Ma'am, please, you need to come and speak to the police."

I wanted to tell her to go away, to tell the police to go away, but I was Georgia Ann Rutherford-Beaumont, and I'd been brought up not to be rude. So I shut off the water and wrapped myself in the robe hanging outside the cubicle.

The woman didn't speak as she led me into an office and pointed at a plastic chair. I dropped down into it, grateful I didn't have to try and stand any longer. The plain, functional furniture was a world away from the elegant decor and relaxed elegance of the public areas of the club, but I was beyond caring.

A grey-haired man perched on the edge of the desk held his hand out to me. I stared at it. What had he touched? The waiter? Had he touched the waiter? After a few seconds, he dropped his hand into his lap and cleared his throat.

"Mrs. Beaumont, you seemed a little confused after the shooting. Do you remember what happened?"

I focused on his face. He had kind eyes. In fact, his whole expression reminded me of my grandfather's when my hamster died. I'd been eight years old, and he helped me bury Mr. Biggles in a shoebox in the yard.

"Was that man shot? I mean, his head... He looked like he was shot. But I didn't hear a bang."

"He was definitely shot. We found the bullet embedded in the wall behind him."

"How is that possible? Did the shooter use a silencer?"

"We don't know for sure, but it seems likely." He consulted his notepad. "You would have been facing the direction the shot came from. Did you see anything? Any movement? Maybe around the tree line?"

"Nothing." I hadn't even been looking out of the window. "I was talking to Monica and Mindy just before it happened, so I was watching them."

The woman spoke up. "Have you had any disagreements with anyone lately? Received any threats?"

She didn't seem as easygoing as her partner. She'd scraped her hair back in an unforgiving ponytail and looked tougher than he did. The way she fidgeted, I imagined she'd rather be out chasing robbers than interviewing a spoiled country club brat.

"No. Why would anybody threaten me? What's that got to do with anything?"

She ignored my question. "It might not have

seemed significant at the time, but we do need to know about anything, no matter how petty."

"I haven't had any disagreements, petty or not. Why does that matter?"

The woman sucked in a breath and gave her head a little shake as if she didn't believe me.

"We've talked to your friends," the man said. "It seems a second before the victim was shot, your head was right in front of his. He may not have been the intended target."

It took a few seconds for that thought to penetrate. At least I was seated when it did. As it was I went woozy, the cops in front of me fading in and out of focus like my husband did after I'd drunk one too many glasses of champagne.

The policewoman stepped forward and shoved my head down. "Put your head between your knees if you feel faint."

I didn't have much choice the way she leaned on it.

My head started to clear, the fuzz receding. Was the cop right? Could the shooter really have been aiming at me? If I hadn't bent to pick up my pen cap, would that be me lying on the floor with my brains splashed across the wall like one of Jackson Pollock's creations?

"B-b-but I can't think of anyone who hates me. I mean I did tell Bettina Rossiter that she was a mean old cow last year at Lucinda Wahlberg's birthday dinner when she called Sophie Marchand fat, but everyone else agreed with me, and Bettina hates everybody anyway. Apart from that, I don't think I've ever had an argument with anybody."

I truly hadn't. Calling Bettina a cow was totally out of character for me, but she'd made Sophie cry, and

Sophie was such a sweet girl. And she fitted in the sample size, for crying out loud. Just because Bettina threw up everything she ever ate, she thought she had the right to belittle people. Probably she'd mellow out if she let herself have a donut. Anyway, something inside me snapped, and I told her to stop being so horrid and apologise. She was so shocked that she actually did.

When Douglas heard about the incident, he told me in no uncertain terms that it wasn't to happen again.

"It looks bad on my campaign if you go around bad-mouthing the wives of potential donors." Donors were his lifeblood.

"I'm sorry. It just came out."

"Well, next time make sure it stays in."

So I'd tamped down any spirit I had left and made sure my interactions at future birthday parties were restricted to buying a suitable gift and making small talk.

The policewoman scribbled something in a notepad. "We'll make sure we talk to this Bettina, just in case. Are you sure nothing else comes to mind?"

Talk about putting me on the spot. "It's not something I've spent a lot of time considering. I guess you should talk to my husband and father. Do you know who they are?"

"We've been made aware of your father's position and your husband's aspirations." Her sneering tone left me in no doubt as to her opinion of politicians. "We've got officers tracking them both down. In the meantime, it would be best if we took you into protective custody for your own safety."

Custody? What? No! "I don't want to go into custody. I just want to go home."

"You don't—"

The policeman cut off the woman with a glare. "Mrs. Beaumont, it's not really custody. It's more like a little vacation. We're just worried that as the shooter missed, he may try again. There's a good chance he knows where you live, and if you go home, it could put your family in danger."

Oh hell, I hadn't thought of that. What if he tried again and shot Douglas by accident? Or our maid or the gardener or the pool boy? What if one of them got in the way like the waiter had?

I couldn't live with myself if I put someone else in that position.

"So what happens? Do you lock me in a cell? Will there be armed guards?"

He gave a chuckle. "No, nothing like that. We'll take you to a safe house. It'll be just like a normal house except it'll have several policemen inside and outside, and because it's not associated with you, the shooter won't know where it is."

That didn't sound so bad. "Will I be able to stop and pick up some clothes? Maybe a few books?"

"I'm afraid not, but we can have one of our people collect your personal items for you."

"How long will I have to stay there?" I had an appointment at the hair salon tomorrow at three and a dinner to attend the day after that. Douglas would be upset if I started missing functions.

"It depends. We've got a lot of leads to investigate." He shrugged. "A few days at least."

A chill came over me. "Do you really think the shooter will try again?"

This time the woman answered. "It's a possibility.

He seems to have got away clean, which suggests he could be a professional. If he is, he'll have to have another go, because if he doesn't kill you, he doesn't get paid."

I leaned forward and stuck my head between my legs again.

CHAPTER 3

IF THIS WAS the policeman's idea of a vacation, he'd have been better off staying at home. The safe house, a small, detached two-storey home in a suburb of Richmond, didn't get any stars from me. Drab green paint peeled from the siding, revealing an equally ugly shade of brown underneath.

In the small front yard, even the weeds looked sickly. My room overlooked the back where a rickety garage took up most of the garden, the two wooden doors open slightly and sagging on their hinges. The remaining space was slabbed with pitted concrete, which served as a home for the two garbage cans, neither of which had been emptied recently judging by the fast food cartons spilling out of them.

It was a dull, nondescript house on a street of equally dull, nondescript houses. If I had to spend much time there, I'd be tempted to shoot myself sooner rather than later and save the hitman the trouble.

I lay back on the lumpy mattress, staring up at the ceiling. The shades were permanently drawn, and the single, bare bulb hung slightly off-centre, as if whoever built the house hadn't bothered to measure up properly. A cobweb fluttered in the draught next to it, its resident mercifully absent. Even the spider had gone in search of better digs elsewhere.

The door creaked as one of the cops peered in. "Everything okay?"

Oh, sure. I'd been shot at, I wasn't allowed to speak to my family, and I couldn't go home. "Fine, thank you."

"I'm making coffee. You want a cup?"

I didn't need caffeine; I needed sleep. I'd been awake for the last twenty-four hours. Every time I closed my eyes I saw the waiter, lying dead in front of me, his brain spilling across the marble floor.

"Have you got any Ambien?"

"Sorry, I can't let you have that. We need you alert in case of any incidents."

"You think something might happen?" My heart sped up at the thought.

He shrugged. "We haven't had any specific intelligence, but we can't rule it out."

"You're going to catch him soon though, right?"

"We're doing our best, ma'am, but you may be here a while."

"Can I speak to my father yet? Or my husband?"

"The line here isn't secure."

"What about clothes? Toiletries? Underwear? I need some of my things."

He looked fresh out of cop school and blushed when I mentioned underwear. "If you write a list, I'll have someone pass it to your family."

As his footsteps receded on the wooden floor, I thunked my head back on the painfully thin pillow, fighting back tears. How could this be happening? I went out of my way to avoid confrontation, yet someone still wanted me dead. During my daddy's time as attorney general, we'd been rushed out of the house twice in the middle of the night, but nobody ever fired a shot. Could one of his haters still be out there, bearing a grudge?

Or what about Douglas's enemies? After all, he'd been involved in several controversial projects recently. Two months ago we had a protest outside the house over his approval of plans to build a wind farm on land occupied by a family of eagles.

I'd always done my duty and stood behind both of them. Had I upset someone by doing so?

I had plenty of time to think over that the next day. The trouble was, I didn't come up with any answers.

On day three, a Monday, the young policeman dragged the largest suitcase from my matching Louis Vuitton set upstairs, filling most of the available space in front of my window. I'd been allocated what a realtor would describe as the third bedroom, but in reality it was more of a cupboard containing a single bed, a tiny closet and a wobbly chair.

Seeing my luggage felt like Christmas had arrived. At least I could spend the day reading the spy thrillers I'd requested and get lost in somebody else's woes instead of my own.

I threw the lid back then groaned. With all the drama, I'd forgotten Manuela, our maid, was off yesterday. Douglas must have packed my case himself, and once again, he'd proven how little he understood women in general and me in particular. Half the clothes were for summer and the others were more suited to formal occasions. I dug down further and found the complete works of Jane Austen, a cookbook and a handy guide on French for beginners.

Chantelle, my nanny between the ages of six and ten, had been an excellent teacher so I had a fairly good grasp of the language, a fact that clearly escaped Douglas. Not surprising, since on our only visit to France he abandoned me in a hotel in Paris while he spent almost the whole time in one incredibly important business meeting or another. The cookbook wasn't going to be much use either as the most nutritious thing I'd found in the house so far was a Pop-Tart.

So, in the afternoon of day three, I found myself sitting on the wooden chair with Mr. Darcy for company. I'd wedged the cookbook under the shorter leg, which was perhaps the best use I could find for it. One of the policemen lent me a jacket to put over my sparkly Versace top and crinkled linen pants, and I wrapped the blankets around my legs for extra warmth.

I was beginning to despair of ever going home when the grumpy policeman who'd brought the pizza last night walked in.

"Your father is insisting on speaking to you." He held out a chunky looking phone, looking distinctly unamused. "He sent a secure phone."

I snatched it off him and pressed it to my ear. "Daddy?"

"Hey, Twinkle."

Twenty-nine years and I hadn't managed to outgrow the nickname he gave me as a baby. "What's going on? They said someone's trying to kill me and brought me to this house, and nobody will tell me anything. I just want to go home."

"I know, but that's not a good idea right now. You're in the best place."

"So they haven't caught him yet?"

"Not yet, but everyone's looking as hard as they can."

"Well, what have they found? Fingerprints? A vehicle? Have they matched the bullet to a gun?"

There was a long pause, and I knew the news wouldn't be good. "None of that. They're still looking for his position, but if the sniper shot from the treeline that's almost five hundred yards away, which leaves a lot of ground to cover. No witnesses. So far, it looks like whoever it was got away clean. Every agency is looking into...possible motives."

"What aren't you telling me?" I knew there was something from his tone of voice.

"It's not important."

"Tell me."

Another pause.

"Daddy, I need to know."

He sighed deeply. "I've been involved in a senate sub-committee on domestic terrorism. Last week, we all received letters threatening our families. The FBI didn't see it as a legitimate threat at the time, but obviously they're rethinking that."

"What about the waiter who died? Is there no way the shooter aimed for him intentionally?"

"The police don't think so. He'd worked at the club for three years, and there's nobody in his background who could afford a professional hit. His only family was a wife and a two-year-old son."

I'd kept it together up to that point, but when I thought of the tiny child who'd never know his father, the dam broke. Tears rolled down my cheeks until the policeman hovering in the doorway handed me tissues to wipe them with.

"That p-p-poor man. It should have been me."

My daddy's voice dropped to a whisper. "I'm thankful it wasn't."

"Can you help his family?"

"Douglas has already offered whatever assistance they need."

"How is Douglas?" I even missed him, and that rarely happened.

"Worried, like we all are. I spoke to him this morning, and he's praying you'll be home soon."

At least now I had this phone, I could call him. "He's not the only one." Another sniffle escaped. "Daddy, I'm scared."

"I know, Twinkle. We all are. I'm doing everything I can to keep you safe."

"Can you tell Pippa what happened?" She was my best friend, my only real friend. "She'll be worried."

"I'll call her."

We talked for a few more minutes, mainly about Daddy's new boat. I knew he was only trying to take my mind off the shooting, and although it didn't work, I appreciated his efforts.

"We'll go out for a sail as soon as you get back, how about that?"

"Sure, Daddy."

"Keep your chin up, Twinkle. I've got meetings for the rest of the day, but if you need me, call my secretary and she'll put you through."

As soon as he hung up, I dialled Douglas. Hearing familiar voices settled the nerves jangling in my stomach.

"Is that you, Georgia?"

"Yes, I'm on a different phone."

"Thank goodness you're alright. We've all been terribly worried. And I can't find my airplane cufflinks. Do you know where they are?"

Cufflinks? He was worried about cufflinks? "I think they're in your travel bag."

"Oh. I didn't look there. How are things in the, er, safe house?"

"A little dull. Would you be able to send me more of my things?" Like all the stuff I asked for in the first place.

"I'm away for a few days, but I can ask Manuela to pack another case tomorrow."

"You're still going to New York?"

"I can't afford to pass up speaking engagements. Not before the election. You said you understood that?"

"Well, yes, but..." We'd had that conversation weeks ago, when he announced we'd have to skip our annual skiing trip. Yes, I could understand his campaign being more important than a week in Aspen, but taking precedence over...this?

He huffed a little, and I pictured him pursing his lips. "I'll only be gone a few days, and from what your father said, you'll still be away. We'll be lucky if you're able to accompany me to the Hearts and Minds charity soiree at the end of the month."

That was two weeks away. I'd go stir crazy if I was stuck here for that long. "I hope I'll be back by then."

"So do I. It'll look poor if I have to attend on my own. Not to mention all the papers calling to interview you. If you're away for too long they'll move onto another story, and that'll be a big opportunity lost."

When he said things like that, I wanted to throttle him. "Douglas, a man *died*. It's not all about me." Or you.

"I'm well aware of that. I've already met his wife and son. Now, that made a great photo op."

"I'm going now." Before I threw the phone against the wall.

"Call me tomorrow, as long as your new bodyguards will let you use the phone."

"Sorry? What bodyguards?"

"The ones your father hired."

"He hired bodyguards? I already have the police here."

"Exactly. I tried to tell him how bad it would look if we were seen to undermine local law enforcement, but he insisted."

Why did Douglas always have to be so negative? "You know what, I'm glad he did. At least someone cares."

"Georgia, I know how stressful this is for us, but there's no need to take that tone."

"Stressful for us? *Us?* You're not the one stuck in a no-star jail cell."

"It's not easy for me, either. Manuela called in sick today."

That was it. I hung up.

CHAPTER 4

NO MATTER HOW much everybody raved about *Pride and Prejudice*, I struggled to get into it. I'd moved onto the tattered couch downstairs, sick of the four dingy walls in the bedroom.

"Would you like a cup of tea or coffee?" I asked the cop sitting in the armchair opposite, his feet propped up on the stained coffee table as he watched baseball on an ancient television scarred with lines of static.

"Wouldn't say no."

The youngest of my four companions trailed me out into the kitchen and leaned against the wall as I put the kettle on.

"Do you take milk and sugar?" I asked.

"Yeah. We all do."

"Even the men outside? I could take them drinks as well."

One was sitting in a nondescript Honda in the driveway and the other sat on a lawn chair in the backyard, bundled up in several jackets and a scarf. He definitely drew the short straw—it was barely above freezing.

The cop nodded. "But you're not to go outside, ma'am. It's for your own safety. I'll take them."

Dammit. I craved fresh air. The inside of the house smelled musty, like it had been shut up for months before we arrived.

"Have you seen anyone hanging around?"

"Not yet. But that doesn't mean you're not in danger."

"Did you know my daddy hired extra bodyguards?"

He huffed a little. "Could hardly miss it. He told everyone at the press conference that he'd hired Blackwood Security. I guess he hoped to deter the shooter from trying again."

"But there are four armed men here already. Will a few more make much difference?"

He shrugged. "Probably not. But I heard from the captain your father's not happy with the progress made so far, so he most likely wanted to feel like he was doing something useful."

The doorbell rang a little after three in an off-key rendition of Beethoven's Für Elise, entirely too cheerful for this tragic little house. I cracked the bedroom door open and listened, stifling a smile as one of the newcomers berated the cop who answered the door for failing to ask for any kind of identification.

At least my new bodyguards were on the ball.

They all moved further into the house, and no matter how hard I listened, I could no longer make out what they were saying. I was tempted to go downstairs, but mother taught me nosiness was an undesirable trait. Twenty minutes later, I heard footsteps on the stairs and pretended to be engrossed in my book.

A knock sounded at my door.

"It's open."

In walked somebody who couldn't possibly be a cop. If he was, he'd have women up and down the country committing petty crimes just so he'd frisk them. He was tall—over six feet—and rather than a uniform, he wore a pair of jeans, hiking boots and a battered leather jacket. When he grinned at me, dimples popped out, and I couldn't help but smile back.

"Hey, I'm Nick. I work for Blackwood Security."

"I'm Georgia."

He just smiled and nodded while I berated myself for sounding like an idiot. Of course I was Georgia. How many other women were in the house?

He stepped further into the room and raised the shades then flicked the catch on the window and lifted it as high as it would go.

"What are you doing?"

"Checking exit routes." He nodded to himself then closed the window again.

"The window? We're on the second floor."

"You never know."

"Can you leave the shades open?"

It was so dingy inside, I was most likely suffering from a vitamin D deficiency.

"The guy nearly hit you from five hundred yards. Giving him line of sight into your bedroom isn't a good idea." He snapped the shades shut.

A second man stepped into the room, not as tall or muscular as Nick, and although he smiled, it didn't quite reach his icy blue eyes.

He stuck out his hand. "Kevin."

I didn't bother to introduce myself this time, just shook a hand as cold as his demeanour. "Pleased to meet you."

Nick turned back to me. "I'll be stationed right outside your room and Kev's going to be downstairs. We're moving one more of the cops outside, so there'll be three of us inside and three out."

I bet the cop would be just thrilled about that. "Is all this really necessary? I mean, are four cops not enough?"

"Your father's concerned, Georgia. He just wants you to be safe."

"Surely the safest thing would be to catch the person who shot at me?"

"Believe me, the cops are trying. They think they've found the car he was driving, but it was stolen and burnt out. The only witness to the theft was an eighty-year-old woman who can't see properly without her glasses, which she wasn't wearing."

I plopped down on the bed. "So there's nothing?"

"She described the thief as a good-looking man with dark hair, but her granddaughter thinks she might have been describing Marlon Brando. Apparently she gets confused and thinks every man over the age of twenty is Marlon Brando."

"So what, I just stay here until somebody figures things out?"

He shrugged. "Sorry."

I dropped my head down on the pillow and closed my eyes. The door clicked as Nick and Kevin left the room.

Maybe if I wished hard enough, this would all turn out to be a bad dream.

Day turned into night, and once again I tossed and turned, trying to avoid the broken springs in the mattress without success. This was worse than prison. At least in prison, I might have had somebody to talk to. I could have learned the basics of breaking and entering and maybe got myself a nice tattoo. Now there was something that would give Douglas a fit. He considered anybody who adorned their skin to be uncouth.

In the morning, a quiet knock at my door summoned me from my bed. I padded over with the blanket wrapped around me as Douglas forgot to send my robe.

It was Nick. "I thought the place looked a bit spartan, so I got somebody to drop a few bits off." He walked in and heaved a black duffle bag onto the bed.

I unzipped it with the excitement of a kid on their birthday. *Please, don't let it be more Jane Austen.*

Trivial Pursuit, travel Monopoly and a few fashion magazines spilled out onto the mattress. I rummaged further and found the holy grail—an eReader! I took it out and kissed it.

Nick grinned, his eyes twinkling. "I thought that might cheer you up."

Digging deeper, I found two sweaters in my size, a pair of jeans, a silk scarf, and sheepskin boots. There was even a small makeup compact—purples and pinks, just my colours.

Nick looked sheepish as I held it up. "I didn't buy that, I swear. My assistant did."

"I think I love her."

He chuckled. "I'll pass that on. There's fresh Danishes in the kitchen if you're feeling hungry."

My mouth watered at the prospect. "I'll be down in a few minutes."

As Nick's footsteps receded along the hallway, I dug through the bag again. Slippers and a hairbrush! At least I could feel human again. Whatever my father paid these people, it wasn't enough.

I spent the afternoon playing Trivial Pursuit with Nick, perched on the edge of my bed while he took the chair, his huge frame dwarfing it. He had a surprising knowledge of both history and current affairs, demonstrated when he won five games to my one.

"How about we switch to Monopoly?" I suggested.

He laughed. "Can't take coming second?"

On the contrary, I was used to it. Always by myself, in the bathroom. Of course, I didn't tell him that. Or that I'd had more fun that day playing board games than I had in the last year with my husband.

Over the following days, Nick brought Jenga, Scrabble and chess. I hadn't played chess since I was a little girl. My daddy and I once had a ritual of playing every Sunday morning after church, although our time together faded away as he became busier with work. Government affairs took precedence over family, that was what mother always told me.

I surprised myself by remembering the rules of the game, but Nick proved to be a master and beat me every time except one, and I was convinced he threw that to make me feel better.

By the end of the week, I'd grown used to this protective custody lark. I'd even go so far as to say I was enjoying it. Sure, the house sucked, but at least I had someone to have conversations with who didn't have an ulterior motive.

If it wasn't for the constant crackle of Nick's radio and the calls he kept taking, his frequent trips to patrol around the house and the fact that he always had one eye on the door, I could almost pretend we were just friends hanging out.

Until day eight. Things changed on day eight.

CHAPTER 5

"FIFTY-SEVEN! BEAT that." I sat back with a self-satisfied smile on my face.

I'd just managed to get "quality," on a triple word score no less, when Nick's radio came to life. I recognised Kev's calm voice.

"Nick from Kev, over."

"Kev from Nick. Go ahead, over."

"Bert and Tim checked in five minutes ago, but Ron hasn't answered."

Ron was one of the policemen who'd been there since I arrived. He liked his tea with three sugars and spent most of the time griping about his mother-in-law. I hated to admit it, but I was glad he'd been stationed in the car outside. It gave my ears a rest.

Nick stood up as Kev continued, "We can see his outline in the front seat. Looks like he's fallen asleep. Tony's gonna go wake him up."

"Understood. Tell him to be careful."

"Roger that."

The front door opened and closed, and Nick took his seat again. I turned my attention back to Scrabble, where I'd picked up some awful letters. What could I make with two Y's, two A's, two P's, and a V? Was "yappy" in the dictionary?

As I contemplated my chances of getting that one

past Nick, footsteps sounded on the wooden floor in the hallway, followed by a soft pop. Nick's hand froze halfway to the board, his fingers clutching the letter Z. What was that? No...it couldn't be...

The bang that came next left me under no doubt.

"Th-that was a gunshot!" All thoughts of Scrabble flew from my head as I leapt up, scattering letters across the floor.

Nick didn't answer. He was already on his feet, bolting the door. Where did that gun in his hand come from? I hadn't seen him carrying it, and I'd admit to looking at his body more than I should have.

A burst of static sounded from the radio clipped to his belt, followed by Kev's voice. "I'm hit. I fired back, but I missed."

My knees went weak as Nick snaked an arm around my waist, shielding me with his body as he pushed me towards the window. Shouting came from downstairs, followed by another gunshot.

"H-h-he's in the house."

"I know." Nick's voice was grim.

A blast of icy air hit me as he slid the window open and lifted me out feet first. I clutched at his jacket as my legs dangled into the darkness.

"Wait! You can't drop me out of the window! I'll die!"

"Sssh. No, you won't. The garage roof's right underneath. Bend your knees when you land, run to the far side and climb down. I'll be right behind you."

"I can't..."

"You can. Hurry, he's on the stairs."

I slipped out of Nick's arms, falling through darkness until I hit the slimy roof. For a second I thought I'd fall, but I scrambled to keep my balance then ran.

Vibrations shuddered through the roof as Nick dropped down behind me. A quiet pop I instinctively knew was a silenced gunshot sounded from the house, then another. A sting ripped along the top of my ear, and I didn't even think about climbing down, just launched myself off the edge. Behind me, Nick fired back, his unsilenced rounds making my ears ring.

I landed on the cracked concrete in the yard, and my ankle bent under me. The jarring pain that shot up my leg made me gasp. Temporarily deafened, I didn't hear Nick land, but his familiar musk surrounded me as he pressed me back into the garage wall.

"Are you okay?" he asked.

"Did you hit him?"

"Don't think so. He ducked behind the wall. Are you okay?"

"My ankle hurts."

He stepped back in a crouch, aimed at the window we'd just came out of and let go a volley of shots. There was an answering echo from upstairs as he ducked back under the cover of the garage wall.

Then a more ominous sound—the soft thud of the gunman landing on the roof above us.

Nick grabbed me and pushed me in front of him. "Run. Go around the side of the house."

All my treadmill sessions in the gym paid off as I sprinted for the corner of the building. My ankle buckled underneath me at one point, sending me down on one knee, but I ignored the pain. It's funny how the threat of imminent death wipes everything from your mind.

When I fell, Nick hauled me up and shoved me behind Ron's car, pushing me to the ground. As I dropped, I caught a glimpse of Ron in the dim glow of the streetlight, and even in the greyness I could see the dark line across his throat where it had been cut wide open. The tang of blood mingled with the stench of faeces and the rubber from the tyre I was squashed up against. I turned away, trying to rid my mind of the sight of him and came face to face with Tony, who'd received the same treatment. The knife had cut deeper, and his head hung at an awkward angle, almost decapitated. The white of his spine gleamed up at me.

I gagged, trying desperately not to throw up. Failed. The remains of lunch erupted onto the ground by the rear wheel, leaving me faint.

Another shot rang out, and the window above my head shattered.

The scream that left my mouth sounded inhuman to my own ears, and I scrambled backwards until Nick grabbed me and pulled me towards him.

"Stay close," he hissed.

A siren sounded. It couldn't be far, maybe a couple of blocks away. As it got louder, muffled footsteps ran down the street away from us, and Nick poked his head around the back of the car.

"He's gone. It's okay; he's gone."

I burst into tears and clutched at Nick for support. Sweat dripped down my back from my exertions, but still my teeth started chattering. I wiped my nose on my sleeve, ignoring the voice of my mother in my head telling me how unladylike that was.

Nick put his arm around my shoulders and pulled me close. "We need to go inside. Can you walk?"

Walk? I couldn't even speak. I was beginning to make an awful habit of falling apart. At least I didn't have mascara on this time.

As I hesitated, Nick picked me up and carried me into the house.

"Is it just your ankle and ear that got damaged?" he asked as he walked.

I managed to nod. How did he know about my ear? I reached up and felt blood running down the side of my face.

"We'll get you seen to. Medics are on their way. The control room called the cavalry as soon as the first shot was fired."

"How do you know?" My nose started running again, but I didn't want to do the sleeve thing while Nick was watching.

"Earpiece." He stopped in the doorway to the lounge. "Fuck."

Kevin lay at his feet, blood bubbling out of a hole in his chest as he struggled for breath. Nick half-dropped me then ripped off his jacket and tore his shirt over his head, using it to press against Kevin's wound.

"Nick, you're bleeding too!"

A hole in his bicep seeped blood, red drops trickling down his arm and splashing into the puddle spreading out from under Kevin.

"It's nothing. I'll get it seen to later. Can you press on this?"

I dropped to my knees and held the shirt down on Kevin's chest as Nick ran out of the room. Seconds later, he came back with a first aid kit.

Kevin's eyes blinked open, unfocused. "Can't. Breathe."

"Hold on, buddy. Help's coming." Nick inserted an IV line into Kevin's arm and passed the bag of fluid to me. "Stand up and hold this."

I got to my feet as flashing blue lights signalled the arrival of the first police car. Two cops jumped out, guns drawn. One paused by the men outside, and the other ran into the house, stopping short as he arrived in the lounge.

"Fucking hell, man. Looks like you had a war here."

Nick glanced up at him. "How long for the ambulance?"

"Two minutes. Maybe less. How many injured?"

"There's two dead out front, another two missing. They should have been stationed outside, one in the backyard, one on the far side of the house. The perp took off towards Sixteenth."

The other cop appeared behind his partner, communicating without words before they both disappeared outside. An ambulance screeched in behind the police cruiser, and one of the cops waved the two medics who leapt out into the house. They took over from Nick, but I couldn't bear to watch as Kevin's breathing grew shallower. I fell back onto the couch and drew my legs up to my chest as I willed myself to stop shaking.

A few minutes later, another ambulance crew arrived.

"Is it just him?" one of them asked, looking at Kevin.

"Yes." The cops had returned. One of them was ashen and the other green. At least I was in good company.

Within ten minutes, the house was playing host to

an emergency services convention. Half of the cops in Blacksburg milled around while there were enough doctors in attendance to run an ER. A gaggle of firemen hovered near the door, seemingly disappointed because there was nothing for them to do. Through them all, half a dozen black-clad men materialised like ghosts. One of them had a few words in Nick's ear. He nodded then turned to me.

"These guys are here to take you to a new safe house. One of ours this time. The shooter found out about this one within a week, which means either someone talked or somebody got careless and picked up a tail. As I'm certain it wasn't me or Kev, we want to avoid involving the local cops this time. The whole department's like a fucking sieve."

What could I do but nod? I'd lost the ability to form coherent thoughts. A man had tried to kill me again, and this time I had the bruises to show for it. Why me? What got someone so upset they wanted me dead?

I stared vacantly into space as a medic strapped up my ankle in a thick, white bandage before handing me a pair of crutches. "Try to keep weight off it for a few days. You've sprained your ligaments."

I hobbled a few steps before one of the black-clad men picked me up, and another grabbed the crutches. I was lifted into a black SUV beside a wiry but tough-looking man with a tattoo of a skull on the side of his neck. Two more men climbed into the front, and another three got into the vehicle's twin behind us. The last thing I saw through my tears before we left was the anguished look on Nick's face as Kev was lifted into an ambulance.

We drove around for almost two hours, and all I

could see was blood. Spilling from Kev, Nick, and Ron, red and sticky. We stopped twice so I could throw up stomach acid at the side of the road, a guard standing over me with his hand on his gun. The car I rode in split from the other as we went on the freeway, off the freeway, through the suburbs, around town, back on the freeway, past the projects, down the highway, and finally into a gated community.

Large houses sat on sizeable lots, barely visible behind high walls. The residents clearly didn't like attention. The car drew to a smooth halt in front of a pair of imposing metal gates, and after a few words from our driver through the intercom, they slid back to reveal a detached home, brick built. It couldn't be described as pretty—too boxy and plain to make the "star buy" in the real estate pages—but it looked solid.

My door was pulled open and another man lifted me up. Apart from the man with the tattoo, they all looked the same to me. Black-clad, hulking and scary— I hoped my father knew what he was doing when he hired them. Nick had saved my life, but was that a fluke?

The man carrying me deposited me into a comfy, overstuffed armchair in the lounge. If nothing else, this place had better furniture.

One of the ninja brigade took a seat opposite and leaned back, fixing me with a penetrating gaze. Even his eyes were black. The way they tore away at my skin, I imagined he could see through to my soul.

And his voice made me shiver.

"Well, Georgia, I think it's safe to say someone very much wants to kill you."

Chapter 6

I COULDN'T HELP the spurt of laughter that escaped. The ninja thought someone wanted to kill me? Yes, I kind of got that part. "He nearly succeeded. One of his bullets hit my ear."

I gingerly reached up and touched it, feeling a sticky scab on the top edge. The medic who'd treated me tried his best to clean the dried blood off my face, but my hair was crispy with the remnants.

The man peered over at me. "It's just a graze."

Anger fizzed through me. How could he be so casual about it? "Well, maybe in your world it's just a graze. But in my world it represents a much bigger problem."

"I understand that. Your problem just killed one of my men and injured another."

I slumped back in the chair, the fight in me evaporating. "Kevin didn't make it?" I whispered.

My hands trembled, and I looked down. His blood was on them, both literally and figuratively.

The man shook his head, teeth clenched.

"I'm so sorry. Did Kevin have a family?"

"A fiancée. His parents. A sister. We'll look after them."

"If there's anything I can do. My father has money..."

"Money's not a problem. Catching this motherfucker, that's our problem. That's what you need to help with."

"But what can I do? I already explained to the police I have no idea who he is."

"It's not only the police who're involved now. Nick and Kevin were on guard detail as a favour to your father, but after tonight this is a bigger battle." He fixed me with his black stare, and I shrank back a little further. "So I'd appreciate it if you went over a few questions."

"I'll do anything you think will help."

I almost regretted my words as the grilling began. Almost, but not quite. Despite Kevin's cold demeanour, he'd been kind. He even brought me a cupcake the other day, with pink icing and silver sprinkles. He said he wanted to see me smile. A tear ran down my cheek as I pictured him as I saw him last, lying on the floor, barely breathing. It was all I could do not to throw up. For the first time in my life, I wished somebody harm.

I hugged a pillow to my chest as the man grilled me, but it offered scant comfort against the onslaught of questions. One after the other, he fired them in my direction. I didn't even know his name—he hadn't introduced himself, and I was too nervous to ask.

"Let's start with your relationship with your parents," he said, drilling me with his gaze.

I shrugged, trying for casual. "Well, they're my parents."

"Are you close?"

"I guess."

"Could you be more specific?" He looked at his watch, leaving me under no illusion as to whose time was more important.

"I mean, I love them, and I guess they love me, in their own way. I've got more in common with my daddy, but he puts so much of his time into being a senator, there's not much left over for me. My mom, well, she goes where he goes. She's always wanted me to conform to her ideals, but I've found it...hard. My life may look golden from the outside, but I've spent many nights wishing for a normal family, one out of the public eye."

My words made painful listening, especially for me. I'd never had to lay myself bare like that, and talking through my upbringing made me realise just how shallow my life was.

"Your father keeps your mother under his thumb?"

"Kind of. It's more that she lives to please him." And enjoys it.

Growing up, I thought that was how life should be. Only once I married Douglas, I realised I wasn't my mother, no matter how much I might pretend otherwise.

"How about growing up? Were they around much?"

"Not really. I had a nanny until I was twelve and a bodyguard until I was sixteen. I spent more time with them than Mom or Daddy. But lots of kids I went to school with had parents like that—I wasn't the only one."

No matter how lonely I might have been, I refused to let him run my family down. Thousands of children weren't so privileged, and I knew I should feel grateful for what I had.

"Have you ever had anything to do with your father's business dealings?"

"Nothing. I couldn't tell you anything about his business, other than he's a senator, obviously. I think he has investments. He gave me a monthly allowance until I met Douglas, and now Douglas gives me money."

The man leaned back and averted his gaze, but I knew what he was thinking. Poor, spoiled, little rich girl.

"It's not that I've never wanted to work," I continued. "I tried to when I graduated from college, but my father and Douglas were both so dead set against it I gave up on the idea. They're both very old fashioned. A woman's place is in the home and all that."

"I see," he said, but it was clear he didn't.

"Look, my father always gets his own way. He has his whole life. I learned when I was a little girl that trying to get him to change his mind is like trying to get a river to flow uphill. Douglas is the same, although I didn't realise that until I married him. He used to be more easygoing, but he got into politics after college and that changed him. I think he spends more time with my father than I do."

"They get on, then?"

"My father always wanted a son, but after me my mother couldn't have any more children. He was thrilled when I married Douglas. At last, he had another man around to endow with the benefit of all the knowledge that a woman couldn't possibly understand. Douglas laps it up and hangs onto his every word. He wants to follow father into the Senate, you know."

"Big ambitions, then?"

"Yes, he spends most of his life working out which butts to lick and the rest of it licking them." The man raised an eyebrow, and I realised how bitter my words must have sounded. I tried to force a laugh, but it came out as a croak. "I'm not a big fan of the political scene myself, despite my family."

"What's your husband's job?"

"He's a management consultant."

"What does that involve?"

A good question and one that I'd asked myself many time over the years. Douglas never really spoke about work. I suspected he thought I'd be confused by any conversation that didn't involve clothes or parties.

"Mostly playing golf, I think. Although he does go to the occasional conference. Sometimes I attend them with him, but I get shuffled off with the other wives while the men discuss the interesting stuff."

"Do you know any of his colleagues?"

"Maybe a few first names, but there are a lot of Georges and Joes around. You'd be better off asking Douglas."

He nodded. "We will. Did your father or Douglas ever mention any threats against the family?"

"You should talk to them about that."

"I'd like to hear your thoughts."

This was the first time anybody had wanted to hear my views on anything. "My father mentioned one threat, but the FBI didn't think it was important at the time. Those risks always exist. They're a hazard of his job."

"How do you know they exist?"

"I'm not dumb. He's been on various committees over the years, fighting terrorism and crime. It's all too easy to attract the wrong sort of attention."

"But you've never heard about anything else specific?"

Well, yes. I overheard lots of things I wasn't supposed to, but I didn't want to discuss those with a stranger, especially because that would mean admitting my tendency to eavesdrop. And besides, if nobody knew I'd heard those secrets, why would they want to kill me? Surely they were far more likely to go after my father if they had a problem with his work or policies? And if my father thought any of that information was important, I was positive he'd have told the man.

"Not really. Occasionally we took a trip that was too sudden to be a real vacation."

"Okay. And Douglas?"

"The first time he got a death threat he told me all about it in excruciating detail. Almost like it was a point of honour that he'd managed to draw attention to himself. He mentioned a couple more, but there's been nothing for a year or two. Either the cranks decided he wasn't worth the effort or the novelty wore off."

"Interesting."

"Are you done yet? My ankle hurts, I've got a headache, and I want to lie down."

"I'll tell you when we're done. Didn't the medics give you painkillers?"

"Yes, some sort of injection." A small fireplug of a man insisted on taking me into the ambulance and sticking a needle in my butt. I'd rather have put up with the ache. "What more do you need to know about me? Basically, I'm twenty-nine, and I've got the most boring life you could possibly imagine. Or at least I did until a week ago."

"Friends? Enemies? Lovers? A secret gambling habit? Drug addiction? Debts?"

My mouth dropped open and I gasped. "How dare you even suggest...?"

He held his hands up. "Look, I have to ask. Make no mistake, we'll find out eventually, but if you tell me, it'll save everyone time. We might not have much of that." He looked at his watch again, driving home the fact that the clock was ticking.

My cheeks heated and I clenched my fists. How dare he be so rude? He'd obviously never been to charm school, but I refused to stoop to his level.

"I have one friend. Her name's Pippa, and she runs the animal shelter I volunteer at." I knew I was snapping, but I didn't care. "Mostly I hang out with a bunch of other country club wives, but I wouldn't say I liked any of them. Everybody's too busy scoring points off each other to be friendly. I don't have any lovers. My marriage to Douglas may not be a fairy tale, but I'm not about to hop into bed with some young stud and throw it away."

"Admirable."

"I've never gambled or taken drugs. I don't drink much, just a glass of wine with dinner and champagne at parties." Which let's face it, I deserved after running around after Douglas all day. "And as for debts, I got access to my trust fund a year ago, and I've barely even touched it. Happy?"

"Deliriously." His voice dripped sarcasm. "Believe me, I'm not asking these questions for fun."

"Good, because I'm certainly not having any."

"What about Douglas?"

"What about him?"

"Does he gamble? Drink? Have an expensive call girl habit? Like to fly a little high every now and then?"

I bit back a laugh. Any one of those would have made him far more interesting than he actually was.

"Douglas won't even play blackjack, because he says the house always wins and he's got better things to spend his money on. The only alcohol he drinks is red wine and Scotch. He has the Scotch shipped in from a tiny island in the Outer Hebrides. He didn't touch drugs while we were in college, not once, even though most of his fraternity dabbled." My hands shook, and I clutched at the cushion on my lap so my tormentor wouldn't notice. Laying out our private lives for a stranger made me want to vomit. "And given that his schedule's too busy to have sex with me more than once a week, I'd say the call girl thing's out too. Is that clear enough?"

"Crystal." The man stood, towering over me. "You can get some sleep now."

What an asshole. "Gee, thanks very much."

CHAPTER 7

THIS SAFE HOUSE might have been bigger and better furnished than the last, but I felt far from comfortable. After the second attack, I wasn't sure I'd ever sleep properly again, no matter how soft the mattress was. I spent the hours of darkness tossing and turning, the image of two dead cops haunting my dreams as well as my waking thoughts.

All the guards were inside the house here. The man with the black eyes had explained the perimeter security. As well as the whole community being secured, there was electronic wizardry all around the house, including cameras everywhere. The windows were bulletproof, the doors were reinforced, and there was a sprinkler system in case of fire. The whole property was surrounded by an eight-foot wall, which had broken glass set into the top of it. He assured me it was a lot more secure than the previous place, but I still couldn't help feeling nervous.

My bags of things had made their way over from the other house, but without Nick there, I had nobody to play games with any more. The men here only talked to me to grunt good morning or the occasional instruction. I resorted to the eReader, but my beloved thrillers had lost their attraction. I'd spent ages wishing for a little excitement in my life, but now I had it, I wanted nothing more than to go back to how things were. Reality didn't match up to the glamour of fiction. Reality left me with insomnia, which coupled with a lack of appetite, made me permanently exhausted. When this nightmare ended, I'd have to try out new genres. Not romance, because that depressed me. Maybe chick lit.

Although it didn't look as if it would be over any time soon.

The killer had disappeared into thin air. One of the Blackwood team gave me an update, which took about two minutes as there really was nothing to tell. After the man ran off, nobody saw him. He'd worn gloves, so there were no fingerprints, and he hadn't left any DNA as far as anybody could tell. They'd run the bullets through the database, and there were no matches on those either.

My phone hadn't made it to the new place, so now I couldn't speak to Douglas at all. He'd be going crazy. Manuela didn't drive so nobody would have picked up his dry cleaning, which meant he had to be running out of clean shirts. And his schedule was packed. He hated attending functions alone, and by now he must have been to four without me by his side.

On the sixth day, one of the men handed over a new phone and allowed me to speak to my father. When I heard his voice, I burst into tears again and reached for my ever-present box of tissues. I'd become an emotional wreck.

"Daddy, it's awful. I just want out of here."

"We're doing all we can, Twinkle. The police and Blackwood are following every lead they can think of. I spoke to a buddy of mine at the FBI this morning as well. They're going to send an agent to talk to you."

Right now, my father was the chairman of the Senate Committee on the Judiciary, and he'd also served on the Senate Select Committee on Intelligence, so he had a lot of contacts. I had no doubt he was strong arming somebody at the FBI to get involved, and while I was usually against the "you scratch my back, and I'll scratch yours" horse trading that went on, in this situation I was grateful for anything he could do.

"Do you really think they'll be able to help?"

"If the killer's a pro, he might be in their database."

"Or somebody else's," I muttered.

"What was that?"

"Nothing."

I'd overheard enough of my father's conversations over the years to understand the US government wasn't whiter than white. My uncanny ability to fade into the background meant he and his acquaintances forgot I was there, and as long as I kept their glasses of Scotch topped up and the plates of snacks coming, I found out all sorts of things I wasn't supposed to know about.

Like the Horsemen.

Were they on the database my father referred to? I could hardly ask, now could I?

My father filled the silence. "Lou Polizzi's a good guy. He'll stop over in the next day or two, as soon as his schedule will allow. The FBI has promised every assistance in this."

I dabbed at my cheeks with a tissue as one of the bodyguards watched from the doorway. Once, I'd have been mortified for crying in front of an audience, but I'd got past caring. "I'm so scared."

"I know, Twinkle. I wish I could be there with you

to look under your bed and in your closet." When I was small, he used to check my room for monsters every night. The thought made me smile.

"I wish you were here too. I could really use a hug."

"Difficult, but is there anything else you need? I can arrange to send whatever you want."

"I don't have much here, and I'm running out of clothes and toiletries. And I'd love a portable DVD player if it isn't too much trouble."

"I'll get someone on it right away."

I felt a little better after speaking to my father, but it really drove home just how miserable I was in the safe house. I'd thought I was lonely at home with Douglas, but nothing compared to this. Day after day without a friendly face was taking its toll. I missed my parents, I missed Pippa and the animals at the shelter she ran, heck, I even missed Douglas and his endless fussing. And Jordi—Pippa's four-year-old son, my godson—oh gosh, it was his birthday next week. The gifts I'd bought him were all safely tucked away in one of the spare bedrooms, and now it looked like I wouldn't be able to give them to him, or attend the Noah's Ark-themed party we'd planned. Even though I'd jokingly complained to Pippa about having to chaperone twenty small children, I'd secretly been looking forward to it.

All I wanted was to go home. I said a quick prayer to that effect, ending it with a promise never to complain again about the number of functions I had to accompany Douglas to.

I wanted my life back.

The next morning dawned cold and crisp. A tiny crack in the drapes revealed a blue, cloudless sky, the sun already high. Despite Blackwood's promise the glass was bulletproof, I still didn't feel safe enough to leave them open after what Nick said about the guy's shooting abilities.

Midmorning, one of the men downstairs called up. "Georgia, you've got a visitor."

Maybe it was the FBI man? I hurried down the stairs and into the lounge, only to find it wasn't Agent Polizzi after all. A blonde-haired lady stood looking out of the window, dressed casually in a pair of ripped blue jeans I imagined must be quite draughty in this weather, and a black ski jacket. Her tan suggested she didn't spend her days at the mercy of the Virginia winter.

She gave me a smile as I approached, and I couldn't help returning it. The men were friendly, but I'd missed having female company.

"I'm Emmy. I brought some things from your father." She pointed at a red duffle bag on the couch.

Oh, amazing! He'd managed to get my shopping. I kept my fingers crossed for fresh underwear because for the last few days I'd been washing my panties in the bathroom sink with shampoo and drying them over the shower rail. Having a conversation about lingerie with my male bodyguards wasn't a low I wanted to sink to.

"Thank you so much. It's kind of you to bring them."

"No worries. Guess you must be pretty bored, huh?"

She spoke with an English accent. What had drawn her to Virginia?

"I am, a little. I suppose it's better than being shot though."

She laughed. "Yeah, being shot sucks too. Nick told me I had to play Jenga with you. He said there should be a set here."

Nick was my hero. "It's upstairs."

"Lead the way."

I headed for my room with Emmy following. "How is Nick anyway? Is he having much trouble with his arm?"

"His arm's fine. They dug out the bullet and gave him a Band-Aid. His girlfriend's pissed, though. He's been trying to convince her that his job wasn't all that dangerous. She fainted when she heard he'd been shot, and he's been trying to placate her ever since." She shook her head. "He's whipped."

I couldn't help but giggle. The thought of a big, strong man like Nick being told off by a girl was funny.

Emmy took a trip downstairs to make coffee while I set up Jenga, then we took it in turns to remove blocks. The whole tower collapsed when Emmy pulled out one near the bottom.

She grimaced. "Best of three?"

"You bet."

I intended to make the most of Emmy's company, even if it was only for a few hours. In some ways she reminded me of Pippa—both were easy to talk to and neither judged me on my appearance.

I had to remember not to judge Emmy by hers either. She may have been dressed like she couldn't afford proper clothing, but underneath I detected a sharp intelligence and something more. A hard edge. I didn't want to cut myself on it.

Yes, I needed to tread carefully around Emmy.

Three games turned into six, and I was winning five to one when my stomach grumbled. Usually time dragged around here, but the morning had flown by.

"Do you want to get some lunch?" I asked.

"Not a bad idea." She glanced at her watch. "I've got a meeting to go to this afternoon, and I'll scoff all the biscuits if I don't eat first."

The refrigerator magically restocked itself each day, and we both grabbed a package of sandwiches. I arranged mine on a plate while Emmy ate from the carton.

She shrugged when she saw me looking. "Why waste a plate?"

Er, because Douglas would have a fit if he saw me eating like that? I knew he wasn't there, but old habits died hard.

After one more cup of coffee for me, and two for Emmy, she stood and stuffed the remains of her lunch in the trash.

"Better get to that meeting. Believe me, Jenga's more exciting."

"Can you come back?"

"I'll try. I'm busy tomorrow, but I might be free for a few hours the day after. Any requests?"

"Chocolate? I could really use some."

She nodded. "Sure, I'll bring a box. I've got tons of the stuff at home."

One of the men meandered in. "Agent Polizzi's on his way up. The guy on the gate just called through."

Emmy grabbed her jacket off the stool next to her

and shrugged into it. "I'll say hi before I go. I haven't seen him for a few months."

"I'm just going to use the bathroom." My hands were sticky from lunch, and if I was going to have to sit through a long interview, I needed to pee first.

Emmy nodded. "I'll let him know you'll be a minute."

I did my bathroom thing and washed up my hands. Today hadn't turned out so bad after all. Fresh underwear and a promise of chocolate—funny how the little things became so important, wasn't it? I smoothed my hair down and checked my makeup in the mirror. Hardly gala ready, but I looked presentable enough considering I wasn't going out anywhere.

I opened the bathroom door, but I hadn't taken two steps out of the downstairs cloakroom when Emmy barrelled down the hallway. She didn't stop as she grabbed my hand and pulled me along with her.

"What are you—?"

"Shut up and run."

CHAPTER 8

"RUN? RUN WHERE?"

Emmy didn't break stride. "Just follow me, would you? I'll explain later."

The hard set of her mouth left no room for argument, and I stumbled after her as fast as my rickety ankle would allow. Pain shot up my leg with every step, but when I lagged behind, she tugged me along harder.

"Don't slow down. You can't."

My breath came in pants as Emmy shoved me through the backdoor and locked it behind us. I risked a glance behind, but there was nobody following, and the house was quiet. She didn't let up as she pushed me across the uneven lawn, and when she paused to punch a combination of numbers into a keypad on the gate in the back wall, I looked towards the house again.

"What's going on? There's nobody there."

"Get through the gate."

"I really don't think we should be doing this. I mean, there's an FBI agent waiting to talk to me."

"No, there's not."

Yes, there was. The man from Blackwood said so, and what's more, my father told me to expect him. Why was Emmy lying? Could she be some kind of double agent sent to kidnap me? Maybe she was the mole? I dug my heels in when she tried to pull me into the service alley that ran behind the property. Who knew where I'd end up?

"I'm not going anywhere." I hung onto the gatepost as she grabbed me around the waist.

"We don't have time for this."

I was about to insist we did when an explosion came from the house. Flames shot into the air, and I lost my grip as a roof tile landed beside me. Emmy used the distraction to bundle me into the front seat of a black Porsche.

"You might want to put your seatbelt on."

She wasn't kidding. I fumbled with the buckle as she sped down the alley, driving like her one goal in life was to have an accident.

"Would you tell me what's going on?" I clutched at the door handle as she swung around a bend, my knuckles white as I hung on. "Please?"

"The man at the house wasn't Lou Polizzi."

"What do you mean?"

"The guy who turned up, he looked similar, prosthetics or something, but it wasn't Lou." She sounded sure of herself.

"You spoke to him?"

"Didn't need to."

"Then how did you know?"

"We worked on a case together a couple of years back. Lou's got this hideous mole on his chin. Kinda fascinating, all lumpy with little hairs growing out of it. You can't help but stare at it. I had to mentally slap myself to stop myself from doing just that."

"What's that got to do with anything?"

"Lou's mole's on the right side of his chin. Always

has been, always will be. Except today it was on the left."

"How is that possible?"

She took her eyes off the road to stare at me, and I screamed as we hurtled up behind a parked car. She swerved with a second to spare, and I closed my eyes. If I was about to die, I didn't want to see it coming.

"Whatever photo our perp worked from when he disguised himself, it must have been reversed."

"Why would someone imitate an FBI agent?"

She snapped her fingers at me a couple of times. "Get with the plot, Georgia. He came to kill you."

Not again. This couldn't be happening.

Emmy spoke matter-of-factly as she continued. "He couldn't get in any other way, not if he wanted to walk away afterwards. The guards were armed and ready. Shooting his way in like he did last time wouldn't have worked."

"So what did you do?"

"I stopped in the comms room on my way to speak to Lou and saw him on camera waiting in the lounge. Asshole was reading a magazine. Cool. He's got balls, I'll give him that."

"How is that a good thing?"

"It isn't, not for us. Anyway, I locked the door remotely and trapped him in there. Wish I could have stayed and dealt with the bastard myself, but he could have had backup, and my priority was to get you out of there." She sounded a little wistful.

"You might have been killed."

"It's a risk. Anyway, to answer your second question, I don't know if anyone got hurt. I turned my regular phones off to stop anybody tracking us, so I haven't had a chance to find out."

"Who would be tracking us? The hitman?"

"Worse. Somebody I work with."

"How could that possibly be worse?" Surely being followed by a hitman was as bad as it got? Especially one who'd come close to killing me three times.

"Because there's a leak. At first we thought it was the police, but it's looking more and more like it's someone at Blackwood. And not just any old leak. It has to be somebody at the top. Only a handful of people knew about that safe house, and even fewer knew you were in it. A leak like that means that I can't use any of Blackwood's resources to protect you. We're on our own."

No. No, no, no. Two women against an assassin wasn't something I wanted to contemplate. "Can't we go back to the police? Or the FBI? What about the real Agent Polizzi? Couldn't he help us?"

"Fifty bucks says Polizzi's dead. When the killer took his place he'd have made sure Polizzi was out of the picture. And you saw the sterling job the police did at the first safe house. The FBI isn't much better. Do you really want to entrust your life to them?"

She had a point. Four cops had been no match for the hitman. Which meant I was screwed. "No. But what other choice do I have?"

"You can trust me."

Could I? All I knew about Emmy was that she liked turkey club sandwiches, drank too much coffee, and she wasn't very good at Jenga. "How can I? I only met you this morning."

"It's a sticking point, isn't it? Well, my name's Emmy Black, I'm thirty-three years old, and I work at

Blackwood on various projects I can't talk about. I've been there for over ten years, and I'm not in the habit of losing clients."

"Have you ever been involved in a situation like this before? I mean, with a hitman?"

"More than once."

"Did you win?"

"I always win. Apart from at Jenga. I suck at Jenga."

My options weren't great, were they? I hadn't been impressed by the police so far, but at least Emmy seemed confident. "If I trust you, then what?"

She was quiet so long I thought she wasn't going to answer. My nails dug into the seat as cars flashed past on both sides. Emmy had made it to the interstate without hitting anything, and now we wove in and out of traffic on our way to an unknown destination.

"I need to find somewhere safe for you to stay while we clean house at Blackwood. If we can find our leak, maybe we can follow the trail backwards to the hitman."

"Define safe? I've already been through two so-called safe houses, which have been anything but."

She drove more slowly when she was thinking, which was a relief. I needed to keep her mind busy. I never drove over the speed limit, and Douglas insisted on driving five miles an hour under it, just in case. All this speed made my heart race.

"I've got an old friend I can leave you with. He's nothing to do with Blackwood, so nobody should be able to find you there."

"And you trust him, this friend?"

"At this moment, I only trust two people. One

works at Blackwood and the other is me. So this is our best option."

At least she was honest. And let's face it, I didn't rate my chances anywhere right now. "I guess I'll have to go with that."

Emmy drove for half an hour before pulling over at a rest area. She fetched a black holdall from the trunk and slid back into the driver's seat with it on her lap.

"What's in there?"

"Emergency kit." She held out a chocolate bar. "Want some?"

I shook my head. My stomach was doing backflips, and it was all I could do to stop myself from throwing up. "It's full of chocolate?"

"Nope. But that's the best bit." She pulled out a phone and turned it on. "I need to make a call."

Trucks rumbled past as Emmy paced on a scrap of grass outside the car. She didn't look happy. I tried to read her lips, but she kept turning her head around, and I figured it would be too obvious if I rolled the window down to eavesdrop. The waiting got unbearable as ten minutes ticked past.

Finally, she climbed back behind the wheel. "Polizzi's dead. A kid found him behind a dumpster a couple of miles from the house."

"How did he die?" I didn't want to know, but at the same time I had to ask.

"Single gunshot to the head. The killer didn't even try to hide the body. He obviously anticipated a quick resolution, and he also came prepared. When I locked him in the lounge, he blew out the front window and escaped. That was the explosion we heard."

"Did he hurt anyone? Apart from Agent Polizzi?"

"Not this time. I'd told everyone to stay back until I got you clear."

"I'm so sorry about Polizzi."

"So am I. He was a good man and a good agent."

We rode in silence as I reflected on the nightmare this had turned into. So far the waiter, four cops, one Blackwood bodyguard and now an FBI agent were dead. Seven people, dead, just because somebody wanted to kill me. It was crazy. Was my soul really worth more than all those others? Honestly? No, it wasn't. My life was nothing, just an endless round of shopping and functions. I felt guilty that I'd survived and the others hadn't. When would it end? How many more people would die before this was over?

"Maybe I should just give up?"

Emmy looked at me, eyes wide. "Georgia, you have one life and one important lesson to learn."

"What's that?"

"You never, ever give up."

CHAPTER 9

I'D BEEN IN a daze for most of the journey, and it wasn't until a plane roared overhead I realised we'd driven all the way to Dulles International Airport.

"We're flying?"

"Nope. Just renting a car, but this is the best place to do it. Wish we could stay in this, but it's a bit too conspicuous." As if to illustrate her point, a couple of guys on the sidewalk turned their heads as we rolled past. "Not to mention the fact its owner wants it back."

"It's not yours then?" I'd wondered how she could afford such a nice car when she wore pants with holes in them.

"No, it's Nick's. I borrowed it."

Being a bodyguard must pay more than I thought. She pulled into long-term parking and left me in the Porsche while she went to the rental desk, taking the holdall with her. I contemplated getting out and jumping onto a plane, but I'd left the house with nothing. No money, no driver's licence, no passport. Where could I go?

Emmy came back fifteen minutes later, except I had to look twice before I realised it was her. Her blue eyes had turned brown, and her hair was styled in a mousey bob with purple streaks. Thick-framed glasses gave her a geeky look. Coupled with the silver spikes she'd put through her ears, they took several years off her.

I raised my eyebrows as she pulled the door open.

"I know, I know. It's not the outfit I'd have chosen for today, but it matches the papers I've got. The earrings don't really go with that choir girl thing you've got going on, do they?"

"Choir girl?"

She looked me up and down. "Yeah, that goody-goody, sweet but boring look. You dress like you want people to admire but not touch."

"Really? That's how I come across?"

"Isn't that what you're going for?"

I'd never stopped to consider it before. Since tying the knot with Douglas, I dressed more to his taste than mine. What would I wear with free rein to do as I pleased? I had no idea.

I still hadn't answered when we transferred over to a dark grey Toyota Camry with a dent in the rear bumper and a foot-long scratch along the driver's door. The backseat sported a dubious brown stain. Please say that came from a beverage and not something else.

Emmy grimaced as she started the engine. "Yeah, I know the car's shit, but at least it doesn't stand out."

We soon reached the city limits. Despite the plasticky smell of the interior, the sub-standard AC and the uncomfortable seat, the Camry did have one advantage over the Porsche: Emmy couldn't drive it so fast. I relaxed a little more with every mile she put between us and Washington, DC.

At that moment, I wanted her to carry on driving to the end of the earth.

An hour later, Emmy pulled into the parking lot outside a run-down strip mall. Darkness had fallen, and garish neon lights blinked on and off in the hope of enticing desperate souls inside. The bail bonds office next to the liquor store at the front gave an indication of the usual clientele.

"Back in a few." She hopped out and jogged inside.

A group of youths hovered a few yards from the car, and I shrank down in my seat. How long did Emmy plan to be? The tallest of the gang moved closer, and I checked the doors were locked. Recent events had left me jumpy, and I watched every twitch of the boy's arms. To me, going to the mall meant a trip around high-end boutiques accompanied by a personal shopper, followed by a manicure and a relaxing glass of wine, not hiding in the car worrying about muggers.

Would things ever be the same again? Right now, I had no idea where I was going, and not just because I had an appalling sense of direction either. Since we left the safe house, I'd been counting my life in hours rather than years. If I survived, would I be able to slot back into Douglas's world when I got home? He'd be furious about me disappearing like this, but surely he'd have to forgive me under the circumstances?

Then again, did I want to go back to how things were before? Being a senator's daughter and a budding politician's wife was all I knew, but now I'd been forced to take a step back, I could see I'd been far from happy. I didn't want to return to the status quo. Maybe I could convince Douglas to loosen up a bit? Allow me to take up a hobby or two? I didn't want to die with regrets, and at almost thirty years old, regrets were all I had.

I jumped out of my skin when Emmy knocked on the window, and I scrambled to unlock the door. She tossed a bunch of shopping bags onto the backseat then poked her head in the front.

"I've got clothes, food, and toiletries. Grab a snack if you're hungry."

I nodded, but made no move to take the food. I still felt sick. Emmy disappeared again, and I resumed my vigil. The gang had moved under a streetlight a few cars away.

Where had Emmy vanished to? What else did we need? I still didn't know what she was up to when she returned a few minutes later and crouched at the back of the car, a couple of the youths glancing in her direction. Please, hurry up. The last thing we needed was for her to get attacked, or worse.

When she rapped on the window again, I chipped a nail in my hurry to open the door lock and bit back a curse. "What were you doing?"

"Swapping out the licence plate. There's another Camry on the other side of the lot, so I've borrowed its identity. Probably the owner won't even notice."

"You think the hitman can track the car?"

"Blackwood can, and Blackwood's got a leak."

"So what do we do? Keep running until you find out who it is, or I die?"

"Please, have a little faith in me. You're not gonna die." She started the engine. "We need to drive for a few more hours then find somewhere to stay for the night."

"Where are we going? Do you even have a plan?"

"I always have a plan. I'm a good little Girl Scout,

always prepared. We're going to Colorado."

"Colorado? But that's hundreds of miles away."

"It'll be fun. Haven't you ever taken a road trip before?" She looked at me then answered her own question. "No, I don't imagine you have."

"What's that supposed to mean?"

The turn signal clicked as she pulled out into traffic. "You strike me as more of an all-inclusive, five-star beach vacation sort of girl. I can't see you roughing it."

People had judged me by my appearance my whole life, and I was getting mighty sick of it. "How can you say that? You barely know me."

"Am I wrong?"

Since I'd been with Douglas, apart from the occasional business trip to Europe, all our summer vacations had been to resorts in the Caribbean. Winters took us to Aspen where my parents had a chalet. But it wasn't like I chose those destinations myself. Douglas booked the trips and simply let me know where we were going. Given the choice, maybe I'd choose a camping trip. Maybe.

"Well?"

My silence gave her my answer.

"I knew it."

"I'm not averse to 'roughing it,' as you so eloquently put it. I'll try anything once."

I didn't like the way she laughed. "Yeah, we'll see."

Emmy said I'd see, and I saw at quarter to midnight when she pulled into the forecourt of a dingy looking motel. A sign outside squeaked in the breeze as it flickered on and off, advertising "V canc es." No wonder they had rooms available—the place looked vile.

"You expect us to stay here?"

"What happened to trying anything once?"

"I was talking about sleeping in a tent, not going out of my way to catch an infectious disease."

"Oh, lighten up. We can play health violation bingo."

At this point, a bullet looked remarkably attractive. But I bit my tongue and followed her into a filthy office, where an obese man wearing a stained vest lolled in a lopsided swivel chair.

"You have a twin room?" Emmy asked.

"Eighty dollars."

Emmy reached into her pocket and dropped four twenties on the counter.

"Sign the register." The man nodded at the smudged book in front of us.

Emmy put down another fifty, and the man replaced the register with a key. Just like in politics, it seemed bribery made the world go round.

"Room seven," the man grunted.

Seven. My lucky number. What a joke.

We retrieved our bags from the car then found room seven at the far end of the building. I grimaced at the scarred door as Emmy fitted the key in the lock.

"Home, sweet home," she announced as she motioned me inside.

I took in the stained carpet, the worn blankets on the narrow twin beds, and the cracked mirror. The room smelled of a mixture of bleach and cigarette smoke.

"You know, on second thoughts, I think I'll just

sleep in the car."

"No, you won't."

"This place is disgusting."

She wrinkled her nose. "It's not five stars, but I've stayed in worse."

"Perhaps you should try vacationing in the Caribbean."

She laughed and dropped her holdall on the nearest bed. "I'll bear that in mind."

While Emmy used the bathroom, I opened up the first bag and found she'd bought me clothes similar to her own. A couple of pairs of jeans, two hooded sweaters and five T-shirts. I dropped the one with the offensive slogan onto her bed. I wouldn't dare to wear that out in public. Another bag held a pair of Converse I didn't believe for a moment was genuine.

"There's toiletries and food as well." She came back into the room, drying her hands on a towel that probably wouldn't have been out of place in a CDC lab.

"Thank you."

"No problem. You hungry?" She tipped a pile of groceries out on the chipped table.

"Not really."

"Try to eat something. We both need to keep our strength up."

I tore open a package of cheese crackers and nibbled on one to keep her happy. The powdery flavour turned my stomach. Emmy bit into an apple as she sat on the bed, leaning against the headboard with her legs stretched out.

"Been a hell of a day, don't you think? How are you feeling?"

I couldn't remember the last time someone asked

me that. "Not so good."

"Understandable. The past few weeks haven't been kind."

"I just want this to be over, one way or another."

"No, you want this to be over the right way. And it will be. You need to hang in there for a little bit longer."

"How long until we get to Colorado?"

"Three days, I reckon. Maybe four if we hit any delays."

Or six with a normal person at the wheel. I forced another cracker down, trying not to gag as I swallowed. "How do you stay so calm?"

"Practice."

"People explode buildings and shoot at you regularly?"

"More than I'd like."

"I'd never even seen a dead body outside the movies, not until that waiter died in front of me." A tear ran down my cheek, and I wiped it with my sleeve. "He died because of me."

"No, he didn't. He died because some asshole shot him. Not you. And that asshole was most likely hired by someone, who also wasn't you."

"But I keep thinking I must have done something. Why else would someone want to kill me? Hitmen don't come cheap, do they?"

"No, they don't. Especially the competent ones. Usually that helps narrow the list of suspects to those who can afford to pay. Problem is, you've got a long list of loaded acquaintances."

"Another disadvantage of being a Rutherford."

"Not quite the bed of roses everyone imagines, is it?"

If people only knew. "It's full of thorns."

Chapter 10

A RUMBLE OF thunder jolted me awake. It was still dark outside, so I couldn't have been asleep long. Rain pounded on the roof and clattered against the window that overlooked the parking lot. When I rolled over, Emmy was standing in front of it, staring through the glass.

"Can't you sleep either?" I asked.

"Not when I'm out on a job. I can't stay out for more than a couple of hours."

"Don't you get tired?"

"I cope."

Something in her tone told me she didn't, not really. "Do you spend much time on jobs?"

She shrugged. "Half my life."

"What about the rest of it?"

"I work in the office. Train. Keep fit."

I shoved my feet into the Converse I'd left next to the bed then stood next to her. The rain was falling in sheets, illuminated by the pink neon sign of the diner opposite.

"What about time off? What do you do for fun?"

She barked out a laugh. "I rarely take time off."

"Everybody needs a break."

"Tell that to the bad guys."

"So you've never taken a vacation? Not even

camping?"

She pushed back from the glass but didn't take her eyes off the storm. The next lightning bolt illuminated fine lines on her forehead, the result of too many frowns. The lack of matching crinkles around her mouth told me she didn't smile much.

"Once or twice. And I took a couple of months out last year, not out of choice. More...circumstances. I got bored. If I don't work, I feel dead inside."

That touched a nerve. What purpose did I have in life? None, that was what. I coasted from day to day in the same routine, pleasing everyone but myself. If I survived this hell, things needed to change.

We fell silent, watching the shifting shadows and the way the clouds swirled as they unleashed their anger at the world. Water splashed up from puddles that grew wider with each passing second. If things got much wetter, we'd need to trade in the Camry for a canoe.

Emmy spread one hand out on the glass. "One day, you'll dance in the rain."

"But I'll get wet."

"And you won't care, because every time a drop stings your skin, you'll remember you're alive."

I thought that through. Whenever a storm broke over Virginia, I took cover, sometimes under an umbrella, but more usually in a warm car or plush building. I'd never taken the risk of walking in the elements. I just wasn't that sort of person.

But what if I could be? What if I embraced everything life threw at me because it made me feel that vital spark I'd been missing?

Five minutes ticked by, then ten.

"You spend a lot of time dancing in the rain, don't you?" I whispered.

Her reply was almost too soft to hear. "Half my life."

One day, I vowed, I would too.

I'd gone back to bed after the chill in the room made me start shivering, and Emmy had crawled back under her blankets too. Two more days of travelling lay ahead of us, and we both wanted to get an early start.

The sooner we left, the sooner we'd get there.

"Do you want me to take a turn at driving?" I asked.

"You feel up to it?"

After our talk last night, I'd woken feeling a tiny glimmer of determination. "I want to help."

"We can swap in a couple of hours then."

Two hours on, two hours off. We'd stopped at a pancake place for breakfast, and just after noon Emmy pulled into a diner for lunch.

My appetite made an appearance, and I ate most of a burger and a plate of fries. Thinking of Douglas's face at the sight of so much saturated fat made me smile a little as I smothered the whole lot in ketchup.

"You seem happier today," Emmy said.

"It's laugh or cry."

"I'm glad you've picked the former. I'm shit at sympathy."

"As long as you're good at keeping me alive, I don't care."

"You're still breathing, aren't you?"

By a miracle, I was. "You think he's following us?"

"The hitman?"

"No, Santa Claus."

She took a sip of her coffee and grinned. "If you're being sarcastic, you must be feeling better."

"I guess I'm sick of giving in. And at least I'm not a sitting duck in the safe house anymore."

Her lips twitched to the side, then she went back to my question. "He'll be trying to pick up our trail, but he won't have managed it yet. I rented the car in a different name. A few people in Blackwood might be able to work it out, but it'll take time then they'll have to start tracking us. I changed the plates, and I've paid cash for everything. The only way he'll find us is if he gets lucky, or we make a mistake."

From the way she said it, I didn't imagine she made mistakes very often. So that meant any screw-ups would be down to me. My blunder, my life. "I'll do whatever you say. I don't want him to find us."

"We could do with changing your appearance, just to be on the safe side. How do you fancy a new haircut?"

Cut my hair? I loved my hair. Although it was long and thick and took forever to dry, Douglas always told me how elegant it was when I did it up to go out. One of my most attractive features—he'd said that many times and happily paid for me to have it styled every four weeks. Hang on. Was it me that loved my hair, or Douglas?

I thought about it. It was Douglas. I'd be quite happy with shorter hair. It might not look so flashy for functions, but it would be a lot easier to look after from day to day.

"I guess a haircut would be a good idea. Maybe

something shorter?"

"That would suit you. A darker colour too, at least for now."

"Should we stop somewhere?"

There was bound to be a hairstylist in one of the many towns we drove through. I just hoped we found a proficient one. Ending up like a scarecrow would only make this ordeal worse.

"I want to get to Colorado first. Mitch will know of somewhere you can go."

"Mitch?"

"My friend who lives near Denver. We're going to pay him a surprise visit."

CHAPTER 11

NIGHTFALL FOUND US in Indiana, perched on stools in a run-down bar. Beer came in bottles and everything on the menu was fried. Emmy's request for two glasses of tap water was met with a scowl from the bartender until she dropped a twenty on the bar—then we got water with ice and straws.

"What do you want to eat?" she asked me.

"What do you think's healthiest?"

"Onion rings. They're a vegetable. And the battered chicken burger might come with some sort of salad." She peered at the plate in front of the guy sitting next to her. "Or maybe not."

The man adjusted his cowboy hat and grinned at her. "You new around here, ladies?"

Emmy gave him a perky grin. "How'd you guess?"

"Never seen two faces as pretty as yours."

My cheeks went pink. He thought I was pretty? Nobody ever told me that apart from my daddy.

"I'm Abe, and this is Ted." The man jerked a thumb at his dining companion.

I smiled at him. "I'm Ge—"

"Jemima," Emmy interrupted. "And I go by Terri."

My face went redder but for a different reason. I'd nearly told two men our names, and we didn't even know them. What if they were connected to the hitman? I was so damn stupid.

"You passing through or sticking around?" Abe asked.

The bartender was busy talking to a man in a checked shirt, seemingly oblivious to us as Emmy glanced in his direction and drummed her nails on her thigh.

"Passing through. What's good to eat in here?"

The pig pointed at his crotch. "You can start with this."

Emmy picked up a steak knife and fork from the bar and twirled them in her fingers. "You want to lay out on the bar? Or bend over the table?"

The knife glinted in her hand, and her eyes had turned to flint. So far, she'd been kind to me, but I sensed she knew how to use that knife and she wouldn't hesitate if the need arose.

Abe must have realised it too, because he shuffled his stool away a foot and held up a hand in apology. "Just tryin' to be friendly."

"I'll make a suggestion. Don't."

We made it through dinner without any more hassle, and once he acknowledged our existence, the bartender suggested a small boarding house down the street. The lady who ran it welcomed us with open arms. Literally. She hugged me like I was her long-lost daughter.

"It's so nice to have company, hun. Gets lonely in this little town. You stayin' the one night or longer?"

Emmy answered for me. "Just one night."

"Headin' somewhere nice?"

The giggle that left Emmy's lips sounded natural, but I knew better. "My divorce finally came through and Jemima split with her boyfriend, the cheating asshole. So we thought we'd do the Thelma and Louise thing. You know, a car, the open road, an adventure."

"Brad Pitt," I put in. Who would be a marked improvement on Douglas.

The lady's double chin shook as she laughed along with us. "Just don't go shootin' nobody."

Emmy's lips curved up in a smile. "I'll try not to."

But I saw her fingers crossed behind her back, and when she opened her bag earlier, I'd glimpsed the pistol inside. No promises.

Our shared room was basic but a heck of a lot cleaner than last night's motel. Sure, it lacked toiletries and a kettle, but you couldn't have everything, could you? I slept soundly and woke early, but Emmy still beat me out to the car.

"Ready for this?" she asked.

"As I'll ever be."

By lunchtime, we'd driven clean across Illinois and into Missouri, a state I'd never visited before. We skirted around the south of St. Louis before picking up I70, which would take us all the way to Denver, Colorado. The rolling hills of the Northern Plains stretched for miles in every direction, and I kept yawning as the car trundled along.

"Tired?" Emmy asked.

"A little. Yes. You must be too?"

"I could do with stopping for a coffee."

I'd drifted off again by the time she pulled into the parking lot of another diner. Until two days ago, I'd never set foot in anywhere so...so...normal. But now I was developing a taste for American food as opposed to the French Douglas favoured.

"Burger with everything," I requested when the waitress came over with her pad.

"Make that two."

"Sure thing, girls." She tucked her pen into her apron and walked off.

"Do you always eat like this?" I asked Emmy.

"Hell, no. My nutritionist would kill me."

Nutritionist? She had a nutritionist? Even I didn't have a nutritionist. Every time I thought I was starting to understand Emmy, she surprised me.

"Better that than a hitman trying to kill you."

"He won't get you. Trust me."

I wished I could. Although I had to admit this trip wasn't the nightmare I thought it would be. Under different circumstances, I might almost have been enjoying myself with Emmy. She wasn't like any other woman I'd met, and I relished her irreverence, wishing I had the confidence to act the same way.

While I finished the last of my fries, she slid out of the booth.

"I need to check in with my contact at Blackwood. Let him know we're still alive."

"Of course. I bet he'll be worried about the hitman."

"No, it's not that. He knows how I drive."

I watched through the window as she paced back and forth in front of the Camry, occasionally gesturing with her hands. Was it good news or bad? Had they found the leak? Or even the man trying to kill me? I couldn't tell from her expression.

"Anything?" I asked, the instant we got back in the car.

She fastened her seatbelt and set off down the road before she replied. "It's not great news."

"Tell me."

"We got him on camera at the safe house, but because of the disguise he was wearing it's hard to tell what he really looks like. He had a car parked around the corner, but that was stolen from a long-term lot three months ago."

"Wait a minute—you think he's been planning this for three months?"

"At least. A paid assassin rarely just walks in and shoots someone. They need to plan their entrance, their exit, every aspect of the operation so they don't leave any clues."

"I didn't even notice. He must have followed me, mustn't he?"

"Don't feel bad about it. He didn't need to get that near, not when he was planning a long shot. The FBI found his nest overlooking the country club. Nine hundred yards away—further than anyone reckoned." She gave her head a little shake. "It was damn windy that day, and he got close. Not many people could have made that shot."

I stiffened in my seat as a memory flashed through my mind. Those words. I'd heard them before.

From my father's lips.

"Dime," I whispered.

This time it was Emmy's turn to sound surprised. "What did you just say?"

"Dime. I think there's an assassin called Dime. The best in the world, or so they say. Could he have been the one who tried to kill me?"

Her voice stayed level but tight. "What do you know

about Dime?"

"You've heard of him?"

"I've heard rumours. Now, tell me what you know."

"Nothing. Just a name and Dime's speciality. The long shot." And I wasn't even supposed to know that.

"Who told you? Not someone from the country club, I'd bet on that."

I let out a sigh. "My father."

"Seriously? Your father told you about Dime?"

"Well, not exactly *told* me."

"Georgia, stop waffling and spill. It could be important to the case. If you've got any information, you need to tell me."

"I overheard him, okay? Nobody ever notices me in the background. I see things and hear things, and I know I'm not supposed to, but I can't help being curious. I don't get any other excitement in my life."

"So, what did you overhear?"

"I'm not sure I should tell you. I mean, it's supposed to be secret. Part of my father's job."

"Look, Georgia, I'm not going to splash it all over the internet. It won't go beyond this car if I don't think it's relevant to the investigation. But if something you've seen or heard means someone with deadly skills and a penchant for murder has taken a shine to you, I need to fucking know. Okay?"

Daddy really wasn't going to be happy with me if he found out. But then again, being in the doghouse was better than being dead.

"It started years ago, back when I was a teenager. Mother asked me to take Daddy a mug of coffee, but when I got to his study he'd fallen asleep at his desk. I only meant to leave the drink and go, but then I saw the file in front of him. The Horsemen."

"Sounds like a bunch of cowboys."

"Oh, they're anything but. The Horsemen is the name the government's given to the world's top assassins. When I first found out about them there were four—Black, White, Red, and Pale."

"The four Horsemen of the Apocalypse," she murmured.

"Exactly. Daddy's head covered part of the writing, but I got that much."

"So where does Dime fit in?"

"Over the years, they expanded. I picked up snippets about them every now and then, mostly after my father's baseball parties. He and his friends would put a ball game on then drink all afternoon, and by evening they barely remembered their own names. As long as I kept their beers topped up and brought canapés, they carried on talking."

"And that's when you heard about Dime?"

"And the others."

She let out a low groan. "There are others?"

"I've heard of at least twelve."

"A dirty dozen of assassins. And you think they could be after us? Why? Did you mention them to anyone else?"

"Never! You're the first person I've told, and if someone wasn't trying to murder me, believe me, my lips would have stayed sealed."

Her knuckles tightened as she gripped the wheel. "Okay, run me through what's in that pretty little head of yours. If you or your father have managed to piss off one of the Horsemen, it would be nice to get some advance warning."

"I think my father's committee is trying to stop them. You know, wipe them out. I doubt any of them are fond of him."

"Details, Georgia. I need details."

I sighed and closed my eyes. How did a simple hobby of listening to my father's gossip come to this?

CHAPTER 12

EMMY WANTED DETAILS? Fine, I'd give them to her. I'd been carrying these secrets around for so long that dying with them, maybe because of them, would be an insult.

"Black's one of the originals, but I don't think it's him after me. He likes to kill with a message, not an anonymous gunshot."

"What do you mean a message?"

"Like the time he crucified a drug dealer. He nailed the man to the outside of his house with bags of heroin stuffed in every orifice. And there was a paedophile found with his own manhood stuffed in his mouth."

Daddy had been on the cognac when he talked about those two. A couple of fingers of VSOP always did loosen his tongue. I'd drunk in every word. While what Black did was obviously wrong, there was a part of me that admired the man for getting justice in a way no one else could. His victims deserved their fate.

Emmy shuddered behind the wheel. "Doesn't sound like a man you'd want to get on the wrong side of."

"The thought that these people are out there terrifies me."

"Tell me about Red."

"Red likes technology. Malfunctioning life support machines, cars with no brakes, heating systems belching out carbon monoxide. He once electrocuted someone with a blender."

"Good thing I can't cook."

"I began chopping my ingredients by hand after that."

"Keeping a knife handy probably wasn't a bad idea."

It was my turn to shiver. "The idea of using it on a person makes me sick."

"But what if it was them or you?"

"I don't know. I don't know what I'd do."

"So that's two. What about the rest?"

"Of the other two originals, Pale makes death look like an accident. I think we can rule him out, seeing as the mess left behind with me would have been pretty freaking obvious. And I've never heard anything more about White since I saw the original file."

"Back to Dime, then. You mentioned him first?"

"Because he shoots people, and the first attempt to kill me fit with that. But the way he came to the house the third time? I'm not sure, when I think about it. The 'up close and personal' thing sounds more like Smoke."

"Go on then, tell me about Smoke."

"He likes to see his victims suffer. You know that 'death by a thousand cuts' thing?"

"I thought that was a legend."

"Maybe it is. Smoke only got up to eight hundred before his victim died, or so the pathologist's report said. I saw it when I cleared away the plate from Daddy's sandwiches."

I had to admit, realising my father knew about these people always worried me, but because I thought they might come after him, not me. Part of his job was to keep America safe and stopping a band of assassins no doubt played an important part in that. So while I was scared for him, I was also proud.

"A failure then. He'll have to try harder next time. Who else is there?"

"I think we can eliminate most of them." I ticked them off on my fingers as I spoke. "Snow likes to poison people, California has only ever killed on the West Coast, and Fuego sets things on fire. His pièce de résistance involved a divorce and a fireworks factory."

When I'd glimpsed that dossier, it was like reading one of my thriller novels. To this day, I wasn't quite sure I believed the story.

Emmy slowed up for a moment as we came up behind a truck, huffing in frustration when she couldn't get around it straight away. Eventually the road straightened up, and she accelerated past.

"Bloody Japanese piece of shit. I'd be faster on a pedal bike."

"You'd be exhausted, though. You couldn't have done seven states in three days on a pedal bike."

"Fair point. At least we've only got two left to do. We should be there tomorrow." Emmy stretched back in the seat and yawned.

"Do you want me to drive for a while?"

"After the next stop. There's a town up ahead. In the meantime, you can keep me awake with your stories."

"You don't think they're true?"

"Most of them sound a little far-fetched, you have to admit."

I was convinced some of them were real, at least the ones where I'd caught sight of official-looking reports. But the tales where my father and his cronies let their mouths run while they drank Scotch and puffed away on cigars they weren't supposed to be smoking in the house? Those could well have been embellished somewhat.

"Okay, they do sound ridiculous, don't they? I wonder if the Horsemen know each other? Maybe they sit around and compare notes?"

"Assassins' coffee mornings." She glanced at me and chuckled. "They could gossip while they sharpen their knives and compare the latest guns."

"Or maybe they live in dark caves and only come out at night."

Emmy shook her head. "That's vampires."

"Who says they can't be both? I don't suppose they have a rule book."

"Have any of the victims been found with fang marks?"

"One of Smoke's victims had puncture wounds, but the FBI couldn't work out where they came from. And I don't suppose they ever will, seeing as nobody's mentioned Smoke in years. I think he might be dead."

"At least that's one we can knock off the list, but you said there were twelve. That still leaves four."

"It's not Player. He specialises in character assassination."

"Like, how?"

"He strangled one poor woman during the act itself then framed her boyfriend."

When I'd overheard Daddy on his conference call, I'd tiptoed along the hallway until I got to the downstairs bathroom then thrown up until there wasn't anything left in me.

"Sick. At least it's not him after you."

"Thank goodness for small mercies, eh?" I couldn't help the modicum of sarcasm that crept into my voice. Having my head blown to smithereens might have been the better option but only marginally.

"Sorry. I know this can't be easy, talking about all this. But forewarned is forearmed. If we've got a clue as to who might be after us, it'll help us prepare."

I didn't want to prepare. I wanted to go home, put on a pretty dress and sip faux champagne at Monica's baby shower. I wanted to be by Douglas's side at dinner and smile politely as he made small talk. Now I'd had a taste of excitement, I longed for my boring life back. But three quarters of the way to Denver, with a woman I both respected and feared, it didn't look like that would happen any time soon. I took a deep breath and told her about the last three Horsemen.

"Okay. There's Valkyrie."

"Unusual name."

"Isn't it?"

"Did you ever see *Apocalypse Now*? You know, the movie? Where they play 'Ride of the Valkyries' from the helicopter?"

"I don't watch war movies. All the blood makes me feel queasy."

"It's epic."

"I'll take your word for it. Anyway, that's not where the name came from. Valkyrie's first known victim was a soldier accused of war crimes who was found impaled by an arrow stuck into a print of Edward Robert Hughes' 'The Valkyrie's Vigil.' In Norse mythology, the Valkyries are war goddesses who choose who lives in battle and who dies. Did you know that?"

"I slept through that lesson at school."

"You should read more."

"I'm out living life instead."

Ouch. That dig hurt. She must have realised it because she reached a hand over and squeezed mine.

"Sorry. That was uncalled for. Besides, you seem to have found plenty of excitement in your own home."

"My parents' home." Douglas's conversations about Maslow's Hierarchy of Needs and the BCG growth-share matrix weren't nearly so interesting.

"Close enough. Valkyrie?"

"There was speculation the killer was acting as the Valkyrie in the picture, hence the name. But I've never heard of Valkyrie sniping anybody."

"Okay, Valkyrie goes to the bottom of the list."

"Then there's Lilith."

"After the demon in Jewish mythology? I know that one. Think I saw it in a movie once."

"Although she's more likely to be from Eastern Europe. Daddy's friend believes she murdered a congressman a few years back."

"Which one?"

"I forget his name. He died in a hunting accident."

"Congressman Page, from Oklahoma."

"You know about it?"

"It was all over the TV. Served him right for hunting out of season."

"Only Lilith was hunting him."

"You saw that in an official report?"

"No. One of Daddy's friends made a comment about it while they were watching a hunting documentary."

"So he could have been speculating?"

"I suppose it's possible."

"Who does that leave? Who's the twelfth? Because

so far, none of these guys seem to fit."

"Ace might. From what I've heard, he's a jack-of-all-trades. He's shot, stabbed, bludgeoned, and choked his way onto the list. And last year he set a car bomb. The link between each killing was the playing card he left at the scene."

"We didn't find any playing cards."

"Maybe that's only because he didn't kill me yet."

Emmy wrinkled her nose and braked for a slower vehicle. "We'll leave him as a possible. But I'm not sure. Didn't you say this group was supposed to be the best?"

"Apparently so."

"Your attacker's failed three times now, so I doubt he'd make it into the Horsemen. He's a wannabe."

"I heard Daddy whispering on the phone the other day about the Horsemen having a problem. Perhaps it was something to do with this whole situation?"

And that would mean my father knew more than he'd told me. Was that why he hired Blackwood? The possibility he'd kept me in the dark made me want to run to the other side of the world. If I couldn't trust my own family, who could I trust?

"I'm sure it's all just a coincidence. Lots of people fight crime every day—the cops, the FBI, the sheriff's department. They don't all have deranged shooters after them."

I held onto that thought. "Do you think he'll give up? If he can't find us?"

"Not if he wants to get paid. Also, he's got his reputation to consider. He can't charge the big bucks if he gets known for fucking things up. No, he'll keep coming. He'll be kicking himself for ever taking the job, but he'll be determined to finish it."

Great. Just great.

The motel we stayed in that night was marginally better than the first, but still shabbier than the boarding house. And there was no sweet, motherly lady to serve us pancakes before we left for the road, either. Emmy stopped at a gas station and came back with another bagful of cookies to keep us going, along with the ubiquitous bitter coffee.

"Will we get to your friend's house today?"

"It's more of a cabin. Yeah, I think so, as long as we don't hit any delays."

"A cabin?"

"Up in the mountains. Fresh air, solitude, peace and quiet. You'll love it."

"I'm not sure I want to be in the middle of nowhere. What if there's a problem? Who do I call for help?"

"Mitch will look after you. And it's not that isolated —it's far enough out of town that nobody'll stumble across it, but close enough to be civilised."

I settled back in my seat and tried to be positive. At least nothing could be as bad as that first motel.

Although when Emmy pulled off the road and onto a small dirt track just as daylight began to fade, I rethought that.

"Is this even a road?"

"What, you've never seen potholes before?"

They were so big a family of five could have set up home inside one and been quite comfortable. I clung onto the seat to save myself from hitting my head on the window as the Camry jolted along. Just when I thought it could get no worse, Emmy jerked the wheel left and trundled up a near-vertical path.

"Almost there."

"We'd better be, or I won't have any teeth left."

I closed my eyes as Emmy skirted around tree boughs and splashed through the mud patches. Please, I'd survived three murder attempts and travelled halfway across the country—don't let me die in an overturned car because someone didn't make it a priority to maintain their driveway.

Then the engine stopped.

"Are we here?"

"We're here."

Thank goodness.

CHAPTER 13

WHEN EMMY SAID cabin, I'd pictured a small log affair in the middle of the woods, somewhat primitive, although I'd been hoping for indoor plumbing at least. This cabin was in the woods, but there the similarity ended. The huge, A-frame building stood two storeys high, taller than some of the trees around the edge of the clearing. A wide balcony spanned the underside of the eaves on the second floor, chalet style, looking down the mountain. I couldn't wait to see the view in daylight. The grey curtain of darkness falling over the trees didn't do it justice.

Under the balcony, a wide porch held a swing seat and barbecue, both covered up for winter. I bet in the summer, with the trees in leaf and the sun shining, the place would be paradise on earth. I'd even forgive the state of the driveway.

"What a fantastic house," I breathed.

"It's quite something, isn't it? Mitch designed it himself."

"Is he home?"

Apart from the Camry's headlights and the soft glow of the moon, the place was in darkness. I couldn't see any other vehicles, either.

"Doesn't look like it. Sit tight while I check."

Emmy hopped out of the car, climbed the steps up

to the porch, and knocked on the front door. When nobody answered she walked around the side, peering in each window until she disappeared out of sight behind the house. A few minutes later, she came back.

"He's not here. The garage is empty, and he's turned everything off."

My heart sank at the thought of going back over all those holes. "Now what? Do you think we'll find a place to stay nearby?"

"I picked up the spare key he keeps hidden. We can go inside and wait for him."

"Won't he mind?"

"I'll deal with him."

Well, okay then. As long as she was sure. I trailed up the steps behind Emmy, pausing to admire the carved wooden wolf's head mounted next to the door.

"Are you coming inside? I want to get the door shut."

"Yes, of course."

I hurried past and found myself in a huge, open plan room which took up most of the cabin. Emmy had lit a cylindrical lamp on a side table, and I took in the decor. A central area held a collection of comfortable-looking sofas and behind it the kitchen took up half of the back wall, divided from the main room by a waist-high counter.

Emmy pointed at two doors next to the kitchen. "Bathroom and guest room. You can sleep in there."

"What about you?"

She looked upwards, where a loft spanned the full width of the cabin. A set of narrow stairs hugged the wall. "I'll borrow Mitch's bed."

While the centre of the cabin was double height

with beams stretching the full width, I spotted another loft at the other end, accessed by a matching staircase. That one must open up onto the balcony at the front. Emmy followed my gaze.

"Is that another bedroom?" I asked.

"No, it's Mitch's studio."

"Studio?"

"He paints. He reckons the light's best up there." She rubbed her hands together. "Bloody hell, it's freezing in here. I'm gonna sort the heating out."

She was right about the chill. My breath puffed out in clouds, and I gave an involuntary shiver. If I didn't get shot, there was every chance I'd succumb to hypothermia. I stamped my feet and rubbed my hands together as Emmy rummaged in the kitchen.

"Could you turn the main lights on? The switch is by the stairs to the master bedroom."

I skirted around a sideboard and did as she asked. As spotlights blazed down, I got my first proper look at the walls.

"Oh my goodness." The words escaped before I could stop them.

Canvases covered every wall. Watercolours of dark, dramatic landscapes with boiling skies gave way to detailed pencil studies of birds and animals. Cheerful acrylics of busy streets led to oils depicting dark, hellish scenes of otherworldly monsters. Above the mantel was a diptych, the left hand panel depicting an angel perched on a fallen tree trunk, looking into the distance. The figure on the right adopted the same pose, but there was no mistaking the devil's horns and whip-like tail. They drew me closer, mesmerised.

The detail was something to behold, the hair almost

life-like. But when I looked past the sparkling halo, I gave a start.

"Emmy?"

"Yeah?"

"This is you. The angel above the fireplace."

"I know."

"And the devil?" He'd captured her strong features perfectly.

"Also me." She shrugged. "Me and Mitch have had our ups and downs."

"He painted all these?"

A nod.

I shivered again and not from the cold this time. While half of the paintings were a delight to look at, the rest bordered on disturbing. I walked further into the room. On the wall above a dining table, seated for four, I saw a picture I recognised. A majestic eagle, soaring above a snow-covered mountain.

"I have a print of this. Douglas bought it for me for my birthday a few years ago."

"Doesn't surprise me. Mitch has to make his money somehow, and he rarely sells the originals."

It took a few seconds for her words to sink in. Then I leaned forward and peered at the brush strokes on the canvas, each one perfectly placed. "Are you telling me your friend Mitch is Mitchell Gray? As in *the* Mitchell Gray?"

"That's his name."

"But he's a world-renowned artist. You're telling me he lives by himself on this mountain?"

"He's not that famous. Not like Van Gogh or Picasso."

"He's famous enough. His prints sell for thousands

of dollars."

She shrugged again. "Don't go all fan girl. It'll give him a big head."

Somehow I doubted that. When Douglas gave me the painting, I did my research. Mitchell Gray was a notorious recluse who never gave interviews or made public appearances, so I supposed his living arrangements shouldn't really have surprised me. I couldn't even find a photo of him. He released several limited edition prints a year, and they all sold for top dollar, more with every passing season. Most of them were landscapes, and he was famous for the emotions he managed to paint into each picture.

The eagle in my picture was on the hunt, hungry for prey. I focused again on the devil Emmy and shuddered. That evoked emotion all right, but it wasn't one I enjoyed feeling.

"I promise I won't ask for his autograph or anything." Not unless the right moment arose. "Do you know when he'll be back?"

"Nope. His cell phone's off. We'll just wait."

When Emmy described Mitch as a recluse who lived up a mountain, I'd imagined one of those crazy old men who shunned all human contact. You know the type— the wild-eyed, long-haired ones who shot their own food as well as any strangers who made the mistake of straying onto their land. Finding out the owner of the cabin was in fact a well-known artist set my mind at ease a little.

Despite some of his paintings being slightly odd, he

was probably a normal person. After all, he had a very civilised home.

I opened up the refrigerator, but apart from two bottles of beer and what looked like a shrivelled lemon, the shelves were bare.

"Try the freezer," Emmy suggested.

I knelt to rummage through. A sports ice pack, a wine chiller something unidentifiable wrapped in cling film—did the man ever eat?

"Anything?"

"Not much." I pulled a second drawer open. "Hang on. There's a package of microwaveable spaghetti bolognese."

"That'll do. Give it here."

We ate at the table below the tableau of paintings. It reminded me of La Gallerie, the high-end restaurant-slash-art gallery in Richmond, except the paintings were better. Creepier, maybe, but better.

"What if Mitch doesn't come back tonight?" I asked as I rinsed the dishes. There was still no sign of him.

"We wait longer."

I covered a yawn with my hand as I shuffled off to the guest bedroom. It had been a long day, and I couldn't wait to fall into bed. At least, until I opened the door and something black ran across the floor.

I'd have won gold in a hurdles race the way I ran backwards and leapt over the coffee table. A gun appeared in Emmy's hand before I could blink.

"What is it?"

"Spider!"

She burst out laughing. "That's it? A spider."

"It's not funny. It was one of those hairy ones with the fat bodies."

"You want me to shoot it?"

"Stop it. It's not my fault I'm terrified of them."

"It's, like, a millionth of the size of you."

"They bite."

She rolled her eyes and tucked the pistol into her waistband. "I'll deal with it. No more screaming."

Did I scream? I hadn't even realised. This whole trip left me jumpier than a frog on triple espressos.

A minute later, Emmy emerged. "I've put the spider out of the window." She gave a little smirk. "It's safe now."

I tried again, careful to check each corner of the ceiling in case any more spiders were lurking, and under the bed too. The room was basic but comfortable. Warm too, now Emmy had sorted the heating out. The double bed had clean sheets, but they smelled musty, like nobody had slept there for years. Maybe ever. The small nightstand was empty, and the narrow closet held only a few hangers. For the first time in weeks, I slept with the drapes open. I wanted to see the outside world when I woke up. If the hitman followed us all the way here, I figured the flimsy material wouldn't help much anyway.

I woke with the sun in the morning, but Emmy still beat me to the kitchen. When I stumbled out of my room, she was already fiddling with the coffee machine.

"Do you want a cup?"

"Yes, please. I'd love one."

I'd put on yesterday's jeans, but she wore a pair of men's boxer shorts and a grey T-shirt that reached almost to the bottom of them.

"Are those Mitchell's clothes?"

She nodded, took a sip of coffee, then pursed her lips and blew on it.

"Won't he mind?"

"He'll get over it."

"Have you heard anything from him?

She shook her head. "The fridge was empty, he'd turned everything off, and there was three weeks' worth of mail in the box. He planned to be away for a while."

"So what do we do?"

"Stay here. Fifty bucks says he'll be back within a couple of days." She glanced at her watch. "He'd better be. I need to get home and fix up this mess."

"I'm sorry for being a burden."

"It's the fucking traitor at Blackwood who's the burden, not you."

"I know you're just being kind, but thank you all the same. Leaving your life must have been as difficult for you as it was for me."

"Don't worry about it. It's not the first time, and it won't be the last. At least I'm not sleeping in a tent and shitting in a hole in the ground on this trip."

"You've really had to do that?"

She grimaced. "Yeah, and it's not pleasant, especially if your travelling companions are all men. Even if the hole's really big, they still can't manage to aim into it."

"Reminds me of home." I'd even left a sticky note by the basin to remind Douglas to put the seat down, but he still couldn't manage that simple thing.

"Maybe this trip won't be so bad for you then." Emmy laughed as she pushed her chair back. "I'm going to take a quick trip into town. We need food."

"Will it be safe for me to stay here on my own?"

"Yes, at the moment. He won't have caught up with us yet. Nobody followed us."

"In that case, I might go back to bed. I haven't slept properly for days."

"Rest's important. If Mitch turns up, tell him I'll be back soon."

"How will I know him?"

"Brown hair, brown eyes. Last time I saw him his hair was short, but that could have changed. He always looks grumpy, so don't take it personally. Plus, he'll have a key."

Duh, of course. It's not as if he'd have to stop and knock on his own door. "I guess I'll see you soon, then."

"Any requests? I've already got chocolate and Jenga on the list."

"A bottle of red wine. I need it."

CHAPTER 14

HE GOT OUT of his Land Rover and stood at the bottom of the driveway, staring up at his mountain. Three weeks had passed since he'd been home, and he took in the changes. A fallen tree branch. The buds forming on the scrubby bushes. A faint smell of skunk. The mailbox stood at his side like a sentry, and he flipped the lid open. Empty.

Emmy was here, he knew it. He melted into the woods at the side of the track then wound his way upwards like a wraith until he stood in the shadows next to the cabin. A dim light glowed from inside. Not one of the overhead lights, but maybe the table lamp next to the couch—the sort of light a person left on in case they woke at night in unfamiliar surroundings.

Well, she'd be waking up tonight, that was for sure.

He ran over, his footsteps silent as he climbed the steps to the front door. Years of practice had made him adept at moving noiselessly over difficult terrain. The lock was well-oiled and the key made the faintest click as it turned, then he slipped inside. Warmth seeped into him from the central heating that she'd left on high. She always did like things hot.

Now, where was she? He glanced up at the loft. If he was her, that was where he'd choose to sleep.

He avoided the squeaky fourth step as he crept up

the wooden stairs. There was no door to the loft, just a waist-high railing that ran across the front of the room. He liked being able to see down into his house from there, king of his own castle. And the light from downstairs seeped up, bathing the room in a faint wash of yellow that allowed him to see straight away someone was asleep in his bed. A woman—face down, one arm underneath the pillow and the other stretched out by her side.

Fucking Goldilocks.

His rubber-soled shoes made no sound as he crossed the room to the bed. Putting a knee on the mattress, he was on her in an instant. One hand grabbed her hair and snapped her head back. She flipped over in the blink of an eye, but he already had a knife at her throat.

"Losing your touch, bitch."

"You're losing yours," she hissed back.

He felt a sharp pain at the bottom of his ribcage and glanced down to see the knife she was holding, angled up so a flick of her wrist would drive it into his heart.

"Shall we call this round a draw?"

Damn her. "Fuck you."

He retracted his knife then waited as she did the same with hers. An Emerson CQC-7B, he noted. Some things never changed.

Once she'd folded it, he leaned forward and kissed her roughly, their tongues tangling and teeth clashing. His fingers twisted tighter in her hair as she clawed at his back.

"Hey, Valkyrie," he rasped.

"Hello, Smoke," she whispered back.

He kissed her again, but this time she bit his lip and

pushed him away. "I can't do this. I'm giving monogamy a try."

"Not even for old times' sake?"

She shook her head. "Things have changed."

"How much?"

She twisted, rolled so she was on top. That always had been her favourite position. "Not that much." She sprang off him and dashed across the room.

Two minutes. Two minutes he'd been back, and she was already up to her tricks. He was getting too damn old for this, he thought, as he took off after her, cursing under his breath. She vaulted the railing at the front of the loft and ran across the exposed beams, perfectly in balance, then cleared its opposite number into the studio at the other end of the cabin. Shit. Good thing he had a head for heights.

Mounted on the wall next to his favourite easel was a pair of Japanese katanas. Hand-forged and dating back to the Kotō period, they'd cost him thousands. He groaned as she grabbed one of them and danced backwards.

"Let's see how much you've lost your touch, old man."

"I'm only three years older than you." He snatched the other sword, hefted it in his right hand.

"You're retired. That makes you old."

He slashed at her, and she leaped backwards, skidding on the wooden floor. But she kept her balance and whirled the sword in front of her, cutting the air in a figure-eight motion as she slowly advanced towards him. Time had a nasty habit of dulling the senses, and while he'd gone rusty, he could see she was still razor sharp. Fuck it.

"Why did I teach you how to use a sword?"

She gave him that perfect smile—the one that made him lose his mind. "Because you like me."

"I'm rethinking that."

She leapt towards him and the swords clashed, metal on metal grating through the air. Her blade got perilously close to one of the only decent paintings he'd done in the last year.

"Watch the canvas, would you? Can we continue this downstairs?"

Without answering, she shot backwards and slid down the smooth wooden banister while he took the stairs three at a time as he thundered after her. She was ready for him as he reached the bottom, and forced him back up a couple of steps before her sword struck the finial and checked her swing for a second.

He leapt over the safety rail into the lounge and got behind her, slicing dangerously close to a kidney before she slashed back at him. She missed as he moved and knocked the pile of mail all over the floor instead. Before she could try again, he ran across the room, grabbed a dining chair and threw it at her. She dodged, and the chair slammed into the coffee table, sending a pile of precariously stacked Jenga bricks flying.

Jenga? Why the fuck was she playing Jenga?

No time to think about that right now. He bounded over the couch, and the air turned blue when she trod on one of the bricks as she followed. Never one to dwell, she picked it up and hurled it at him, but he ducked and it bounced off the television. Dammit—that flat-screen was almost new.

Still, it wasn't like he couldn't afford a new one.

A shaky voice called out from the guest room.

"Emmy? Is everything all right out there?"

"Everything's fine. Don't worry."

"I thought I heard a crash?"

"There's a spider. A big one. I'm trying to catch it. Best you stay in your room."

Xavier rolled his eyes, swallowing down laughter as the bitch jumped onto the kitchen counter and ran along it, stabbing down at him while he swiped with the sword above his head. Somehow in the melee, the coffee machine fell onto the floor with a crash loud enough to make his ears ring, although it wasn't as loud as the time he'd blown up a row of six cars on the outskirts of Tel Aviv and perforated his eardrum. He jumped over the mangled remains, picked an apple out of the fruit bowl and launched it at her. She flicked the sword upwards and chopped it neatly in half.

"Fruit salad for breakfast?" She flashed that smile again.

"Have an orange."

He tossed the fruit from hand to hand before throwing it. Same result. He glanced across at the fruit bowl. What next? A lime? "Shame there's no watermelon. That would be impressive."

With one neat hop over the refrigerator, she landed back in the lounge area, laughing. "I'll get one tomorrow."

"We're not doing this again tomorrow."

"Spoilsport."

Light glinted off metal as she whipped the blade around again, but he twisted out of the way and the sword hit a vase. Venetian glass was no match for sixteenth-century forged steel, and it shattered into smithereens.

"Stop!"

He raised an eyebrow. "What? You give in?"

"No, I'm fucking barefoot, you idiot."

Shit. He'd been so busy trying to avoid death he hadn't noticed her feet. His observation skills had deteriorated in the same way as his swordsmanship. Fighting forgotten, he dropped the sword on the dining table, picked her up and set her cute ass on the kitchen counter.

"Did you get any glass in you?" He lifted one of her feet and studied the sole.

"No, we stopped in time."

"Good. Can we be more civilised now, rather than trying to kill each other?"

She shrugged. As good as a yes, in her book.

He wrapped her up in his arms and pressed his lips to her temple. "In that case, good morning, Emerson."

"Good morning, Xavier."

He closed his eyes, resting his forehead on hers. "Why do we always fight?"

"Because we love it. Miss me?"

"Always. What's it been? Two years?"

"Two years, four months. And I meant what I said about you losing your touch. Two years ago I'd never have got a knife to your ribs like that." She poked him in the chest for emphasis.

"And I meant what I said about being retired. I've got no need for all that anymore."

"Yeah, you thought." She looked cagey, and he knew this wasn't a social call.

"Why are you here, Emmy? Who's the other woman with you? I don't recognise her."

Emmy glanced around the room, her eyes pausing

on the moulding over the sink, then the light fitting above the couch. "You still playing stalker with your CCTV?"

"It's my fucking house. I can wire it if I want to. Just answer the damn question."

"I need a little bit of help with something."

Before she could elaborate, the woman's voice called out again. "Did you get the spider? Tell me you got it."

"Yeah. It's flat now. Try to get some sleep."

"I thought I heard voices?"

"I can't sleep. I'm gonna watch TV for a while."

Xavier rolled his eyes as Emmy turned back to face him. "What did you tell her my name was?"

"I stuck with Mitchell Gray. She's even got one of your paintings."

He waggled his eyebrows. "Always nice to meet a fan."

She thumped him on the arm. "Down, boy."

"Now, would you mind telling me who the hell she is and why she's sleeping in my guest room?"

CHAPTER 15

XAVIER GOT THE last two bottles of beer from the fridge and carried Emmy over to the sofa nearest the front door. She lay with her head resting on his thigh as she told him the story, starting with the shooting at the country club and ending with her fears of a traitor at Blackwood.

"And she knows about the Horsemen."

That made Xavier take notice. He'd been trying to block out the Horsemen for two years, but now they came back to haunt him. "How?"

"Because of who her daddy is. She sees too much and hears too much."

"Fuck. Senator Rutherford. I didn't put two and two together." He'd been out of this game too long.

"Yeah. Only she thinks he's trying to stop the Horsemen as opposed to merely monitoring them for Hades. We were talking about the sniper's distance, and she thought it might have been Dime."

"What do you think?"

"It wasn't Dime. Dime was at Disneyland with Red and their kid."

"Fuck. Mickey meets the Underworld. You reckon there could be any connection with the others?"

"Honestly? I don't know. The Horsemen strayed so far from its original concept, the whole project is a mess now."

Xav blew out a breath. Back when the Horsemen all knew each other, operations had been much simpler. "It got too big. I couldn't pick half of them out of a lineup now."

"Me neither. Hades-the-second started the problems when he expanded from the original four, and we both know Hades number three is an asshole. Eight was a sensible number, but there's got to be thirty fucking names on that list today, although Georgia only knows a dozen of them."

"The question is, would any of them take on Blackwood?"

Emmy sighed as he twirled a lock of her hair around his fingers. "Who the hell knows? We can rule out a few more of them, at least. White's dead. It wasn't Black, and Pale's got honour. I haven't seen Snow for a while, but she wouldn't have done this either."

"Lilith's got the skills. I heard she hit a man's eye from fifteen hundred yards."

A low groan escaped Emmy's lips.

"What?"

"I don't want to think about Lilith."

"What happened? Tell me?"

"I'm pretty sure I came across her. There was an incident. She could have taken me out, but she chose not to. So she's got some ethics, and from what I understand, her targets are political. Scratch her off the list."

Xavier chose not to push it. If Emmy didn't want to talk, nobody could make her. "What about the rest?"

"There's definitely a man involved, because he came after us at the safe house. I need to call Black. He might have some ideas. This whole job is a bloody nightmare. Usually in an investigation, we'll have a motive and a handful of suspects. Right now, we've got suspects coming out of our ears, no idea whether this is aimed at Georgia in particular or the Rutherford family in general, money, money everywhere and some fucker feeding information to the other side. Maybe I'll just stay here. We can catch fish for dinner and pick berries and stuff."

He kissed two fingers and pressed them to her lips. "I wouldn't say no."

For a few seconds, she lay back with her eyes closed, and he knew she was remembering the good times, as was he. There had been plenty of those, but they'd been mixed in with bad. They'd been young when they first met, too young, both headstrong and hurting inside. And outside too. He recalled the bruises they'd worn like badges of honour as a result of their experimentation with fighting skills. Then there were the marks on her wrists where he'd tied her up and fucked her while she screamed at him to try harder. Back then, she'd only come alive in bed. The rest of the time, she'd acted like the robot Black trained her to be.

But that was in their past. And now he sensed a change in her.

No going back.

"So, you're here. And what exactly am I supposed to do about all this?"

"I was hoping you'd keep an eye on Georgia while I go back to Virginia to plug the leak. I don't completely trust anyone but Black."

"What about me?"

"I'd trust a burning cobra more than I'd trust you."

"I see your judgement hasn't been impaired while we've been apart."

"Will you help?"

He sighed. "Which part of retired don't you understand?"

"The bit where you owe me a favour."

"You and your fucking favours." But he did. She'd come through with a route out of Italy on one of his last jobs, saving him from a run-in with an angry mafia boss's son who wasn't thrilled about the death of his father. "All right, I'll do it. I don't really have much of a choice now that you're here, do I?"

She kissed him softly on the cheek and whispered, "Thank you."

"Any particular requests?"

"I want to know more about her character. So far she's been non-confrontational, and I can't see her pissing anyone off enough for them to want to kill her. Not in cold blood. But she's been jumpy as hell."

"That's probably because of the situation."

"I don't want to rule anything out."

"So you want me to do some digging?"

"Wind her up. See if you can get her to snap. It shouldn't be too difficult—irritating the crap out of people comes naturally to you."

For that, Emmy ended up on her front with his knee in her back. He twisted sideways as her knife appeared out of nowhere and headed for his thigh, then he slammed her hand onto the floor. Good to see he hadn't lost his touch completely.

"Play nice, Valkyrie."

"Asshole."

He held her down for a few more seconds then

exhaled slowly. "We'd better get this mess cleared up. I'll bring your shoes. Is that my shirt you're wearing? And my boxers?"

"They're comfy."

"I'll never wash them again."

"Shut up and get the damn shoes."

Between them, they set about getting the house straight. Emmy swept up the glass while Xavier re-hung the swords.

"Why do I always get the crappy jobs?" she muttered.

"I'd make a crack about you being a woman, but I value my testicles."

Oh, if looks could kill.

Twenty minutes later, Emmy swore under her breath. "The coffee machine's knackered. I need coffee. How am I supposed to wake up in the morning without coffee?"

"There's instant in the cupboard."

She made a gagging noise. "I'll go buy another machine first thing."

Xavier looked at his watch, a Panerai Luminor Submersible he'd bought after he went freelance over a decade ago. "We've got a couple of hours before we need to get up. Are you still trying to murder people in your sleep?"

"Not for six months now."

"Is it safe to share a bed with you? Or shall I take the couch?"

"Depends how brave you're feeling."

He took the couch.

First thing in the morning, Emmy borrowed a phone from Xavier's stash then stepped onto the porch to call Black. Xav paced the great room while he waited for her to come back with news. Would Blackwood have made any progress? How long would he have to put up with this interruption to his life?

He'd admit to being a little bored lately, but babysitting some rich bitch wasn't what he'd had in mind to break up the tedium. There'd been enough of them in Aspen. When he booked a month's stay in the millionaire's playground, he'd planned to split his time between painting and skiing, but in the three weeks he'd stuck it out, he'd fought for space on the black runs with the Silicon Valley crowd, fucked three socialites, got slapped by number three when she saw him talking to a potential number four the next day, and painted precisely nothing.

Then Emmy turned up at his house, the alarm tripped, and he breathed a sigh of relief that he had an excuse to leave.

"And?" he asked when she walked back inside.

He slipped his arms around her waist and kissed her hair. She may take liberties and frustrate the hell out of him, but he'd missed the sneaky little witch.

"Black already thought of the Horsemen connection, what with it being Rutherford and everything. He's ruled most of them out, but there's been whispers about Ace. Hades isn't happy with the amount of collateral damage he's been leaving lately."

"I always thought he was a strange one."

"Yeah. Those fucking playing cards. I mean, who leaves calling cards all over the place? It's so unprofessional."

"Agreed. So, you're going to look for him?"

"It's a possibility."

"Be careful."

"Always am."

CHAPTER 16

A SUNBEAM SLICED across my face as I looked out of the window. Following so many dark days, the blue sky with just a few fluffy clouds skidding across it felt like a new start. The branch of a majestic oak hung low near the window, and a squirrel ran down it. I held my breath as he paused a few feet away, nose twitching. Maybe I could get him some food. What did squirrels eat, anyway?

After a day in the cabin, I'd begun to enjoy the place. While I'd never lived in the centre of town, my homes hadn't exactly been in the country either, and I'd never seen such an abundance of wildlife. Being woken by birdsong rather than an alarm clock was something I could get used to. And yesterday evening, when I'd wrapped a blanket around myself and curled up on the seat next to the hot tub on the back porch, a deer walked past not six feet away. No wonder Mitchell Gray chose this place to paint. It was an artist's paradise.

I could have leaned on the windowsill for another hour watching the birds flitting through the trees, but my bladder reminded me of a more pressing matter I needed to attend to. Emmy had brought back half a dozen bottles of red wine from her shopping trip, and we'd shared one late last night. And when I said shared, I meant she drank half a glass and I drank the rest.

I'd slept like the dead last night, although I did recall a strange dream about Emmy chasing a spider around the cabin in the early hours. Really, I should cut down on the alcohol. And I could do with a headache pill.

Reluctantly, I peeled myself away from the view. The cabin may not have had an en-suite like our bedroom at home, but with the bathroom next door and only Emmy in residence, at least I didn't need to bother getting dressed. Not when I was wearing the same outfit as her—an oversized T-shirt and another pair of Mitchell's boxers. It felt a little strange wearing a man's clothes but surprisingly comfortable. I choked back a laugh at what Douglas would say if he saw me. He liked me to wear something silky from Victoria's Secret to bed, not a tatty grey shroud. I couldn't imagine wearing Douglas's Y-fronts either.

The wooden floor chilled the soles of my feet as I stepped off the rug and tiptoed out of the door. I needed slippers or maybe a pair of thick socks. Hmmm... Did Mitchell have any hidden away in a drawer upstairs?

I was so busy thinking about the merits of underfloor heating, I didn't see the man by the kitchen counter until I got to the bathroom door. When I did catch a glimpse, my first thought was that the hitman had caught up with me, and I let out a squeak that was half mouse, half dolphin.

Then I saw Emmy standing in the kitchen, relaxed as she poured water from the kettle into a pair of mugs, and a blush spread up my cheeks.

Way to go, Georgia.

What should I do? I could hardly ignore the visitor,

but my attire was far from suitable for greeting a stranger. My cheeks burned as I swivelled to face him.

"Ah good, you're up," Emmy said. "Do you want coffee?"

Well, she hadn't bothered getting dressed either. At least I wasn't the only one dressed like a vagrant although the situation was still far from ideal.

"Yes, please."

I straightened up and took a step towards the kitchen, wishing with all my heart I'd stayed in my room. I felt naked without a fashionable dress and smart shoes. My feelings of inadequacy only got stronger as I took in the newcomer. Although he was seated, he looked big—not just tall but with the broad shoulders that only came from manual labour or a serious gym habit. His hair was a delicious mess of molten dark chocolate, with matching eyes half-hidden by a pair of thick-framed glasses. They should've been geeky, but on him... *Stop it, Georgia.*

As I walked over, his lips smiled, but his eyes didn't. "Is there anyone in this house who's not wearing my underwear?"

Emmy didn't bat an eyelid. "Depends on whether you've decided to go commando or not."

His underwear? Oh hell, was this Mitchell Gray? Tell me I was still stuck in a dream. Or rather, a nightmare. I pinched my eyes closed then opened them again. Nope—he was still there.

When Emmy described him as an old friend, I'd imagined someone, well, old. You know the type—straggly hair, unfashionable clothes, a bit of a stoop. This man could have stepped out of a Calvin Klein ad. Except he didn't wear Calvin Klein. He wore Armani. I knew that because that was what Emmy had tossed me out of his underwear drawer last night.

What were the chances of me disappearing into the floor? Not good, I imagined. You know, if the hitman planned to make another appearance, now would have been an excellent time.

I stood there like an idiot as Mitchell stood up in all his manly gorgeousness and held out his hand. Just as Emmy said, he looked grumpy.

"Georgia Rutherford-Beaumont. I'm pleased to meet you."

His hand was dry, his grip firm. As opposed to mine, which was a hot, sweaty mess, just like the rest of me. My hair had an awful tendency to stick out in all directions first thing in the morning, and I could only imagine what I looked like. A witch? A gremlin? Up close, Mitchell's face was flawless apart from an ever-so-slightly crooked nose, as if it got broken once and hadn't been set quite right.

Without a doubt, this was the most embarrassing moment of my life.

"Mitch Gray." His velvety voice resonated through my core.

"I'm sorry about wearing your things. I've been a little short of clothes."

"I don't suppose it was your idea." He glared at Emmy, who smirked.

"Lighten up. Any other man would enjoy watching a couple of women parading around in his underwear."

"Fair point."

She threw a banana at him, which he neatly caught and began to peel. How could she act so calmly?

"I'd better make that coffee," she said. "It's shit this

morning, though."

"Why?"

She pointed at a jar. "Instant."

"What happened to the machine?"

"It malfunctioned. I'm gonna head into town in a minute and buy a new one."

"Oh. Uh, I guess I'd still like a cup." Anything to help wake up.

Mitchell—Mitch—took a sip from his own mug and grimaced. "Get some groceries while you're there, would you?"

"Anything in particular?"

"Grapefruit. Eggs. Enough food for at least a week. You know what I like, but I expect our guest will have her own preferences."

From the way he said it while looking over his glasses, I knew he'd already made up his mind about me. Georgia Rutherford-Beaumont, spoiled rich girl. Maybe I should invent some fad diet to live up to his expectations? Oh, who was I kidding? I'd never dare.

"Okay, grapefruit and eggs. Georgia, do you want anything?"

"Nothing in particular. I'll eat whatever's on hand." Even if I hated it.

I mean, I'd stomached a whole plate of steak tartare at a dinner with Douglas last year then excused myself to the bathroom to throw it up. I was in good company. Half the girls in attendance puked up everything they ever ate.

"In that case..." She grabbed the car keys. "I won't be long."

As soon as the front door closed behind Emmy, I mumbled an apology to Mitch and dashed into the bathroom. I longed for a soak in the tub, mainly so I wouldn't have to face the man outside again in a hurry, but instead, I did the sensible thing and took a shower. With no makeup and no hairdryer, making myself presentable wasn't an easy task. I clipped my damp hair into a knot on top of my head then checked myself in the mirror. Not quite the dragged-through-a-forest-backwards look I'd had going on this morning but not great either.

Now, how could I rectify the terrible impression I'd made on Mitch earlier?

He was sitting at the table when I walked back into the great room, his mug empty by his side. I picked it up and headed for the kitchen. The cabin didn't have a dishwasher, so I could help by washing up.

"You don't have to do that."

That voice. It made me tingle in places it shouldn't.

"I feel bad enough for being here. At least let me make myself useful."

"Emmy told me what happened. I know you're about as thrilled as I am with this arrangement, so let's just deal with it, okay?"

"But the way I'm imposing on you like this... If I could go home..." My safe, dull, existence with Douglas looked more attractive by the second.

He waved a hand. "Like I said, we'll cope. If the situation was reversed, I know Emmy would do the same for me."

"I'll keep out of your way as much as possible."

"Appreciated."

Oh, what a contrast he was to Nick. This residence might be a hundred times more luxurious than the first safe house, but I felt a thousand times more uncomfortable. Nick went out of his way to make me feel at home, like I was a friend rather than an imposition. Mitch? Well, I didn't expect much sympathy from him. All I could do was be helpful so I didn't upset him.

"Would you like breakfast? I can make whatever you want."

"I'm not hungry."

"Do you mind if I eat something?"

"As opposed to what? Starving?"

I took that to mean a no, although not a very polite one. There was one egg left in the refrigerator, and I made it into an omelette with a handful of chopped pepper. No cheese.

Rather than sit at the table with Mitch, I ate at the kitchen counter, although I couldn't help sneaking a few glances as he tapped away on his laptop. He really was disturbingly handsome. Don't get me wrong, Douglas wasn't ugly. But even when we went on our first date, and he dressed up in a suit with a matching tie and pocket square, he didn't take my breath away.

With Mitch, it felt as if all the oxygen had been sucked out of the room.

I'd just washed and dried my plate when Emmy returned, complete with a fancy coffee machine in a huge box.

"Can I help with anything?"

"There's bags of groceries in the car. Would you

mind carrying a couple?"

Mitch ignored us while we shuttled back and forth with enough food for a small army. Was he expecting more guests? I helped unpack and stow everything in the cupboards, arranging the supplies in a logical order. Fresh food at the front, tins and dried at the back. Ooh, Emmy bought flour, eggs and sugar. Did Mitch have a cake pan? I felt a sudden need to bake.

I didn't want to disturb him by asking, not while he had a knife in his hands. It seemed he'd got his appetite back because he'd started chopping up a pile of fruit at the counter. Wow. He got through a banana in two and a half seconds. Did he work in a kitchen when he was younger? He sure knew how to handle a knife.

"You want fruit salad?" Emmy asked. "I got yogurt to go with it."

"No, thank you. I already ate breakfast."

Emmy and Mitch both filled bowls then moved to the couch at the far end of the great room. I tried to hear what they were saying, but their voices were too quiet. No doubt they were talking about me—most probably assessing my chances of getting out of this mess alive. They sat close, obviously comfortable with each other. What was the story there? What history did they share?

Curiosity ate away inside me, but I didn't dare to ask.

After an awkward lunch where Mitch forked down a couple of chicken breasts and a pile of salad and ignored both me and Emmy, she gave me a sympathetic pat on the arm.

"You're not gonna like this, but I need to go."

"Back to Virginia?"

"Yeah. I need to get to the bottom of this issue. But you'll be safe with Mitch—don't worry."

When we'd first arrived at the cabin, my main concerns had been staying alive while I was in an assassin's crosshairs and how I'd placate Douglas if I did eventually make it home. Now, I had the added worry of spending the foreseeable future with a man who wasn't my husband, who appeared to dislike me, but who somehow still made my knees go weak. It promised to be an uncomfortable time ahead.

But I could hardly tell Emmy that, could I? She seemed entirely unaffected by Mitch's presence. Of course, after working with Nick and some of the other Blackwood men I'd met, she'd probably built up an immunity to looks that could melt panties.

"I'm sure I'll be fine. Mitch seems...nice."

She picked up her holdall and hefted it over her shoulder. "Nah, mostly he behaves like an asshole. But underneath he's a good person. Never forget that."

"I'll try not to. Really, I'm incredibly grateful he's letting me stay." I followed Emmy as she walked to the front door. "Will you tell Douglas I miss him?"

"Sure."

"And my parents?"

"I'm going to be kind of busy, but I will if I see them."

"Of course. I'm so sorry for imposing. It's just... I'm a little homesick."

"We all get that way, but the sooner we can fix things, the sooner you can come back."

And I was holding her up. Oh, how I longed to hop in the car beside her and go back to my old life.

"Are you driving all the way?"

"I'll probably jump on a plane at some point."

"Will you let me know what's going on?"

"I'll contact you through Mitch. If I don't get in touch, it's because nothing's happened."

We were standing on the porch by then, and I threw my arms around her in an impromptu hug. Normally, I wasn't the hugging kind, but in that moment it felt like the right thing to do.

After a second, she hugged me back.

"Thank you for everything," I mumbled into her hair. "For saving my life and driving me halfway across the country."

She pulled away and headed towards the Camry. "No problem. I'm only doing my job." She bleeped the locks open. "I'll see you soon, yeah?"

I certainly hoped so.

Chapter 17

SO THAT WAS it. Emmy had gone back to Virginia, leaving me alone with Mitch, a man I'd only met a couple of hours ago. We were now officially roommates.

That thought alone tempted me to take up camping. Funny how the cabin had seemed so spacious when I first arrived, but now the walls were closing in like that scene in *Indiana Jones and the Temple of Doom* when Indy and Shorty were trapped in that awful cave with all the bugs outside. Only I had a hitman rather than scorpions waiting for me.

Okay, maybe camping wasn't such an attractive proposition.

Anyway, this couldn't be worse than college, could it? I'd had a roommate there. Yes, she'd been the bulimic, bitchy vice-captain of the cheerleading squad, with a penchant for borrowing my things without asking and a tendency to bonk other people's boyfriends, but she'd been a roommate nonetheless. And I'd survived, hadn't I?

An image popped into my head of Mitch in a cheerleading outfit, complete with pom-poms, and a snort of laughter escaped. He gave me a quizzical look over the top of his laptop, brows pinched. Nope, not helping.

I retreated to the furthest sofa and flicked through an architectural magazine from the shelf under the coffee table. The homes were spectacular, but I couldn't concentrate. Nor could I stop sneaking looks at Mitch. Once, he caught me and scowled, and I hastily switched my gaze to the window. Whoops.

By late afternoon, I'd read the same five chapters of a book on the political history of Israel six times over, and I could take the strained silence no more.

"I'm going to cook dinner. Do you have any requests?"

If I kept busy, it would be easier not to think about him.

"No, I don't. Make what you like. Emmy bought me TV dinners, so I'll eat one of those later."

"But I can easily do dinner for two." Oh hell—that made it sound like I wanted to sit down to a cosy, candlelit meal. "I mean, it's no trouble. All I need to do is double the quantities."

"Like I said, do what you want."

Ugh—Mitch might be very nice to look at, but he was exasperating. A simple yes or no would have sufficed, but he'd already fixed his eyes back on his computer. Well, I'd just need to make something delicious, wouldn't I? And even if I said it myself, I could damn well cook. Douglas expected every meal to be a masterpiece, and when we first married I'd taken cooking lessons. I could prepare three courses for twelve in my sleep.

After a quick rummage through the cupboards, I decided on risotto. Emmy certainly had gone overboard on the vegetables when she went shopping. And, let's see...trifle for dessert.

Dessert solved everything.

"Do you have any truffle oil?" I asked absentmindedly once I'd plated up the risotto an hour and a half later.

Mitch tore his eyes away from the screen to give me a bemused look. "Do I seem like the kind of guy who has truffle oil?"

"Um..."

"I live halfway up a mountain in a log cabin."

"You have a hot tub and an Italian coffee machine." He didn't exactly rough it.

"I'll give you the hot tub, but Emmy bought the coffee machine."

"Only because the other one broke."

"She bought that one too."

So I was right about them having a history. Enough of one for her to buy him an expensive household appliance, anyway. "Have you known Emmy long?"

He sighed and gave a non-answer. "Long enough."

I set the food out on the table, sans truffle oil, and he finally shut down the laptop and gave me his attention. Then I wished he hadn't. Intense eyes bored into my soul, and I didn't want to think what they might find there.

"I hope you like risotto."

"Thanks." It came out grudgingly.

"It's honestly not a bother. My husband, Douglas, likes me to cook him a proper meal every day, unless of course we're attending a function or dining out, so I'm used to making dinner."

He took a forkful then pierced me with his gaze

again. "And what do you like?"

"Sorry?"

"You said that's what your husband likes. What do you like?"

What did I like? Growing up, of course, we'd had a housekeeper, but when I'd started college, perhaps the only time I'd ever been free to be myself, I preferred to veg out on the sofa with a bowl of instant mac and cheese than spend the afternoon baking dinner rolls. But that was in another lifetime.

"It doesn't matter what I like."

He gave me a sharp look but didn't comment, just returned to his plate. Silence reigned for the rest of the main course. I didn't mind. It wasn't as if I knew what to say to him, anyway.

I saved room for trifle, and once I'd cleared the plates away, I set the bowl on the table. I'd taken my frustrations out on the whipped cream, so it was beautifully light and fluffy.

Mitch took one look and pushed his chair back. "I don't eat dessert."

"Sorry. I shouldn't have assumed." Douglas loved my desserts. Time and time again he told me a meal wasn't complete without one.

But Mitch turned his back and climbed the stairs to his loft, leaving me alone with enough pudding for six people. His light clicked off a few minutes later. Feeling more miserable than I had since I left Virginia, I scooped a portion of trifle into a bowl. Then another. And another. I ate almost the whole damn thing then felt utterly sick as I threw the last dregs away in disgust. What was wrong with me?

I shouldn't let a man affect me like that. What did it

matter what Mitch thought of me? I just had to make the best of the situation and stay alive until I could go home. If Mitch hated me, so be it.

Oh my... I sat up on the sofa at seven in the morning, drenched, trying to erase the image of a muscled chest from my mind. Since the shooting, my scrappy sleep had been plagued by nightmares about headless waiters and black shadows chasing me, hour after hour until I woke in a cold sweat. Except today. Today I was a sweaty mess. I'd never seen Mitchell Gray without a shirt on, but my mind took liberties and decided to fill in the blanks.

Luckily, he was nowhere to be seen when I scooted to my bedroom with lank hair plastered to my head, cursing myself for falling asleep while I watched the TV. I glanced up at Mitch's loft, but there was no sign of him. Thank goodness. I'd learned my lesson yesterday and pulled on a sweater and jeans before venturing out again. Hell, I'd have worn a muumuu if I'd had one.

Only when I felt vaguely human again did I make my way to the kitchen and attempt to use Emmy's coffee machine. It had more buttons than a fighter jet. Where had she gone to buy it—Denver or the moon? I picked up the little manual she'd left next to it and found it was all in Italian. My mistake. She'd obviously popped over to Rome. I flicked through the pictures, trying to work out where the coffee went. I'd found the little metal cup thingy on the draining board, but where did it fit?

Warm breath on my neck had me clutching at my

chest.

"Need some help?"

"Where the h... I mean, where did you come from?" I hadn't even heard Mitch approach.

"I was painting."

I struggled to regain my composure. "No, I mean, well, yes. I can't understand the instructions. They're in Italian."

He sighed, reached over and plucked the manual from my fingers. I caught a whiff of expensive cologne and inhaled deeply. Good heavens, was I actually smelling him? I got a hold of myself and took a step back, thankful he didn't seem to have noticed.

He flipped through the booklet then took the metal thing from my hand. "It slots in here."

I blinked in surprise. "You speak Italian?"

"The fruits of a misspent youth."

The machine was soon hissing away, and Mitch fetched a grapefruit from the refrigerator.

"Want one?" He held it out.

"Ugh, no." I loved oranges, and lemons and limes certainly had their place in moderation, or in gin, but grapefruit? They were Satan's idea of a joke.

"Suit yourself." The blade of the knife flashed as Mitch chopped the fruit into segments and dropped them into a bowl, then he leaned back against the counter, bowl in one hand and fork in the other, as he watched me prepare my breakfast.

I poured granola into a bowl, dropped my spoon on the floor, picked it up, and rinsed it, all the time wishing he'd move away. His gaze made me uncomfortable, as did his silence.

"Have you lived here long?" I asked. Anything to

break the spell.

"Define long."

He wasn't going to make this easy, was he? "More than a few years?"

"In that case, no."

"Um, do you have any plans for today?"

"Yes."

I tried once more. "It looks like it's going to be a beautiful day."

He glanced out the window. "It does."

Mitch was so frustrating! Why couldn't he just have a conversation? I narrowed my eyes at him then remembered I was a guest in his home. Not even a guest, really. More of an intruder. I had no right to be annoyed. In fact, I should be grateful he was letting me stay at all. Trying not to let my irritation show, I schooled my face into expression number one, blank, and sat down at the table.

He continued to watch me. I said nothing.

Five minutes later, he finished his grapefruit and dropped the bowl on the counter then climbed the stairs into his studio. Although the room only had a railing, like the sleeping loft, he'd set up a series of easels along it which meant I couldn't see him.

Alone once more, I leaned back in my seat and blew out a breath. I didn't understand that man. I was fairly sure I didn't even like him. But there was something, some aura that drew me towards him, like a moth towards a raging bonfire. Or a funeral pyre.

After I'd cleared the table, I meandered around downstairs, all the while keeping an eye on the studio for movement. There was a bookshelf behind the sofa containing a truly eclectic collection of books. At least seven languages from what I could tell, although several of the tomes didn't use the Roman alphabet. What were they? Arabic? Persian? Most were non-fiction—memoirs, travel, history. I spotted *The Art of War* by Sun Tzu—hardly bedtime reading, unless he was an insomniac, of course. In that instance it might work quite well. At the end of one shelf, I found a couple of dog-eared paperbacks, and selected a second-rate spy thriller to borrow.

I settled down in one of the armchairs to read, but every so often I'd catch myself glancing up at the studio, hoping for a glimpse of Mitch. What was my problem? Why should I care what he was doing? The book. That must be it. I was bored with the book. I wasn't even halfway through, and I already knew who did it and why.

Ten minutes later, I couldn't help looking again. This time I got up and moved to the couch underneath the studio floor, thereby removing all temptation to ogle things I shouldn't. I forced myself to read page after page, and it was with a sigh of relief that I turned the last one. Task completed, I threw the book down on the coffee table with a satisfying thwack and prepared to lever myself up.

"Good book?" Mitch asked from just behind my ear, making me jump. When had he come down the stairs? Was he human or part ghost?

The hint of a smile that flickered at his lips suggested he found me amusing for some reason. Or did I have something on my face? Yogurt, maybe? I resisted the urge to wipe my mouth and stood my ground as he studied me.

Which gave me the chance to take a better look at

him too. He hadn't shaved, and the faint shadow around his jaw made him even more attractive. His tousled hair, his high cheekbones, the faint look of expectation on his face. Wait. What was that for? Oh yes, he asked me a question. Probably I should answer it.

"Yes, the book was wonderful, thank you. I hope you don't mind me borrowing it?"

"Borrow away. When I read it, I thought it was shit."

Douglas abhorred foul language, and I'd always been extremely careful to mind my mouth while I was near him. Douglas would also never voice a strong opinion like that. A true politician, he changed his opinions the way most people changed their socks, depending on whose company he was in, and was always careful to keep as close to the middle ground as possible. For that reason, I wasn't used to undisguised crudeness, and that was why my mouth dropped open.

"Open your mind before your mouth," Mitch said.

I snapped it shut. "What?"

"It's a quote by Aristophanes. You just reminded me of it. It means you should be open-minded and think things through before speaking."

How dare he judge me? "I am open-minded."

"Sweetheart, you're a spoiled little rich girl. You don't know enough about how the world works to be open-minded."

Oh, how I itched to pick up the book and throw it at him. Or better yet, the coffee table. That would leave a nice dent in his chiselled jaw. But I couldn't do that because, after all, his view was one the world shared. The senator's daughter who had it all and wanted for nothing. But honestly? If I stripped away the bullshit I fed everyone, including myself? I hated it. Hated it all.

And I'd also look like the most ungrateful witch this side of Kansas if I admitted that little fact to anybody. Mind you, what did that make Mitch? The Tin Man? I swallowed back a laugh.

"I'll take your assessment on board."

"What's so funny?"

"Nothing."

Nothing at all.

The next day was more of the same. We ate breakfast. If I asked a question, I got a non-answer, a sarcastic comment, or occasionally a rude one. Thankfully, Mitch disappeared into his studio all day again. It was easier to put up with this hellishly awful situation without his creepy stare following me around.

To take my mind off him, I did what I always did in times of stress, and baked. I'd done a lot of baking over the years. I'd even won contests for it. Make me angry, you got a quiche. Make me cry, you got cupcakes.

Today, I did what I could with the ingredients available, and by the time he emerged from his studio in the early evening, the kitchen counters were stacked full.

"What the hell is all this?"

I glanced up. "That's a lasagne." I smiled sweetly. "I thought you might be hungry."

"And the rest of it?"

I shrugged. "Snacks."

"Fuck me," he muttered under his breath as he

picked up a serving spoon and dolloped a lump of lasagne onto a plate.

A part of me hoped he liked it. The other part of me hoped he choked on it. My public persona forced expression number three, polite indifference, onto my face as I took a seat opposite.

He forked the whole plateful down without a word, and for that I was grateful. Now I'd got used to the quiet, I realised life with Mitch was easier without words. When he finished, I put on a smile and cleared his plate away like the well-trained wife I was.

"Would you like a cookie? I made three kinds. Or some cake?"

When he answered, "Yeah, just gimme whatever," I wanted to hurl them at him, plate and all.

CHAPTER 18

XAV LEANED ON the railing of the balcony outside his studio, cup of coffee in hand. The early morning sun hadn't yet burned off the last wisps of mist, and they hung in the trees like the spirits local legend said haunted these woods. He loved these kind of mornings. The crack of a twig as a deer walked through the forest, the distant burble of the mountain stream that ran through the property. Up above, a red-tailed hawk soared high above the treetops.

But alas, the peace wasn't to last. He picked up the cheap cell phone sitting on the table and dialled.

Three rings then, "Yeah."

"You home?" He spoke softly out of habit. Well aware of Georgia's propensity to eavesdrop, he'd checked she was still asleep before making the call. There was nobody to hear his words but the sparrow perched on the railing a few feet away.

"About two hours ago," Emmy replied.

"Any news?"

"The journey was shit, thanks for asking. And no, I haven't had any sleep."

He laughed. "I can tell. And?"

"So far, the fucker's got away clean. The charge he used to blow out the window was Russian, which means it could have been anyone."

Xav was all too aware how easy it was to buy Russian-made arms on the black market. Hadn't he done the same thing many times before? "What about the cameras?"

"We've got his height, skin colour, and a vague face shape. That's all."

"Did anyone speak to him?"

"Isaiah, when he answered the door. The dude's accent said New York, but what does that mean? I mean, we've both got American accents when we want them and neither one of us is from the same bloody continent."

"*Benzona.*" He swore in Hebrew out of habit. "This could run and run."

"Don't I fucking know it."

"And how's the equine situation?"

"Interesting. There's an issue with one of the horses which may not be salvageable. Mr. H is talking about euthanasia."

"Who?"

"It's not certain yet. If he plays his cards right, he might survive."

Ace. The weird asshole with the playing cards. Xav didn't know much about him, but from the whispers he'd heard over the years, Ace hailed from Europe, most likely Spain. Not only that, he enjoyed his job a little too much and loved to show off his skills.

"Does that have anything to do with this problem?"

"That's the question we're all asking. The naughty pony broke away from his handler and disappeared. We're all listening out for the pitter patter of hooves."

"Shit."

"Have you been getting in plenty of target

practice?"

"I hate you more with each passing day."

"Aw, but I brought you a pretty lady. How are you getting on?"

How indeed? He'd split his time yesterday between painting and watching Georgia on his laptop screen as she poked around his home. Cute. She thought she'd been subtle, but even if the cameras hadn't been installed, she'd left enough things out of place to reveal her curiosity.

But afterwards, when he'd gone downstairs to act like an asshole again? In between the flashes of anger in her eyes, he'd detected a deep-seated hurt that made him want to wrap her up in his arms and hold her until it went away.

What the hell was that all about?

"She's too damn nice to have made enemies of her own. I've behaved like a total shit for two days, and the meaner I am, the sweeter she gets."

"You're sure?"

"Yesterday, after she asked if I had family living nearby, and I reminded her we don't all have rich daddies around to spoil us, she started cooking. There's cookies and shit everywhere. I'm gonna have to start working out more if she keeps that up." He poked his abs, checking he hadn't grown a spare tire overnight. "When she handed me a plateful, her mouth was smiling but her eyes said she wanted to poison me."

"Did you check she hadn't?"

"All that stuff's well and truly locked away, believe me."

"So you agree with my take on her?"

He looked into the distance, where a pair of pigeons

squabbled over a tree branch. "That she's non-confrontational? Absolutely. She never says what she thinks. You can practically hear the cogs turning, see what she's thinking from her face and eyes, then she shuts it down and says something totally different."

"I know what you mean. And that takes years of practice. A lifetime, maybe."

He took a long gulp from his mug. "So where do we go from here?"

"How's the coffee?"

"The coffee's good. Answer the question."

"So far, the list of suspects is into three figures and growing every day. Her husband turned over all the threats he's received—twelve of them—but getting details from the senator is proving more difficult."

"He's not cooperating?"

"*He* is, but we keep hitting walls with the US Capitol Police. They have the records, and he sent any letters he received to them as well. They just insist they've followed proper procedure, yadda, yadda, yadda, and that they can't hand information over to a private agency."

"Keep trying."

"We are, believe me. And we've still got this *fucking* traitor."

"No progress there?"

"Mack's working around the clock, as is Red. Neither of them has slept in days, and Mack's fiancé's full-time on it as well."

"Have I met him?"

"No—he's another computer geek. Something'll give, sooner or later."

A long sigh escaped him. "It's the later I'm afraid

of." Georgia drove him crazy, but not for the reasons Emmy thought.

"But you can keep her for a while?"

He rolled his eyes, even though Emmy couldn't see. "You make her sound like a pet."

"More of a pet project. Somebody needs to teach her to stand up for herself. Her husband's a prick."

"I got that impression from speaking to her."

"We've got guards on him and the parents twenty-four-seven until we fix the leak, and so far, Douglas has complained Isaiah's tattoos don't fit with his public image, and Joe's hair is too short. Makes him look like a thug, apparently."

"Does the man have any redeeming qualities?"

"If he does, we haven't found them. Georgia's dad asked if you could pass on that everyone's doing what they can and to hang in there. Her mom asked you to tell her that they both love her and everything will be all right. Hubby wants to know where the dry cleaning tickets are because he's having trouble finding them."

He imagined Emmy shaking her head in incredulity at the other end of the line. "Asshole. I'm not asking her."

"With you on that. Although if I did know where they were, I'd let myself into the house again and burn them."

Xav chuckled. "I'm still not asking her. Have you been looking at the husband?"

"Oh come on, give us a little credit. Not found anything yet apart from the fact he likes porn, but that's nothing unusual. As well as being a prick, he's a sneaky little weasel. Mack's still unravelling email trails and bank accounts. He's got an alibi for the country club shooting, and if he decided to hire in help, I don't know where he'd have got the money. He doesn't earn as much as he'd like everyone to think, and he's got ten thousand dollars of debt on his credit card."

"Life insurance on Georgia?"

"Half a million, five years into a ten-year policy. Nothing spectacular. Either it's not him or he's fucking careful."

"I suppose he'd have to be, given that he wants to be in the White House."

"Oh yeah, get this. You know how little girls practise writing out their imaginary married name to see what it looks like?"

"Women do that?"

"Yeah. Well, not me, obviously, seeing as I didn't plan on getting married until five minutes before I did it, and even then I was so fucking drunk I wasn't sure whether I had or not. But yeah."

"Who says romance is dead?"

"Hey, my beloved gave me a customised set of throwing knives last week. Romance isn't dead."

But somebody else would be. "Your point was?"

"Oh, yeah, when I went through the Beaumont house, I found a sheet of paper in his desk drawer where he'd written out 'President Beaumont,' like, a hundred times."

"You're kidding?"

"Nope. It was right there between his dirty magazine collection and a handful of articles about Barack Obama's 2008 election campaign."

"I'm tempted to shoot him just for being an asshole."

"You and me both, Xav, you and me both."

He hung up the phone, the situation leaving him with mixed emotions. Frustration because the investigation was getting nowhere fast, and now he was stuck with Georgia for the foreseeable future. His carefully constructed existence was about to be turned on its head.

But also relief, because he'd get the chance to prove he wasn't the douche she'd first thought. And that worried him. Not that she'd thought he was a douche, but because he *wanted* to prove that he wasn't. Having feelings for a woman was dangerous.

But not as dangerous as the flicker of anticipation that sparked to life inside his belly. He'd missed this life. The game. The thrill of the chase, although he was more used to being the hunter than the hunted.

He'd never lost, and he didn't intend to start now.

CHAPTER 19

OVER THE NEXT two weeks, I settled into life on Mitch's mountain, and as I did so, I noticed the changes in him. Although he remained quiet and slightly moody, after the initial few days, he stopped with the rudeness and sarcasm.

We fell into a routine. At sunrise, I'd hear the door slam as he left the cabin, followed by footsteps on the stairs and the hiss of his shower when he returned an hour later. One morning, curiosity got the better of me, and I dragged myself out of bed a few minutes after he left, curled up on the sofa with a book, and waited for him to come back.

And I wasn't disappointed. When he walked through the door, he lifted the bottom of his shirt to wipe his sweat-soaked face, giving me a perfect view of his abs. Eight perfectly defined squares of muscle I wanted to trace with my tongue. *Mental note: Set the alarm clock for this time every morning.*

"Running? You go running?"

He dropped the hem, and I stifled a groan.

"It's important to stay fit."

I thought of my country club membership and the rows of treadmills I'd avoided whenever possible. Since I got to the mountain I'd done more eating than moving, and my clothes were getting tight. Funny how maintaining a size-four figure became less important when there weren't other women around to monitor my waistline.

"I always found motivation a problem in the gym."

"Then don't go to the gym. Get outside in the fresh air. Do you want to come with me tomorrow?"

Well, that idea had pros and cons. The possibility of Mitch flashing his chest again had to be weighed up carefully against the embarrassment of collapsing from exhaustion before I got halfway around.

"Maybe."

He chuckled. "Let me know."

After he showered, Mitch ate breakfast, usually a pile of grapefruit washed down with coffee, then disappeared into his studio. It was the one place in the cabin I'd never been, and although I longed to creep in there and poke around, it seemed too personal somehow. Odd, seeing as I'd been into his bedroom several times to collect his laundry, and that didn't feel awkward. But Mitch didn't volunteer to show me his paintings, and I didn't ask. He kept that side of himself private.

While Mitch worked, I'd curl up on the sofa, usually with a book, but sometimes with the TV on. The signal flickered a little, and he didn't have all the channels, which made reading even more attractive. My favourite sofa was the big squashy sectional at the front of the cabin—I could curl up in it like a nest, and it had a pleasant view over the front...well, it was hardly a garden. More of a clearing. Every so often Mitch would clomp around in the studio above, reminding me I wasn't alone.

And that was my biggest problem—loneliness. The

only person I had to talk to was Mitch, and he seemed quite content to be on his own. I knew painting was his job, but I found myself waiting for the evenings when he'd finish work so we could eat dinner together. A bowl of soup, or a stew, maybe a quiche. And it wasn't just the company I craved. It was *his* company, no matter how much I tried to convince myself otherwise.

By the end of the second week, I'd worked my way through half of Mitch's book collection. Since I was a child, when I devoured classics like *Nancy Drew* and *The Hardy Boys*, I'd been a voracious reader, and getting through two novels in a day wasn't unusual. Once I finished all the fiction in English and French, I moved onto the non-fiction. The biography of Benjamin Franklin proved more interesting than I thought, as did a book on Queen, the band, not the monarch. The manual on how to build a shed? Not so much. But if someone gave me a piece of wood and a saw, I thought I'd have a good shot at being able to make a dovetail joint. I'd even started reading Sun Tzu.

I'd also used the peace of the cabin to do a lot of soul searching. In some ways I felt trapped on the mountain, but I also felt a freedom I'd never had before. For the first time my life didn't revolve around Douglas and his needs, wants and whims, or my father and his politics. I didn't have to get up early to put on makeup and do my hair. If I wanted to wear jeans all day, I could. If I wanted to have cornflakes for lunch, I could. If I wanted to spend the entire afternoon doing nothing but reading a book and staring out of the window, I could. I didn't miss the formal dinners. I didn't miss the lunches with my pretend friends. And I didn't even miss date night.

No, I had two hands, and with Mitch tormenting my dreams every night, I'd learned how to use my fingers to bring myself more pleasure than Douglas ever had.

I squinted at the recipe book at the beginning of week three then rocked back on my heels.

"Mitch?"

"Yeah?" He was spending a rare morning downstairs, albeit engrossed in his laptop.

"What's *backpulver*?"

"What?"

"I wanted to try some new recipes. I found this cookbook but it's in German. At least, I think it's German." Luckily, it had pictures.

"Oh. Baking powder."

I'd given up asking how Mitch knew so many languages. When I'd asked about the Arabic books he told me he'd been on vacation to Sharm El Sheikh once and picked up a few words from the tour guide.

"When you next go into town, could you pick some up, please? I've almost run out. And *pistazien*?"

"Pistachios?"

"Yes, those."

"You realise there are only two of us, and most of what you're making's going in the garbage?"

I knew that. I'd thrown away almost a whole cake yesterday. How could I expect him to understand it wasn't the food itself I craved, it was the process of making it? It helped me relax. But if Mitch didn't want me cooking so much, I'd have to manage without.

"Sorry, you're right. Don't worry about it. But could you...?" Oh hell, now this was embarrassing. "Could you pick up some tampons?" The stress had made my periods go haywire, but I had to be due one soon.

Well, that got a reaction. His eyes widened, and a few seconds later, he pushed his chair back. "Why don't you come with me and get them yourself?"

A trip out? Was that possible? "Is that safe?"

"Emmy said nobody followed her here, and if she said that, nobody did. And when I went into town, I told Patsy in the grocery store my girlfriend was staying with me, and you'd had trouble with an ex bothering you. And when I say I told Patsy, that means the whole town knew by next morning at the latest."

"So you don't think the hitman's around?"

"If a stranger asked about you in Wolf's Corner, I'd have got seventeen phone calls, 'just in case.' It's a small town thing."

I wished he'd told me that before. On the nights my dirty dreams woke me up, I couldn't get back to sleep again from imagining the man who wanted me dead creeping through the woods in the dark.

"Thank goodness."

"So, are you ready to go?"

Most definitely. The thought of getting off the mountain for an hour or two had me dancing towards the door. Then I remembered my shoes and tugged the pair of Converse out from under the side table.

"If we're going to a supermarket, can I get shampoo?" I'd been rationing myself so far.

"Get what you like." His eyes paused on my face. "You need a visit to the salon as well."

Well, Mitch, you sure knew how to make a girl feel

pretty. "Thanks." It came out flat.

"I meant you should consider a change of style. Long, blonde hair doesn't exactly fade into the background."

"Oh. Of course." And come to think of it, I recalled Emmy suggesting the same thing.

"And your new name is Vivien."

"Vivien?"

"My mother's favourite movie was *Gone with the Wind*."

He ushered me out of the door as I took in that new piece of information. It was the first thing he'd told me about his family. The first indication he'd given that he had one. Who was Mitch?

Five minutes later, I sat beside Mitch as he steered his Land Rover down the mountain. Going down proved a lot easier than coming up, especially when you weren't in a Toyota Camry.

"Is Wolf's Corner far?"

"A fifteen-minute drive."

Wolf's Corner called itself a town, but that made the motley collection of streets and its handful of stores sound more impressive than the reality.

"It's not very big."

"People just drive to Denver if they want to buy anything serious."

"Are we far from Denver?" I knew we were in Colorado, obviously, but the specifics of the location had evaded me.

"About an hour and a half."

So we weren't quite as isolated as I thought.

Our first stop was Daisy Mae's Hair and Beauty. The peeling paint on the dusty storefront made me pause outside the door.

"Is Daisy Mae experienced?"

Mitch pointed at his own tousled mess. "Does it look like I know?"

"I guess not, but..."

"I haven't heard any horror stories, if that's what you're asking, and most of the women in town go there."

In that case, I was probably safe. But the place was a world away from what I was used to. Back in Richmond, I had my hair cut by Sven, who used to be a Hollywood A-lister's personal stylist. He'd start off by critically examining my hair, sucking in a breath every time he spotted a split end, before prescribing me the latest must-have treatment that he swore would fix the problem. Then he'd demand the scissors from his assistant and snip, snip, snip, soon my hair would be cut just the way he wanted it.

So when I sat down in the worn but comfortable chair in Daisy Mae's and she asked me what style I wanted, I was at a loss.

"Um, what do you think?"

"Not my hair, honey. Do you want to page through some magazines? Maybe pick out a few looks you like?"

She left me with a dozen, and I leafed through, discounting anything too fiddly. Picking my own hairstyle was more difficult than I thought. Mitch had left me some cash then gone to the hardware store, and there weren't even any other customers I could ask for a second opinion. After flipping through each page twice, the style that stuck in my head was a shoulder-length bob with a side fringe. It sure would dry faster than my long layers.

But Douglas had always told me to keep my hair long. Did I dare go for such a radical change? He'd hate it.

Then I thought back to the conversation I'd had with Mitch a couple of days ago, after he'd disappeared outside for an update with Emmy.

"Is there any news?" I'd asked.

"Nothing concrete. They're still hunting down leads, but the problem is volume. Your father made a lot of enemies over the years."

He'd only ever tried to do right, but for every group of people who supported his policies, a handful of others hated them. Politics was a difficult game, and it seemed now he'd made a wrong move.

"I miss him."

"He said to keep your chin up, and he's doing everything he can to help catch the man."

"Emmy saw him?"

"She met both your parents. Your mom said she hopes you're remembering to take your vitamins, and don't worry because she's had your favourite boutiques keep aside a selection of new season dresses in your size. I guess I should buy you some vitamins."

I stared down at my stomach, which was developing a definite pooch. "She should probably take those dresses off hold. How about Douglas? What did he say?"

"No message from Douglas."

"Nothing?"

"Apparently not."

Well, Douglas could stuff his long layers somewhere unpleasant, couldn't he? I held up the picture to Daisy Mae.

"Can you do it like that?"

"Sure can, honey. That'll suit a pretty thing like you. Do you want a touch of colour?"

When I walked out an hour later, my hair shoulder-length and chestnut brown with copper highlights, Mitch did a double take before he recognised me.

"Well? What do you think?"

He didn't say anything, just grabbed my hand and pulled me close.

I tried to move away. "What are you doing?"

He turned and smiled at me. Not one of his half-hearted efforts, but a proper ear to ear smile showing a row of perfect white teeth, which stood out against his tanned skin. For a second my knees went weak. He was beautiful. And I needed sunglasses.

"Our cover story is that you're my girlfriend. So I'm holding your hand." Far from letting go, he tugged me against his side and started down the street.

Without much choice in the matter, I let him lead me along. Douglas had never held my hand in public. He always said open displays of affection were something a budding politician should avoid unless the occasion demanded it. But when Mitch did it, it felt...nice. Safe.

"Where else do you want to go?" he asked me.

I shrugged. "Wherever you want."

He stopped dead in the middle of the sidewalk and swung me round to face him. "No, *Vivien*, I'm asking what *you* want. Where do *you* want to go?"

"Uh..." This wasn't how things worked. In my life,

somebody else decided where we were going and I went. I bit my lip. What should I say? What did he want me to say?

He leaned in close and lowered his voice. "Look, Georgia, it's not a difficult question. You moved into my house with nothing, so I'm sure you need to shop. I'll ask again. Where do you want to go?"

"I could do with some clothes, I guess? And maybe some books?"

"Better. See, that wasn't so hard, was it?"

I guess not.

There was only one clothes store in town, a relic of the past that fitted perfectly with Daisy Mae's. In Rose's Clothes, the eponymous owner, an efficient-looking woman in her early forties, helped me pick out approximately twice as many clothes as I'd intended to buy, plus a silver necklace and a purse, "Because they look just darling with that outfit, so pretty."

As Mitch, who'd sat patiently on a rickety chair by the door as I tried on item after item, handed over his credit card, I whispered a hasty thank you. "I promise I'll pay you back as soon as I can."

"Consider it a gift."

"No, really, you don't have to do that."

"This is one occasion where you don't argue back. You say thank you, you smile, and you carry on looking beautiful."

CHAPTER 20

DID MITCHELL GRAY just call me beautiful? I barely had time to process his words before he whisked me out of the door and down the street again. He sort of did, didn't he?

"Bookstore next?"

"Wherever you... Yes, please."

It wasn't like any bookstore I'd ever seen before, more a room in a small house at the end of the street, stuffed from floor to ceiling with second-hand books in every genre imaginable. An old man sat on a high stool next to the cash register, and his eyes jerked open when Mitch rang a small brass bell on the counter.

"Ah, young Mitchell. You've finally brought your girl in to meet me."

"I have. This is Vivien."

The old-timer held a surprisingly steady hand out, and I shook it.

"Nice to meet you."

"Pleasure's all mine. I'm Clive. Been running this bookstore for thirty years, and my daddy owned it before me."

"Vivien's a bookworm. She's come here to make me a poor man."

Clive guffawed as he waved a hand at the stacks. "And I'll be happy to help her with that." He slid off the stool in slow motion. With both feet on the floor, he reached my chin. "What kind of books you looking for, missy?"

"Do you have anything by Lee Child?"

"Thought you'd be more of a romance girl."

"Romance has always passed me by."

The selection was surprisingly good, and I picked out a dozen paperbacks, enough to keep me going for a week. As Clive rang them up, Mitch looked over the titles.

"Thriller junkie?"

"Guilty pleasure." I lowered my voice so Clive couldn't hear. "Although now I'm living in one, they've lost a bit of their magic."

"Nothing compares to a good thriller."

He stared out the window as he spoke, and I got the feeling he wasn't talking about books. Another secret? How many did he have?

Our final stop in Wolf's Corner was the grocery store. Mitch wheeled the cart while I picked up the items off the list, including the tampons, much to Mitch's relief.

"Didn't you want baking powder and pistachios?"

"I thought you didn't want me to make so much food?"

"If you need to cook, you cook."

The way he phrased it gave me pause. Not if I wanted to cook, but if I needed to cook. He got me. He understood I wasn't cooking because I wanted to eat all those cakes and cookies, but as a way to keep my sanity. And his empathy alone made my need to bake from dawn to dusk recede just a little.

"Maybe I'll get a small pack of each."

When we got to the register, I met Patsy. She had to be in her fifties, but she dressed like she was twenty and her leathery skin contrasted starkly with her bleached blonde hair. She kept touching her fingers to her mouth. I imagined she was far more at home with a cigarette between them.

"So this is Vivien? What a darling little thing you are." She paused to cough then turned to Mitch. "I can understand why her ex would be after her. She's a real catch. Must be hard to let that go."

Mitch lit up his mega-watt smile then put his arm around my shoulders and pulled me into him. I stumbled then ended up plastered against his side. "Yes, she is a catch. I won't be making the same mistake."

I barely breathed while Patsy packed the groceries into bags. Even so, the smell of Mitch's cologne invaded my nose, along with the undeniable musk of male. My left hand had landed on his stomach, a wall of rock hard muscle under his checked shirt. I moved a hand over his abs, trying not to be too obvious about it. Whoa. He should be the subject of his own paintings. Women would pay a fortune.

Alas, he let me go to pick up the grocery bags, and I trailed him out to the Land Rover where he stacked them in the back.

"While we're in town, do you want to get lunch? It'd give you a few hours off cooking."

"Whatever you want."

"Vivien, we've spoken about this."

This decision making thing was all new. Did Mitch

want lunch? He wouldn't have suggested it otherwise, right? "In that case, yes, I'd love to go for lunch."

The diner at the other end of the street looked like it opened in the fifties and nobody had touched the decor since. Mitch slid into one side of a booth, and I perched on a red plastic seat on the other with the scarred Formica table between us. Honestly, if Douglas could have seen me, he'd have sent me straight to my therapist.

But Mitch? Mitch simply handed me a menu. "Nothing's healthy; everything's good."

He wasn't wrong. Burger. Cheeseburger. Cheeseburger with bacon. Double cheeseburger. Double cheeseburger with double bacon. Not a salad in sight. My arteries hardened just from reading the list.

I gasped as Mitch slipped his hand into mine then a shadow fell across the table. I looked up to find a waitress staring daggers at me. Nancy, according to her name badge, looked to be in her thirties and wore her uniform a size too small, so her ample breasts spilled over the top. Right into Mitch's face.

"What can I get ya, darlin'?"

"The usual, thanks."

"And you?" She sounded annoyed. What had I done to upset her? I'd only been in town an hour.

"A bacon cheeseburger with fries, please, and a diet coke."

I got her back as she turned to Mitch. "Coming right up."

Once she'd left, he let go of my hand and let out a reedy sigh. "Sorry about that."

"What did I do?"

"Nothing. Nancy hasn't taken well to the idea of me

having a girlfriend. I wouldn't have brought you if I'd known she'd be here. She normally works the evening shift."

"Oh. Was there something between you?"

He shook his head, lips curling up in amusement. "Only in her head. She must have asked me out a dozen times."

"And you haven't been tempted?"

"You saw the way she was with you? I don't go for that."

I was very tempted to ask what he did go for, but what business was it of mine? Instead, I picked at a corner of the menu where the laminate was coming loose. Mitch was different today. More friendly, more open. Was it because of our audience? Or was he bipolar or something? Whatever the reason, I needed to take advantage of his willingness to talk if I wanted to learn more about him.

"Do you come into town often?"

He answered without hesitation, his voice light. "Once or twice a week, usually. More if I need something specific."

"And you stay at the cabin the rest of the time?"

"Mostly."

Nancy interrupted with our drinks. She carefully set Mitch's coffee in front of him then dumped my coke so it sloshed over the edges of the glass. I sincerely hoped Mitch didn't leave a tip. I glared at her wiggling ass as she sashayed away then returned to the conversation.

"Don't you get bored?" Because I sure did, although granted I didn't have painting to keep me busy.

"Honestly? A little of late. When I first moved in, I craved the solitude, but now it's too quiet."

Wow, an actual answer from Mr. Tall, Dark, and Moody. I almost couldn't believe it.

"Why don't you try inviting the neighbours over? You know, for a soiree?"

Mitch choked on a mouthful of coffee then wiped his mouth, laughing.

"What's so funny?"

"The idea of me throwing a party."

"Why not?"

"In case you hadn't noticed, I'm not exactly social."

"But you could be. It's not hard. I mean, when Emmy first took me to the cabin I expected you to be a strange old hermit, but you're actually quite normal."

He laughed harder as I clapped my hand over my mouth. "Oops. Forget I said that last bit."

"I'm not normal, Vivien. Far from it."

"Okay, so maybe a party's a bit ambitious. How about attending an event in town? What do they have out here? Hoe-downs?"

He looked beautiful when he laughed. It was just a shame it was at me.

"Let's just say I don't play nicely with others."

"So what will you do? Stay on your mountain alone? Or leave?"

"I don't know. I'm not sure where I'd go."

"Where did you live before? Didn't you say you've only lived in the cabin for a few years?"

He stared off into the distance, past the counter where Nancy hovered hopefully. "Anywhere and everywhere. I didn't have roots. The cabin's the first home I've ever owned. How about you? What's it like where you live?"

Ah, social strategy number three—the subject

change. I'd used that technique many times myself. I longed to ask Mitch about his travels, but I did the polite thing and answered.

"As you know, I share my home with Douglas. Rybridge is a very sought-after area—good schools, near to the mall, well maintained. Six bedrooms is too many, really, but the kitchen has top-of-the-line appliances, which suits my love of cooking. And the pool's lovely in summer." Good heavens, I sounded like a realtor.

"That's the place where you eat and sleep, but it doesn't sound like you live there."

He got me. Just in a few words. Tears pooled in the corners of my eyes, and I quickly blinked them back. No, I'd never loved that house. Douglas just went out and bought it without any consultation whatsoever. It was too big, somehow cold and impersonal despite the interior designer's best efforts.

Luckily, I was saved from further discussion by Nancy's arrival. She arranged Mitch's double cheeseburger neatly on the table with a napkin and cutlery and asked if he wanted any extra condiments. When he shook his head, she dropped my plate in front of me, flicked her hair, and strode off.

Mitch rolled his eyes. "See?"

We both laughed, and it felt good, better than crying certainly. In fact, despite his denials, Mitch seemed like a normal person right then.

My burger tasted delicious, although I harboured a secret suspicion that Nancy might have spat in it. Mitch's had twice as much ketchup and extra fries, and Nancy stopped by four times to check everything was okay with his meal. The fourth time, he only had a few fries left, and when he suggested he probably wouldn't have eaten it all if there was a problem, I had to laugh, although I quickly turned it into a cough.

We didn't talk much while we ate, but it wasn't like the awkward silences of our first meals in the cabin. When the time came to leave, Mitch slung an arm around my waist and held me close as Nancy glowered from the counter. His fingertips brushed my hip and the rush of heat downwards was like nothing I'd ever experienced. I gave an involuntary shiver.

"Are you cold?"

As I'd kept on the down jacket I'd just purchased from Rose, I couldn't even claim that excuse. "Not really. I think it's just the temperature difference between inside and outside."

"Well, let me know if you are, and you can have my sweater."

Who was this new Mitch, and what had he done with the old one?

And more importantly, which would win out when we got back to the cabin?

CHAPTER 21

XAV CLIMBED THE stairs quickly, adjusting his cock in his pants as he went. Every time he ventured near Georgia the fucking thing stood to attention, and it was driving him to distraction. He needed to paint. Painting calmed him. Painting left him empty. When he got angry, his paintings were dark and edgy, sharp brushstrokes and blurred faces. Sorrow brought landscapes, bleak and melancholy, as if the paint had been poured straight from his heart and the canvas wept with him. Happiness, the rare whispers of it he had, cascaded out in a riot of colour, his feelings transferred to the people brought to life in front of him.

Since he'd retired, since he'd come to hide in his little cabin in the mountains, since he'd shunned human interaction, his paintings had been flat. Dull. Sterile. He'd always dreamed of a life where he could do nothing but paint, but the sad reality was that without the other side of him, he had nothing to express, no inspiration. Over the past two years, he'd painted all right, starting out every day with a fresh canvas and fresh hope, but in that whole time, he'd only painted a handful of pictures he considered good enough to sell. Most of his work had ended up on the bonfire behind his cabin, the earth permanently charred black as he burned his dreams.

Until she came.

The half-finished painting awaited him, and he sat on the padded stool and picked up his palette. At this rate, he'd have to put in a rush order for more paint.

Over the past few weeks, the empty husk he'd become had taken on new life, new energy, new emotions. There was lust, something he'd felt on occasion, but this was stronger, more intense. He felt jealousy, of a husband who treated Georgia like dirt and yet still held onto her. He felt hatred of the man sent to kill her and dread that he might not be able to keep her safe. And—the thing that scared him most—a little flicker he thought might be love.

All he'd drawn for the past few weeks was her, relying on his memories of the time they spent together to make her live on the canvas and paper littering his studio. He'd drawn hundreds of quick sketches, a number of detailed ones, and worked his feelings into several paintings. All of them were good enough to sell, but none of them would ever leave his possession. They were his and his alone. They were as much of her as he could have.

He hid up in his studio, him and his paintings and his drawings and his feelings, because spending time with her was just so damned frustrating. He'd given in today and taken her with him into town, but keeping his hands off her had taken all of his legendary self-control. It lapsed a couple of times, and in the grocery store, when she'd relaxed into his arms and melted against him, it was all he could do not to throw her over his shoulder and march her straight out of there.

Even if she wasn't married, he was no good for her. The life he'd led was everything that scared her, everything she was trying to escape from at the moment. He growled in frustration and gently dabbed titanium white onto the canvas to highlight the contours of her face.

Twelve hours later he finished. He'd painted her looking into a mirror, her reflection staring back at her. What did she see? Was it the same woman he did? He assumed not, because if she did she'd have a much higher opinion of herself. She deserved to be treasured.

Leaving the painting to dry, he looked at his watch. Nearly three a.m. He needed to sleep, something he hadn't been doing well lately because she haunted his dreams as well as his waking thoughts.

Before that, though, he needed to call Emmy. He hadn't spoken to her for a few days, and he wanted an update.

"Do you know what time it is?" she growled.

"Yes."

"Is it an emergency?"

"No."

"Then why the fuck are you calling me now?"

"Because I couldn't wait until morning to hear your dulcet tones."

She laughed. "Flattery will get you everywhere, you bastard."

"So, anything?"

"There's good news and bad news."

"Spit it out."

"The good news is we found our leak. The bad news is it didn't get us any closer to the killer."

At least part of the problem was solved. He should have felt relief, because that meant Georgia could go back to Blackwood's care, but he didn't. All he felt was a hollow ache in his chest.

"So, who was it then?"

"Shit…"

Emmy sucked in a breath, and he knew that while he'd been eating a cheeseburger with Georgia and watching her try on outfits, Emmy had been doing what she did best.

"You remember Nick's PA, Nadia?"

"Blonde? Sharp nose?"

"That's her. It seems she was a little resentful about not earning as much as me, Dan and Mack, so she decided to make a bit extra on the side."

Shit indeed. "How did you find out?"

"She paid cash for a car. Dan saw it in the car park but didn't recall seeing any payment out of her bank in the file Mack pulled together. So she did some digging."

"You put so much trust in all those girls."

"And then one of them kicks us in the teeth. Sloane's devastated."

"She's your PA, right?"

"Yeah. They hung out together most weekends, even had a holiday planned for summer. She had no clue Nadia felt like that."

"Nadia isn't the first traitor to hide their true character."

"That doesn't make it any easier to take. Sloane's been in tears all day, and Nick's been switching between fury and guilt. He got shot because of that bitch."

"And Nadia?"

"Is no longer with the company." From the way Emmy said it, Xav suspected Nadia was no longer with the human race, either.

"What did you get out of her?"

"Everything and not enough. Initial contact was in person—he was waiting in her apartment one evening with a bag full of cash and his face in the shadows. All she could tell us was that he had a West Coast accent and a chunky build."

"The accent's nothing, and we knew the build already."

"Precisely. After that, contact was by burner phone, and he left payments in a locker at the train station. We're going through CCTV, but from what we've found so far, he was careful. We haven't got his face yet."

"Is it worth me talking to Nadia?"

He had to offer, despite being sure Emmy would have got everything out of her. After all, he'd been the one to teach her to interrogate someone in an efficient and effective manner, and she'd been an excellent student.

"You insult me and yourself. Didn't I learn from the best?"

"I had to ask. I want this bastard dead."

"As do I. Anyway, you can only talk to her if you've got a submarine."

Yes, it was as he suspected. She was no longer breathing.

"Fine. What now?"

"We're still going through video, bank records, phone taps, you name it. The FBI is pissed over Lou, and they're putting a fair effort in too. Your name came up, but I respectfully suggested they'd be wasting their time with that particular avenue of investigation."

"Appreciate that."

"James threatened to demote the chief of the

Capitol Police to private if he didn't cooperate, so we've finally got access to their records. Just in time—the senator's getting impatient, and Georgia's mother's on Prozac. Much as I'd love to, we can't pin anything on the husband other than the tendency to behave like a dick, but it's not as if he hides that."

Xav fell silent as he processed Emmy's news. The painting he'd just finished taunted him. "What about Georgia?"

"It's probably safe to bring her back now, so if she's driving you nuts I can come and take her off your hands."

Emmy might as well have taken a knife to his chest with those words. He didn't want Georgia to go. Every day she was in his home was a day he breathed a little easier.

"She's no trouble. Far from it. She's quiet and she cooks a lot."

"Well, ask her what she wants. But if you're happy to keep her, and she's happy to stay, it'd certainly make our lives easier."

When he hung up the phone, Xav sat out on the cold balcony, thinking. If he asked Georgia whether she wanted to go home, even to a safe house, he was almost certain her answer would be yes. He'd been a complete shit to her when he first arrived, and even though there was a reason for it, she didn't know that.

And after that, he'd barely spent any time with her, not because he didn't want to, but because it killed him to be near her and know she could never be his.

So he came to a decision. He hated himself for it, but he wasn't going to ask her.

CHAPTER 22

I DIDN'T KNOW which version of Mitch made it back to the cabin when we came back from Wolf's Corner, because when we arrived, he disappeared up to his studio, and I didn't see him again for the rest of the day. Even for dinner, which left me peeved as I'd used some of my newly bought ingredients for a pie, including making the puff pastry from scratch and that took ages. In the end I gave up waiting, covered his plate in tinfoil and left it on the side with a note.

I lay awake for hours, thinking over the day. It seemed crazy, what with the threat of death hanging over my head and all, but I'd felt happy. Mitch showed me a different side, relaxed and caring, and it was something I liked a lot. Too much, in fact.

Every touch of his seared into my skin like fire, and when I closed my eyes, I could still feel his hand resting on my hip. It was wrong, and I knew it, but Douglas had never made me feel that way. Douglas reminded me of a Volvo—reliable, but expensive and boring, whereas Mitch was a Ferrari—gorgeous to look at and temperamental, and oh so easy to lust over. I could only imagine what the ride would be like, and in the privacy of Mitch's spare room I went the same colour as a Ferrari doing exactly that.

And when my dreams finally came, I did too, as

Mitch plastered me over a scarlet car hood and thrust into me, forbidden but impossible to resist. I woke up in the middle of a damn orgasm, that was how bad it got. How was I supposed to face him and act all normal when inside I was drowning in a sea of wanton-ness? The next morning, I stayed in my room for an extra hour, hoping he'd have disappeared into his studio by the time I came out, but no such luck.

"Just in time for breakfast," he announced.

"Breakfast?"

"Pancakes. You like pancakes, right? Everybody likes pancakes."

"You're cooking?"

"Don't sound so surprised. I fended for myself for years before you came along."

At least it wasn't grapefruit. I peered over at the counter, taking in the mess he'd made. "Is it a special occasion?"

Without my smartphone I'd lost all concept of time. Each day melded into the next on the mountain, and only the leaves swelling on the trees hinted at the passing season.

"Nope. But you always cook me food, so I thought I'd return the favour."

"Thank you." What else could I say? "I don't think anyone's ever cooked for me at home before. Well, apart from my mom and the housekeeper."

Too late, I realised my slip of the tongue. Home. I'd called the cabin home. At least Mitch didn't seem to have noticed. His face bore a look of concentration as he poured pancake batter into the pan, nudging the edges with a spatula so it didn't stick.

I took a seat at the table as I gathered my thoughts.

Despite all its shortcomings, I felt more comfortable out here in the woods than I had in six years of living in Rybridge. The cabin was warm and cosy, and I enjoyed having nature on my doorstep. I liked not having to be at anyone's beck and call. And, most of all, I liked Mitch.

"Seriously? The pr...your husband's never made you breakfast before?"

"Nope. You're the first man ever to cook for me."

"Good. I like coming first."

Well, that was one thing he and Douglas had in common.

"Do you need a hand?"

"Everything's under control. Just relax."

I tried. I failed. How could I relax as I watched him in the kitchen? For a big man, his movements were incredibly graceful, his actions precise. Muscles rippled in his back as he reached into the top cupboard to get the bottle of maple syrup. The man definitely needed to wear tighter shirts. Or no shirts. No shirts would work better.

"How hungry are you?"

"Ravenous."

He raised an eyebrow, but stacked four pancakes onto the plate then added a healthy side of chopped bananas.

"Let's see if you get through this lot."

Mitch's gaze no longer made me squirm, at least not in a bad way, and we managed a proper conversation. Not about anything of consequence, only about Wolf's Corner and the area in general, but it didn't matter because I barely listened to the words. I was just hooked on the sound of his voice, the low vibrations that stroked my core.

"Are you full?" he asked, as I gave up halfway through my fourth pancake.

"Mmm hmm." I couldn't eat another mouthful without bursting. "Are you going to paint now?"

"Not today. I thought we could test out those new hiking boots you bought from Rose. If your ankle's up to it, that is?"

A second day of adventures. I'd hop if I needed to. "It'll be fine. I only get the odd twinge now."

"We'll go slowly."

Slowly, quickly, I'd take Mitch any way I could get him.

After I'd changed into suitable clothing and tied my hair back, Mitch insisted I relax on the sofa while he packed a picnic. I tried to see what he was putting in his backpack, but the counter was too high.

"Have you packed chocolate?"

"Two kinds."

"And something to drink?"

"Yeeeeessss."

"Okay, I'll be quiet now."

His chuckle got me smiling, and it wasn't long until we left. My breakfast had gone down, along with the swelling in my foot, enough that I could walk rather than waddle as we followed a narrow, well-worn trail away from the cabin, twisting between the trees as it wound its way up the mountain. If I'd thought the clearing was pretty, the higher reaches were stunningly beautiful.

"I can see why you decided to move here."

I got another of his equally beautiful smiles in return.

The forest was a mix of evergreen and deciduous trees, the skeletons of majestic oaks punctuated with the sharp green of pine. Buds were beginning to burst into life, and I bet in summer it would be stunning in a different way—sunlight trickling through the leaves rather than the stark vista of winter. As we climbed, the crystal clear waters of a stream tumbled in the opposite direction. That was the gentle rushing I heard from my room at night when the wind was quiet.

"Are there fish in the stream?"

"A few. Most aren't big enough to eat."

"What about other animals? Do you go hunting?"

"Occasionally, for deer and rabbit."

"I don't think I've ever eaten rabbit." Maybe at a dinner some place. I rarely studied the menus. Half the time, I didn't want to know what I was eating anyway.

"There's some in the freezer we can have for dinner if you want."

"In those little packages at the back?"

"No, that's beef. There's another freezer in the garage."

"What garage?"

"It's along a track behind the cabin. Used to be a barn."

I needed to get out more. What else didn't I know about?

As we walked and climbed and climbed and walked, Mitch stopped every so often to point out interesting things I'd have walked right past otherwise. A tree where a woodpecker had been, a deer peeping through the trees, tracks from a bear.

Wait a second? A bear?

"Holy shit!" I clapped my hand over my mouth. I didn't mean to say that, honestly. "There are bears?"

He laughed. "A few. Relax, they don't usually approach humans."

"Usually? Shouldn't you have a gun or something, just in case?"

"I have a gun."

"You do?"

"Of course. Somebody's trying to kill you. I've been carrying a gun since you arrived."

"Oh. Right. Do you know how to use it properly?"

As an artist, Mitch spent most of his time indoors. I didn't want him shooting his foot by accident. Or my foot.

"Yes, Georgia, I know how to use it."

"Can I see? I've never shot a gun before."

Douglas stood firmly in the camp of the tighter gun-control lobby. More than that—he wanted them banned completely. "Law-abiding citizens don't need guns," he always told me. "They only lead to people getting hurt."

Mitch reached behind his waist with one hand, which came back holding a scary-looking pistol.

"It's a Colt Model 1911."

"Is it loaded?"

"No, I thought if the hitman came, I'd just throw it at him."

Duh. I was so full of stupid questions. "Can I hold it?"

He held it out, and I took it gingerly. Whoa, it was heavier than I thought.

"Use two hands. And for fuck's sake keep it pointed

away from both of us."

I aimed at a tree a few yards away, careful to keep my fingers away from the trigger. "It feels big. Chunky."

"That's because the grip's customised for my hand."

"It's all very James Bond."

"Not really. Most people in these parts carry a gun."

"Doesn't that worry you? I mean, guns kill people."

"No. Guns don't kill people. People kill people."

He stowed the gun safely back in his waistband as we carried on walking. He was right, when I thought about it. Thousands of people used guns to hunt for food and for self-defence rather than cold-blooded murder. Banning them entirely seemed a little drastic. The bad guys would still find a way to get hold of them anyway, like with drugs, which, incidentally, Douglas thought should all be legalised so they could be taxed to the moon. Not to fund rehab, mind you, but so big business could get tax breaks.

And Mitch was right, I'd been so conditioned to accept other people's views, I didn't have any of my own.

What did *I* think?

CHAPTER 23

WE AMBLED SLOWLY upwards for another hour before we arrived in another clearing. Not big, maybe sixty feet from end to end, but achingly beautiful. At one end, the stream formed a waterfall into a pool. How deep was it? Hard to tell, even though the water was so clear. I could see every detail of the bottom, including the school of tiny fish that darted behind a rock as I peered down at them.

"This is amazing," I breathed.

Mitch smiled, enhancing the landscape still further. "It's my favourite place. I like to come up here in the summer and paint."

"Do you swim in the pool?"

"Sometimes, but even in August the water's cold."

Even if it was freezing, I'd swim there too. I could just imagine standing under the waterfall like a girl in a shampoo commercial, Mitch walking towards me through the water wearing... No—I mustn't! I shook my head, trying to clear my wayward thoughts.

Mitch raised an eyebrow, and I arranged my face into expression number one—blank. Only the whole mask thing was getting more difficult. I was out of practice.

"Are we going to eat here?" I asked.

"That's the plan."

He shook out a plaid blanket and spread it on the ground then unpacked the food. As I suspected, it made an interesting selection.

"A jar of olives?" I turned it over in my hands.

"I like olives."

"With peanut butter and jelly?" I picked up the sandwiches and looked at them dubiously.

"Yeah." His face fell. "Can you tell this is a first for me?"

"You've never been on a picnic?"

He shook his head. "It's not a very 'guy' thing to do."

"What about with girls?"

"I've never felt the urge to take a girl for a picnic before."

"Not even a girlfriend?"

"I've never had anybody serious. I've always been too busy with work."

Really? He was in his mid-thirties. Like, how? I'd seen the way women reacted to him, even just in town. Surely it wouldn't have been that difficult for him to date a girl, even if he was busy at work? And Emmy? They seemed so close.

I risked asking, even if I didn't expect an answer. "What about Emmy? Didn't you ever date her?"

"Not sure I'd describe her as a girlfriend. Back when we were together, she wasn't in the market for a serious relationship."

"What about now?"

"Now she's married."

Oh. I racked my brain, but I couldn't recall her mentioning that. "So you never brought her up here?"

"Not for a picnic. We ran up here and she pushed

me into the pool."

I burst into laughter and he glared at me. "Seriously? She pushed you in? What did you do?"

"Pulled her in as well, then she tried to drown me. It was December, and it was cold enough to turn my balls blue. The woman's crazy."

"From what I've seen of her, she certainly is that."

Throughout the picnic, I kept waiting for the old Mitch to appear, for him to make a snarky comment or grumpy remark, but all I got was charm. And information, just a little.

"You own the whole mountain?" My eyes widened at that revelation.

"Bought it eleven years ago. One visit and I knew I wanted it."

"I didn't think you'd lived here that long?"

"I haven't. Back then, there was a shitty old house and no electricity. Took another five years to get that place built." He pointed down the mountain. "But I only used it for vacations until I retired."

"Retired? Haven't you always been an artist?"

"I didn't paint for a living, just a hobby."

"So what did you do?" There were so many things I didn't know about him.

"I worked in liquidations."

Not quite what I was expecting, but there was good money in legal work, wasn't there? "I admire you for following your dreams. It must have taken a lot of guts to leave a steady job to paint."

"It was the right decision at the time."

"And now?"

"I've got a lot of thinking to do about my future."

And I had a lot of thinking to do about mine. Sitting

cross-legged on the blanket, leaning on a moss-covered rock, I found myself confiding how my own life hadn't turned out the way I hoped. Until then, I'd never told anybody but my therapist my misgivings about my marriage to Douglas, or the despair I felt when I thought of my future. And Dr. Nielsen basically told me I was being silly about the whole thing.

But not Mitch. He listened quietly while I talked, eyes fixed on mine, and I saw no pity or ridicule in his, only empathy. That made me well up, and I looked away.

He scooted closer and gently turned me back to face him, using his thumbs to wipe my cheeks. "Don't cry, little flower. You're brave to talk about things. It's a big step."

"But what can I do? What options do I have? At the moment, it's either option A: Get shot, or option B: Go back and live with Douglas. I'm not sure which one's less appealing."

"You forgot option C."

"Option C?"

"Do something else. You're stronger than you think, and when this is over you'll have your whole life ahead of you."

Was that even possible? Could I really take my own life back? A tiny seed of possibility took root in my mind as Mitch reached over and squeezed my hand. "You're too damn kind, Mitchell Gray. Not what I was expecting when I first met you."

"So what did you expect?"

"Well, you weren't exactly compassionate."

"That was a test."

"What do you mean, a test?"

"From Emmy. She wanted to see if you were hiding any bitterness under that sweet shell."

I took a second to let that sink in. If that was true, it meant this was the real Mitch, and I wanted that more than anything. It also meant Emmy was more calculating than I first thought.

"Did I pass?" I whispered.

He brought my hand to his lips. "You passed."

A fleeting second and he dropped my hand in my lap. Did I imagine his touch? From the fire that rushed up my arm, I didn't think so. I sat in a daze as Mitch got to his feet and began to clear the picnic away. What did that kiss mean? A friendly gesture? An attempt to break me out of my sorrow? Or...something more?

"Georgia, come here."

"What?" I looked up to see Mitch on the far side of the clearing, balancing two empty coke cans on a fallen tree.

"Come here. Try something new."

I scrambled up and brushed bits of moss off my back, hoping it hadn't stained. Oh, what did it matter? Who cared if I got dirty? Not me. Not anymore.

"Try what?"

He didn't answer, just drew the gun from his waistband once more, aimed, and fired. One of the cans flew into the air as I clapped my hands over my ears.

"That was loud!"

"Because it's a .45. It's got stopping power. Here—your turn."

"I can't..."

He positioned me in front of him, nestled into his body, and wrapped his arms around me. "Hold the grip."

My hands shook as I held them out, and not because I was about to fire a gun for the first time. I held where he showed me, and he put his hands over the top of mine, taking some of the weight of the gun.

"Now, let's line up the sights. See that notch at the back?"

I could barely focus at all, not with his warmth seeping into my back. "Uh, yes?"

"You need to line the pointy bit at the front with the centre. Keep it level."

"Like this?"

He pressed his cheek against mine and followed my line of sight. "That's it. And when you're ready, squeeze the trigger."

I did, too quickly, and he laughed.

"You've got to keep your eyes open."

I cracked a lid and saw the can I'd been aiming at still sitting on the log. "Oops. Can I try again?"

"Sure."

Mitch helped me again, and this time the can pinged backwards. "I hit it!"

"Don't wave the gun around, for fuck's sake." He stiffened his arms, holding mine still.

"Sorry."

"It's okay. You'll learn. You want another go?"

"Yes, please."

For ten minutes, I shot at the cans, caring less about hitting them than the feel of Mitch around me. If only the weather was warmer so we could lose the thick down jackets we both wore. A sigh passed my lips. I'd turned into a hussy, but that no longer bothered me in the way it should.

Then Mitch stepped back, leaving me bereft. "We

need to get going."

"Can't I just have one more shot?"

He pointed at the sky, and I noticed the clouds gathering above us, black and angry. "Not unless you want to get wet. We're in for a cloudburst."

Together, we threw the remainder of the picnic stuff into the bag and started the trek back. With every minute, the sky grew darker, and I broke into a jog to keep up with Mitch's longer strides.

"You okay?" he asked.

"Yes. Just keep going." Would we make it back in time? I didn't want to test out the waterproof capabilities of this jacket.

Mitch got a few feet ahead as I hopped over a small rock and landed awkwardly, causing my already delicate ankle to twist under me. I muffled my squeak and tried to put the pain out of my mind as I hobbled along as fast as I could. This wasn't fun anymore.

"Are you...? Fuck, you're hurt. Why didn't you say something?"

"I'm fine."

"You're not fine. You're hopping."

"It's just a little sprain. I'll put ice on it when we get back."

He swapped the backpack onto his front and patted his shoulder. "Jump up."

"Come again?"

"I'll carry you the last bit."

"Don't be silly. I'm far too heavy."

"Either you get up or I'll throw you over my shoulder." It came out as a growl, an actual growl, and I knew he was serious.

"Okay, okay. But if you hurt your back, don't blame

me." I used a boulder to help me scramble on board, and he set off at a jog. Until that moment, I hadn't appreciated his incredible strength. He carried me like I weighed nothing.

The first fat drops of rain fell as he ran across the yard onto the back porch, quickly followed by a deluge as the heavens opened.

I was laughing as I slid back down to earth, both physically and metaphorically. Mitch turned as I landed, and I ended up facing him with my arms around his neck. If I stood on tiptoe, our lips would touch. I'd never felt temptation like it. Mitch was chocolate fudge cake and champagne after a month on the cabbage soup diet. I looked into his eyes, close enough to see the flecks of gold that danced in the rich brown. Did he feel it too?

What should I do? Should I...?

He made the decision for me, letting out a low groan as he gently removed my arms.

The spell was broken.

I bit my lip. Shit, that was close. A bolt of lightning glinted off my wedding ring, providing a timely reminder of all the reasons why getting close to Mitch was a bad idea. I was married. For better or for worse, I was married. Mostly worse.

Mitch unlocked the back door without speaking and ushered me inside. Then he went off to paint.

Chapter 24

A KNOCK AT the door woke me from my troubled sleep the next morning. Was that Mitch? Stupid—who else would it be? I desperately smoothed my hair down and prayed I didn't look too much of a mess.

"You can come in."

The door cracked open as I wriggled up to a seated position and pulled the quilt up to my chin.

"I thought you might like coffee." He placed a steaming mug on the nightstand next to me.

How did he look so good at that time in the morning? I could scare small children, whereas he could have stepped into a photoshoot in his dark jeans and fine wool sweater. Even though his hair was a mess, it was a mess I itched to run my fingers through. And now he was sitting on my bed. I burned the image into my retinas in case I didn't get to see it again.

"I'm going out to get some shooting practice in. I didn't want to scare you with the noise."

"Can I come with you?"

"No, you sleep. I won't be far away, and I'll be back in a couple of hours."

My heart sank as he knocked me back, before pounding out of my chest as he leaned forward and kissed my forehead. Then he was gone.

Sleep? How on earth was I supposed to sleep after

that?

I wasn't. Half an hour later, the spot on my forehead still burned, as did the blood coursing through my veins. Every nerve ending tingled. My fingers crept into the pair of Mitch's boxer shorts I still wore, because now I never wanted to wear anything else, and with him playing across my mind, I teased myself into the mother of all orgasms. Holy stromboli. Five minutes later, I still couldn't move my legs.

They were even wobbly when I teetered out to breakfast with Mitch, over an hour later. I grabbed the back of the chair for support as I willed myself to act normal.

"Is your ankle okay? You're walking funny."

"Am I? No, it's fine. Good as new."

He raised an eyebrow but said nothing. What if he knew what I'd done? Did he realise how I felt? My cheeks began to burn as I flushed red.

"Are you too warm? Shall I turn the heating down?"

Oh shit, he did notice. "Perhaps just a notch or two?"

He got up and adjusted the thermostat. "So, what do you want to do today?"

I couldn't possibly tell him what I wanted to do today. It would probably get me arrested. "Whatever you want."

"Nuh-uh. Your choice. You come up with an idea."

Brain...wouldn't...function. I stumbled to the kitchen and busied myself making a cup of coffee, just so I wouldn't have to look at Mitch. Idea. I needed to think of an idea. Funny how easy life had been when I'd coasted along without a choice. Back then, if I got asked how I'd like to pass a morning, it would have been a decision between the spa or the country club. Maybe shopping. None of that appealed any more. I wanted to travel. I wanted to get a job. I wanted to adopt a dog, ride on a motorbike, take that kickboxing class Pippa tried to talk me into last year. I wanted to dance in the damn rain.

"Georgia? Why are you crying?"

"I don't know. I guess... I feel like my life's been wasted. Everything so far."

He padded towards me, and I tried to look at him. He'd gone all blurry.

"Flower, don't get upset. The rest of your life will be what you make of it. Don't waste today."

I tore off a piece of paper towel and wiped my nose. Great—how ladylike was that? "I want a dog and a vacation."

"That might be difficult right now. Anything a little easier?"

"Does Wolf's Corner have a kickboxing class?"

He burst out laughing.

"What?"

"How did we get from a dog and a vacation to kickboxing?"

"It's just one of those things I was always too scared to do."

"I don't think it does have a class."

"It's okay. I've got books left. I'll just read."

"Oh, Georgia."

Mitch turned and jogged up the stairs to the loft, leaving me alone. Okay, so I was having a moment, but I didn't mean to scare him off. I wiped my eyes with my sleeve and tried to paste on a smile. Faking was getting ever harder.

A minute later, he came back and tossed me a pair of shorts. "Put those on, and a T-shirt."

"Why?"

"Because I'm going to teach you a few things about how to look after yourself."

"Kickboxing? You know kickboxing?"

"Close. Krav maga."

"Krav ma-what?"

"Kickboxing's for show. Krav maga's for the real world."

"But—"

"Go change."

Mitch's shorts were ridiculously big, but I cinched up the drawstring to hold them up. Hardly country club attire—I'd get my membership revoked if I turned up looking like this. But for the clearing outside Mitch's back deck, they were perfect, if not a tiny bit chilly.

"I'm cold." I hugged my arms around myself as my breath steamed in the air.

"You'll soon warm up."

"So how do you know this krav maga?"

"I took classes in college."

"Where did you go to college?"

"I'm not Ivy League like you."

Another thing I'd wasted. My Harvard education. "That doesn't matter."

He beckoned me forwards. "In krav maga, you fight dirty. Style doesn't matter, form doesn't matter. Winning matters. We'll start with the three main points of attack." He pointed at himself. "Eyes. Throat. Groin."

I stared at the impressive bulge in his jogging pants, unable to tear my eyes away. "I'll try to avoid that one."

"No, you won't. You need to practise."

"What if I hurt you?"

"Trust me, you won't. I'm a big boy."

Didn't I know it?

Hours flew by as he showed me how to gouge his eyes, grab his throat and kick just behind the groin to send a shockwave through his whole body. I had to get in close, and after a while, touching him no longer felt so foreign.

As demonstrated when I sat on his back with his arm bent behind him and pumped my fist in the air. "Gotcha."

"Well done, flower." He sounded a little weary.

"Are you tired?"

"Let's say I'm a bit out of practice myself."

I hopped up and held a hand out, wincing at the purple bruise already blossoming on his arm. I'd done that, but he insisted it didn't matter.

"Thanks for teaching me."

"I'd say it was a pleasure, but that wouldn't be entirely true."

"Can I make it up to you with lunch?"

"I won't turn down that offer."

Mitch took a shower while I threw together a frittata and salad. It was the least I could do after I'd tried to kill him this morning. I couldn't help smiling as I cooked, thinking of the first day in a long time where I'd achieved something I was proud of.

"You look happier," Mitch commented as we sat down to eat.

"I feel happier."

When I got back home, I'd be signing up for self-defence lessons right away. Maybe even krav maga, if I could find a class nearby. And I wouldn't be spending so much time at the country club. It was bad for my sanity.

My smile faded away along with that thought. Going home. I didn't want to go home.

"So, what are our plans for this afternoon, boss?" Mitch asked.

"Nothing strenuous. How about a movie?" I was getting better at this decision-making thing. Progress.

And that progress was how I ended up curled up on the sofa with Mitch, a bowl of popcorn and a bag of M&Ms between us. He'd gotten the peanut ones, which were my favourite, and I'd eaten far too many of them. I felt sick. Or maybe lovesick, I wasn't sure. Mitch being in such close proximity sure wasn't helping.

"You want more wine?"

I glanced over at the bottle on the table next to us. There was only a teaspoon left in the bottom, and I didn't want to get any tipsier than I already was.

"Better not."

As Mitch didn't have many DVDs, we'd made a quick trip into town after lunch and picked out a selection. His action flick was better than I expected, but I felt a little guilty for inflicting the rom-com we were watching on him. Except when I said watching, I meant I was staring blankly at the screen and daydreaming about Mitch.

What if I had kissed him yesterday? What would have happened next? Would he have kissed me back? Or pushed me away? I shouldn't even have been contemplating it, but I couldn't help myself.

I forced myself to think of Douglas instead, of what I had back home, but all that did was remind me how unhappy I'd been there. I didn't want to go back. Staying here was out of the question, but Mitch's option C looked more attractive with every passing day. I didn't need a big house. My trust fund would pay me a monthly income, and I could use my accountancy degree and get a job. People always needed accountants, right? After all, the only certainties in life were death and taxes. Ugh, death. Why did I have to stir up that thought? I shuddered, trying to block it out.

"Cold, flower?"

"A little." Why didn't I just tell him the truth? "And I'm scared. Mostly scared. About what's going to happen in the future."

Rather than answering, he got up and took the bowls to the kitchen. Why did I tell him that? I bared my soul, and he left? I heard a click as he turned up the thermostat, then he came back carrying a blanket.

"Don't be scared. I won't let anything bad happen to you. I promise."

He spread the blanket over both of us, then wrapped an arm around me and pulled me close. I dropped my head onto his chest and exhaled. His body heat seeped into me, and the steady beat of his heart against my cheek soothed my own racing pulse. Gingerly, I traced my fingers across his abs, feeling the muscles rippling underneath, then squashed myself tighter against him. He didn't say a word, and neither did I. Mitch made me forget everything, so much so that I had to remind myself to breathe.

In and out.

In and out.

We didn't move until the credits began to roll. I had no idea what happened on screen. We could have been watching a rom-com, a slasher flick or a documentary on deep sea fishing. I couldn't have told you.

"Movie's ended," Mitch said.

"I know."

"Want to watch another one?"

"Not if it means you moving." Did I just say that out loud? I was going to have to work on my mouth to brain filter.

He clicked off the TV and hooked our legs up onto the sofa then curled both arms around me. I breathed his scent in as one hand slowly stroked up and down my back.

"Sleep, flower," he breathed.

So I did. On a sofa too short for either of us, wrapped up in Mitch, I slept better than I ever had in my life.

CHAPTER 25

HOT. SO HOT. I kicked at the quilt wrapped around my legs and threw my arms out, knocking the covers to the floor. The moon glinted off the mirror on my closet door, highlighting the fact I was fully dressed. I flopped my head back and sighed. Mitch must have carried me to my room. The clock glowing on the nightstand told me it was one a.m.—he'd obviously gone to bed as well.

Late or not, I needed to get the bitter aftertaste of the wine out of my mouth. My furry tongue was crying out for a toothbrush. As I tiptoed to the bathroom, the faint glimmer coming from Mitch's studio turned everyday furniture into monsters, casting eerie shadows across the floor. When I looked up, a dark figure passed in front of the light. So he hadn't gone to sleep. He was painting again.

What kind of passion made a man want to get up in the middle of the night and work? I puzzled over it as I brushed my teeth. I couldn't imagine showing the same kind of enthusiasm over accountancy. Analysing a balance sheet in the early hours was more likely to send me to sleep, not keep me awake—annual accounts were an insomniac's dream, especially those prepared under international financial reporting standards. Now, those were really tedious. I shook my head as I dropped my toothbrush back in the holder and left the bathroom.

Yes, the light was still on. Maybe Mitch had got inspired by the storm? I glanced sideways out of the window at the clouds passing in front of the moon, black and angry. That sky...

"Oof!" The air rushed out of my lungs as I hit an unexpected obstacle.

"Georgia?"

"Sorry." I rubbed my nose where I'd caught it on his shoulder.

He dipped his head and brushed it with his lips.

Then I kissed him.

I tried to kid myself it was because of the wine, but I was a dirty liar. I kissed him because I wanted to. I wanted *him*. More than anything I'd ever wanted in my life, I wanted Mitchell Gray.

And when he kissed me back, his rough tongue said he felt as desperate as I did. I pressed myself against him as he attacked my mouth, harder, harder, until he hit the wall behind. My fingers tangled in his hair all of their own accord, and a stranger's moan escaped from my throat.

What was wrong with me? This wasn't what I did. I never took what wasn't offered; I just politely accepted whatever I was given. I was having an out-of-body experience. Some other woman was rubbing herself against Mitch, climbing up him and wrapping her legs around his waist. Undoing his shirt. Biting his lip. Because it certainly couldn't have been me.

He ripped his mouth away from mine, and the sound of tearing fabric filled the air as he shredded my shirt. Shredded it. The clip on my bra didn't cause him any problems, and that lacy scrap of fabric sailed across the room too.

Old insecurities came to the fore and my hands reached towards my chest, ready to cover myself. I'd always been embarrassed by my size, not helped by Douglas suggesting I might like implants as a Christmas present the year before last. But the way Mitch looked at me made my arms drop back to my side as he began to feast.

"Flower, you taste like honey."

First one nipple, then the other—he gave them equal attention. What moisturiser had I put on today? I needed to buy a whole vat of it. I buried my head in the crook of his neck and groaned as my panties got disturbingly damp. His cock was growing by the second, and I writhed against it, trying to get the friction I craved.

Mitch tilted my head back and eyes dark as smoke met mine, swirling with the same desire that grew within me.

"You remember what I said earlier?"

"When?"

"When I promised I wouldn't let anything bad happen to you."

"Yes?"

"I lied."

I stayed silent, not sure where he was going with this.

He smiled, not his kind smile, not his cheesy grin, but a curve of his lips that showed confidence bordering on arrogance. "Because this is happening, and *perakh*, you have no idea how bad I can be."

Good heavens, I almost came right then.

I clung to him as he set off up the stairs, kneading my ass as he went. Five seconds later, he threw me on his bed. Six seconds, and his shirt came off. Seven seconds, he kicked his jeans to the side. Hot damn, he was enormous. Eight seconds, and his weight pressed me into the mattress, trapping me exactly where I wanted to be. I snuck a hand down, stroking along his length, smooth, worryingly long, and...circumcised?

He bit my earlobe and I squealed, in surprise rather than pain, and let go.

"All in good time, flower."

"But I want you now." I fumbled with the button on my jeans, but it was stiff because they were new, and my fingers wouldn't cooperate.

Mitch moved my hands away and pinned them either side of my head. "I'll take care of it."

"But—"

"Shhh."

He kissed me again, and I forgot everything. My name, my problems, that a world existed beyond that loft in Mitch's cabin. Then I heard a snick, and a chill washed across my legs. What was Mitch doing?

Cutting. He had a knife in his hand, and he was cutting me out of my freaking jeans. I should have been appalled. I should have been horrified. But instead, I felt the first twinges of an orgasm in my stomach as he sliced through the last remnants of denim, then the elastic on my panties, and tossed the vicious-looking blade onto the nightstand.

Fire burned through me as he dropped smoking hot kisses down my body, before his lips fastened around my happy spot and he sucked. Sparks shot through me, and it was a good thing his cabin was in the middle of nowhere, because if any neighbours heard my scream, the police would have arrived to join the party.

I was still floating right up next to the stars when Mitch slid one finger inside me, then a second. He hooked them as he stroked, finding that little bundle of nerves that had eluded Douglas for our entire marriage. His tongue didn't let up either. I'd only taken a couple of gasping breaths when my back arched off the bed and I came again, something I'd never quite believed to be possible outside of romance novels.

I lay there, unable to move, as Mitch pumped his hand up and down his shaft a few times.

"Uh, is that going to fit?"

That cocky smile came back. "You're dripping, *perakh*. I could drink from you all night, but I'm gonna fuck you first."

Oh my...

And then he was inside me, long, slow movements at first until I adjusted to his size. My fingers raked his back, and his hands were everywhere, squeezing my breasts, stroking my thighs, clasping my chin as he forced me to keep looking at him.

"I want to see you, flower."

My eyes began to close again, lost in a haze of pleasure.

"Open them."

I tried, managed it, and he held my gaze as he moved faster, harder... And then he was gone. What the...?

"Gonna come on those beautiful tits of yours, Georgia."

He was *what*?

And then he did.

I'd never watched a man come before, but seeing it, knowing I'd done that to him, sent another shockwave through me. And as I fell back to earth, I couldn't resist dipping a finger in the mess and licking it, just to see what it tasted like. What *he* tasted like. A little salty, a little sweet. All Mitch.

And now his smile grew wider, and I understood why he wore it. He really was *that* good.

Sweat glistened on his chest as he gathered me against him in a tangle of arms and legs. Old Georgia would have rushed for the shower in horror at the mess. Mitch's Georgia merely sighed in satisfaction.

"You're my fire, Georgia. You make me burn."

He peppered light kisses across my jaw.

"I... I don't have any words."

"Don't speak then. Just be."

He arranged me so my head lay on his shoulder, using it as a pillow, and one of my legs draped over his. The smell of filthy sex drifted around us, so thick I could taste it. And it was fucking delicious.

Then we slept.

CHAPTER 26

THE SUNBEAM SHINING through the skylight above Mitch's bed settled on my face, and as I opened my eyes and blinked a few times, everything we'd done the previous night came back with startling clarity.

What had I been thinking? I was married, for goodness' sake! My wedding ring was still firmly on my finger, the one resting on Mitch's chest as he breathed slowly in and out. I'd given into a temptation I shouldn't have, no matter how juicy it was, and now I had to live with myself.

I scrambled out of bed and saw the tattered remains of my jeans on the floor. Fuck. Fuck! I half-ran, half-fell down the stairs into my own room and slammed the door, locking it behind me, partly because I didn't want Mitch to come in and partly because I needed to stop myself from running back to his bed.

Oh hell, oh hell, oh hell.

Yesterday had been surreal, from sunrise until dusk, from my adventures with krav maga to the comfortable companionship of watching a movie with a man I adored. A man who wasn't my husband. But I'd let things go too far when darkness fell. I'd got carried away in a world that wasn't mine.

I collapsed on the bed, breathing hard, head in my hands. A delicious soreness between my legs reminded me just how bad I'd been the night before. I'd messed everything up. Everything. After all, it was me who kissed Mitch and not the other way around. The thrill that he'd kissed me back turned into horror as realisation dawned. Mitch and I were stuck here together, potentially for weeks, and it was going to be hell because I couldn't give in to my feelings again. It just wasn't right.

And what was I going to say to Douglas? I'd never be able to look him in the eye. He was undoubtedly waiting at home for me to return, going to work, paying the mortgage, ensuring Manuela looked after the house, and I'd betrayed him. Yes, I'd been having second thoughts about spending the rest of my life with my husband, but I should have at least talked things through with him before I leapt into bed with another man.

But what a man. Even just thinking of Mitch, of what he did to me, had me fidgeting on the bed. I couldn't help myself. I was stuck in a nightmare all of my own making, and I couldn't end it until either my would-be killer caught me or someone caught him. Frustration got the better of me, and I punched the pillow. Stupid Georgia. Stupid, stupid Georgia!

I glanced up at the loft as I crept next door to the bathroom. Still no sign of Mitch, thank goodness. I shed a tear in the shower as I grabbed a sponge and washed off the lingering smell of him. I'd have kept it forever, if it didn't make me want to cry over what I couldn't have.

For the first time, I wished I hadn't ducked to pick up my pen at Monica's baby shower. That it had been my head smeared across the tiles as forensic officers photographed the scene. Because that would have made things a whole lot simpler.

When Mitch finally padded down the stairs, shirtless and looking like he'd just been fucked, which of course he had, the kitchen was in a flurry of activity.

"Good morning," I said going for perky and sounding more like a robot. "I've made French toast, crispy bacon, waffles, and there's fresh coffee in the machine."

He sat on a stool, elbows propped on the counter, and sighed. "I'm Jewish."

A memory flitted back of the smooth hardness I'd felt last night. Oh shit. I stared at the bacon, sizzling in the pan. "I'll get rid of it."

"It's cooked now. Eat it if you want to."

"I won't buy it again. I—"

"Georgia, it doesn't matter."

My mask slipped further and the sobs started. "Mitch, I'm so sorry, I wish I hadn't... Well, no I don't, but I shouldn't have, well, just... Douglas."

He got up and took a step forward, and I shrank back. If he put his hands on me I'd be a goner. When he saw my reaction, he settled back against the counter, relaxed to an outsider, but I saw the tension in his arms.

"No, I'm sorry. I shouldn't have let it get so far. You're vulnerable, and I took advantage of that."

I wanted to tell him that I wasn't vulnerable, that I was a woman and I had needs, and I'd wanted him every bit as much as he'd wanted me, but I couldn't get the words out. I hung my head and stared at the floor.

He stepped closer but stopped inches away. Nothing touched me but his whispered words. "It won't happen again, I promise you that, but I'll never regret it. Just know that if circumstances were different, I'd be doing everything in my power to make you mine."

He snagged a piece of French toast from the plate and walked upstairs to his studio as my tears flowed.

He wanted me, and I wanted him, but we couldn't *have* each other.

As his footsteps receded, I went back to the bread dough I was kneading, all my anger and frustration about the whole awful situation being transformed into a plaited loaf with an egg glaze.

The next few weeks became an exercise in avoidance. Mitch worked out and painted, and occasionally I heard the sharp crack of his pistol as he honed his skills in the woods behind the cabin. Every other day, I'd sit in silence next to him as we drove to the small retirement home in Wolf's corner to drop off my latest batches of baked goods. When I wasn't cooking, I huddled on the sofa with a book or watched TV. I was using Clive's more like a library now, returning batches of books to make space for new ones, but sometimes staring blankly at a screen was easier than studying words on a page.

Oh, we tried to act normal, but it wasn't easy. I visited Rose's for new jeans, and Mitch pushed the cart around the grocery store while I bought everything but pork and shellfish. We even went to the diner once, but after I snapped at Nancy that she might want to pay me some attention as well as Mitch, we didn't go back.

And Mitch never touched me. Not once. Withdrawal symptoms left me a quaking mess, a woman who lay awake for hours before waking up in a cold sweat. I was a junkie, and Mitch was my drug. How I wished for another fix—a kiss, a touch, or even a smile, but I got nothing. I wished so hard that things could be different between us. What if I'd met him years earlier, before Douglas? Would we have stood a chance?

Just when I thought things could get no worse, they did. Mitch's phone rang while we were ignoring each other over breakfast, and I saw Emmy's name flash up on the screen before he snatched it up and strode outside. What did she want? Could I go home yet?

I knew the instant Mitch walked in that the news wasn't good. Deep frown lines marred his otherwise perfect face.

"What's wrong?"

"No more than before."

"Well, something is. What did Emmy want?"

He sighed. "She reckons they've identified the shooter."

"And? Who is he?"

"Just a man. It doesn't make a difference to you."

"Call me crazy, but I'd like to put a name to the man trying to kill me."

"Fine. Fritz Randall."

"That's it? That's all you're going to give me."

"That's all you need to know."

He turned away and walked towards his studio.

No. No way. He did not get to walk away from me. "What? You think because I'm a woman I can't take it? What gives you the right to know? It's not as if you're some freaking ninja like Emmy. All you do is paint stuff. It's my life, and if this Fritz person gets anywhere near me, it'll be my death, and you won't even give me any information. I'm stuck in this damn cabin, on this damn mountain with a man who won't even hold a proper conversation, and I just want to go home."

He stopped. Turned. Advanced towards me. "You really want to know, flower? Really? Fine, I'll tell you. Fritz Randall used to be in the South African Special Forces Brigade, then he went freelance after he got a dishonourable discharge."

Mitch reached me, and I thought he'd stop, but he kept coming. I had no choice but to back up, one shaky step at a time.

"You know why he got a discharge? He got turned in by members of his own unit for killing one too many civilians." My ass hit the kitchen counter, and Mitch pressed his hips into mine, pinning me in place. "He crossed the boundary when he raped a woman and her eight-year-old daughter in Angola then shot them both, her husband, and their two other children."

The kitchen faded into blackness, and the inside of the cabin was still fuzzy when I came to in Mitch's arms on the sofa. "I wish you hadn't told me now."

He picked me up and set me on my feet, rolling his eyes. "Fuck my life."

"Are you s-s-sure this is the man who's after me?"

"Emmy says ninety percent."

"S-s-so now they know who he is, they can find him, right? Right?"

"It's not as easy as that. If he doesn't want to be found, it'll take a while. He's ex-special forces. He used to hide for a living."

"So what happens now?"

"Emmy does her job, and we carry on as we are."

So we did. Two people living in the same house making small talk about the weather and taking it in turns to do the dishes. I carried a pile of books into my bedroom, and the squirrel in the tree outside kept me company while I avoided any novel containing shooting, romance or men with brown hair.

My life was in limbo. I couldn't go home and work things out with Douglas, one way or another, and I could barely stand living with Mitch. Every night before I went to sleep, I said a quick prayer for something to give, for something to happen to resolve this mess.

But when it did, I regretted every word.

CHAPTER 27

"I'D LIKE TO try knitting," I'd informed Mitch a couple of days ago.

"Knitting? Are you old enough to knit?"

"Don't be so ageist. Letty at the retirement home showed me how to do the stitches, and I picked up a book from Clive."

I remembered my grandma knitting when I was a little girl. I'd sit on her lap and the needles would fly back and forth, clicking away, and two days later, there'd be a cosy sweater or maybe a cardigan. I couldn't see Mitch in a cardigan, but I did have the vague idea of making him a scarf as a thank you for putting up with me for all these weeks.

So far I'd made three attempts. One ended up with a hole in it. Another, I somehow picked up extra stitches as I went so the scarf looked more like a triangle. The third simply slipped off the needles. It turned out I wasn't very good at knitting, but I'd become proficient at unravelling.

Frustration got the better of me, and I threw the pile of wool at the wall. It missed and bounced off the TV, needles and all. I hadn't cracked it, had I? Tell me I hadn't cracked it.

Only when I looked properly at the screen, I stopped caring about the crack. Or the knitting or the damn scarf. Why was Pippa on the news? Were they doing a feature on animal shelters? I fished the remote out from down the side of the sofa cushion and turned up the sound.

"...and we've just received the sad news that the body of Jordi Sullivan, who was in the car with his mother, Pippa, when it was carjacked two days ago, has been found next to I-95 following a statewide manhunt. We understand that Pippa herself has now been released from hospital and is working with police to catch the man who did this. The police ask that anybody who sees their vehicle, a dark blue Honda Accord with the licence plate number 5157EK, does not approach but instead calls 911 immediately..."

Jordi was dead? No, he couldn't be. I flipped through the channels until I found another news bulletin. A solemn reporter huddled under an umbrella outside Hope for Hounds, the animal shelter she ran, wearing expression number nine. Grief.

No, no, no. Jordi's dad had never been on the scene, and that boy was Pippa's whole world. She must be... I couldn't even fathom what she must be feeling. How did one come to terms with losing a child? I needed to do something. I was supposed to be her best friend, and I hadn't even spoken to her for months.

Mitch was upstairs painting, but I spotted his phone on the table. I knew if I asked him he'd say no to a call, but not speaking to Pippa wasn't an option, not when her son had just been killed. Mitch would have to deal with it if he found out.

I snuck out onto the back porch. 3669. That was Mitch's PIN. I'd seen him type it into his phone a few times and memorised it out of habit. It had always struck me as odd that someone who eschewed contact with the outside world should have the latest smartphone, but at least it had a good signal. I tapped Pippa's number in from memory and prayed she picked up.

"Hello?" Her voice trembled.

"It's me, Georgia."

"Georgia? Oh my goodness, where are you? Did you hear what happened?"

"I can't say where I am, but I just saw the news. I'm so sorry. So, so sorry."

She broke down in tears, great racking sobs that tore me apart down the phone line. "It was h-h-horrible. I pulled up behind this guy's car at a stoplight, and he got out and tapped on the window. He was smiling. I thought he was going to tell me I had a bulb out, but then he pointed a g-g-gun at me."

"Did he hurt you?"

"Just wrenched my arm when he threw me into the bushes, but when he took off with the car, Jordi was still in the back."

I had no words. Instead, I cried with her, covering my mouth with a hand so Mitch didn't hear.

"The police said he wouldn't want a k-k-kid, that he'd let him go, but now he's dead."

"Do they have any leads?"

"N-n-not yet. I can't even remember his face. All I can see is the gun."

"I wish I could be there to give you a hug right now."

"So do I. When are you coming back?"

I picked at a splinter in the railing. "I don't know. They haven't caught the man who's after me yet, although they say they're getting closer." I had to believe that. "I miss you and the dogs."

"We'll be waiting for you."

"Do you need help with the dogs? You could call my father. Or Douglas..."

We both knew when those words left my mouth it was a stupid thing to say.

"Douglas isn't going to help with the dogs, Gee."

"I guess I was just clutching at straws. Have you seen him?"

"Only on TV. He keeps popping up on chat shows talking about how much he misses you."

Another stab to the heart. Having my relationship broadcast to the world wasn't my favourite thing, but there was no denying Douglas cared, in his own way.

"I'll be back to see both of you soon, and I'll save up the hugs."

"I-I-I could really use them."

I hung up the phone and erased the call from its memory, just in case. I could do without a lecture. Looked like he cleared it out regularly himself—the only recently dialled numbers were the USPS office in Wolf's Corner and the grocery store. What else did he have on his phone? I couldn't resist flipping to the photos.

Me. He had me. On the sofa, in the woods, busy in the kitchen. When did he take these pictures? I hadn't even noticed. And those ones? He'd photographed me while I was sleeping? I didn't know whether to be creeped out or flattered. Then I saw them. A dozen or so shots of me naked and plastered against his chest, and all the memories of that night came flooding back. Not only the sex, but the way he'd held me afterwards and made me feel like I meant something.

I must have stood there for ten minutes before the sound of the back door brought me to my senses.

"Everything all right?"

I slipped the phone into my pocket and arranged my face in a smile before I turned. "Fine. I was watching the squirrel."

"Do you want me to bring you a jacket?"

"He's disappeared now. I was just going to make lunch. Do you want sandwiches?"

Mitch held the door open, and I walked past, the phone burning away at my side. Had he noticed it was missing?

"Sandwiches sound good. I'll be back in a minute—I left my sweater in the car yesterday."

Thank goodness. The instant he closed the door behind him, I returned the phone to its place on the table. Phew. That was too close.

Bread. I needed bread. And butter, and those beef slices I bought in town yesterday. Anything to keep busy while I digested the news about Pippa. The thought of not seeing Jordi again shredded me, so I could only imagine how hard the news must have hit her.

"Knitting not going so well?" I looked up to find Mitch staring at my sad little pile of wool, bundled on the floor where I'd left it.

"I don't know how Letty does it. She makes it look so easy."

"Just don't give up. You'll be making blankets and all that shit in no time."

He gave my shoulder an affectionate squeeze, the first time he'd laid a finger on me since the news about

Fritz. That made me feel even worse.

"I'm considering crosswords or sudoku instead."

"They won't keep you warm at night, flower."

I knew exactly what would keep me warm, but I couldn't deal with that right now. I gave Mitch my back instead, putting all my efforts into making the perfect sandwich with a salad garnish.

"...and anyone with information should call the police emergency number."

I turned away from the screen in frustration. A day later, and the police still had nothing on Jordi's murder. Nothing. They hadn't even found Pippa's car. Every hour the news played the story, but it was just the same information re-hashed, sometimes with a different talking head or a change of camera angle for variety.

At one point, they showed a picture of Pippa walking out of the hospital next to a policewoman, and I shed a few tears. There was only one reason she'd have been there: A visit to the morgue. How utterly, utterly horrific it must have been to identify the body of her own son. Part of me wanted to jump straight onto a plane back to Virginia, but the coward that hid within vetoed that idea, leaving me disgusted with myself. I'd learned an awful lot about my own character during my stay on Mitch's mountain, and I didn't like most of it.

As I lay in bed that night, I mulled over my options again. Things had been quiet for so long. Maybe Fritz had given up and found somebody else to kill instead? How did these contracts work? Did hitmen take on more than one at a time and slot them into a project plan? Maximise their earning potential? It would make good business sense to have several jobs going on at the same time, certainly.

Or perhaps he got bored and went home? While I hid out with Mitch, Fritz could be sunning himself by the pool in South Africa, waiting for an easier offer to come along.

I'd managed away from Douglas for so long, but now my best friend was in trouble. Staying in Colorado wasn't an option. Especially when I knew how bad Pippa was at admitting she needed help. I'd seen it time and time again with the dogs—she'd rather work all hours herself than ask volunteers to take some of the load.

My sigh filled the little bedroom. I needed to speak to Mitch about this. After all, it was my life, and he kept saying I should make my own decisions.

CHAPTER 28

FOR HALF THE night I lay awake, planning what I'd say to Mitch. I needed to break the news I wanted to go home gently rather than sounding ungrateful for everything he'd done. At a time like this, I really needed Pippa to bounce ideas off, but that was out of the question.

I also needed to pick my moment, and that morning, as Mitch stomped down the stairs from the studio wearing a scowl, wasn't it.

"I've spilled my thinners, and it was my last bottle. You coming into town with me?"

"Uh, yes, okay. Just let me grab my jacket." Picking up the groceries would allow me to delay the conversation I didn't want to have by an hour or two.

Market day in Wolf's Corner meant the town was busier than usual. People from neighbouring towns drove in to shop from the stalls that lined the main street, selling everything from fresh food to arts and crafts. Thanks to Mitch's generosity, I always had cash in my pocket, so I took the opportunity to browse while he went to the hardware store I'd learned also kept a small stock of hobby paints. Maybe this would be my last trip to Wolf's Corner, if my talk with Mitch went as planned. That thought saddened me more than I thought it would. I'd fallen a little bit in love with the town and its inhabitants, Nancy aside. They'd all been so friendly and welcoming to a stranger who'd arrived with nothing.

At the first stall, one of the local farmer's wives greeted me with a happy grin.

"Vivien! I've got more of those chilli beef burgers you and Mitch like so much."

I mustered up a smile of my own as I stooped to scritch her Labrador's head, something else that reminded me of Pippa and the dogs she doted on. "Could you give me half a dozen?"

Even if I might not be around to eat them. At the next table, I picked up some of the craft beer Mitch was fond of then cast a critical eye over the baked goods. I'd harboured a secret wish to set up my own stall but never plucked up the courage to mention it to Mitch. Now I never would.

A picture frame caught my eye, sandwiched between handmade greeting cards and a knitted teddy bear. Two metal dogs on the front held paws, and shiny bubble between said "Best friends." It would be perfect for Pippa—she loved that kind of kitsch. The lady selling it threw in a card and gift-wrapping for free, and I hoped it might cheer Pippa up just a little.

Hot breath on my neck informed me of Mitch's return. I'd given up wondering how he materialised silently out of nowhere like that.

"Can we make a quick stop at the post office?"

"What do you want to post?"

"Just a gift for a friend. Her son died recently."

"How do you know?"

"It made the news. She got carjacked, and the man killed her son. She's so upset by it, and I want to cheer her up."

His eyes narrowed. "How do you know she's upset?"

Shit. Me and my big mouth. "Well, I imagine she would be. Losing a child must be tragic for anybody."

"You didn't say you imagined she'd be upset. You said she *was* upset."

Fine, I'd tell him. It didn't matter anyway, seeing as I planned to go home. "I talked to her, okay? She's my best friend, and I could hardly ignore her after something so serious happened."

His mouth set in a hard line as he gripped my arm and pulled me towards the car, and I tripped over my own feet.

"Let go. You're hurting me."

He loosened his grip slightly but didn't slow down. "When did you call her and where from?"

"Why does it matter?"

"Just answer the fucking question, will you?"

Mitch had made me feel almost every emotion over the last few weeks, but until now, fear hadn't been one of them. I tried to twist out of his grip, but he opened the Land Rover door and shoved me inside.

"Answer the question, Georgia."

"Yesterday. No, the day before. I borrowed your phone. You were painting, or I'd have asked first." Only a tiny white lie.

"Fuck. What time?"

"Uh, I can't remember."

"Try harder."

Why was he being like this? "Before lunch. Just before lunch."

He fired up the engine and skidded out the parking

space, transmission whining. The Land Rover wasn't designed to be driven in such a violent manner. Mitch was going as fast as Emmy. My knuckles turned white as I gripped the edges of the seat, praying he wouldn't wrap the vehicle around a tree.

We were on the bumpy road that led to the driveway when a ringing phone caught my attention. Not Mitch's—that had been bouncing around on the dashboard the whole ride. So where was it?

The answer was, in Mitch's pocket. He pulled out a second phone, tapped the screen while he negotiated a tight bend then wedged it in the ashtray.

"Speak to me."

Emmy's voice crackled into the cab. "Mack's tagged Fritz going out of Dulles, destination Denver. He's on a British passport, name of Peter Smith."

"When?"

"Yesterday lunchtime. Colorado could be a coincidence, but my gut says no."

"Your gut's right. I just found out Georgia made a call the day before yesterday."

"Why? Who to?"

"A friend of hers got carjacked, and the bastard killed her kid. It made the news."

"Pippa Sullivan?"

Mitch looked at me, and I nodded.

"That's her."

"So he killed the kid and used the mother as bait. Drastic, but I guess he got impatient."

It took a second for her words to sink in then the world fuzzed out. "You mean Fritz killed Jordi to get to me?"

The phone crackled again. "Oh, you've got Georgia

with you? That's handy. Yes, Georgia, I'd say that was the likely scenario."

"Stop the car!"

"I'm not fucking stopping."

"Well, I'm going to be sick." I could feel the bile rising up my throat.

"Then you can pay for the damned valet afterwards."

What was wrong with Mitch? I'd made a mistake, and yes, it was a huge one, but now he was just...scary. Who the hell *was* this man?

Emmy's voice interrupted my sniffing. "Where was the call made from?"

"Cabin." Mitch drove up the verge to get around a slower car, and I caught the look of shock on the driver's face. It matched my own.

"Bollocks. So if he's not there already, he'll be with you damn soon."

"We've got to assume that. I'll secure Georgia and get ready for him."

Secure me? What did he mean, secure me?

"I'm on my way with a team. We're on a chopper halfway to the airfield, but I doubt we'll get there in time."

"Then you can help clear up the mess."

Mitch hung up and slowed a fraction. "Get in the footwell."

"Why?"

"Dammit, Georgia, do you have to question everything? Because the windows aren't bulletproof, and if Fritz is here and he sees you, he'll shoot you."

"Oh."

He gave me a shove. "Do it."

I squashed myself down as small as I could get, and the tops of the trees flew past as he hurtled up the driveway, past the cabin and onto the track beyond. I'd never ventured along it before, not even on our occasional hikes. The car went dark as we shot into what I assumed was the garage then strip lights flickered on overhead.

"Mitch, what's going on?" I tried to sound normal, but the quake in my voice gave me away.

"Well, right now, because you got the sudden urge to make a phone call, we have a highly trained assassin on his way to try and kill both of us."

That time, I couldn't keep my breakfast down, I half-fell out the car and vomited next to the back wheel.

"We don't have time for that, Georgia."

"Shut up!"

Mitch turned his back on me and strode to the side wall, and seconds later, the dusty boards slid sideways, revealing a hidden space where metal glinted under a row of spotlights.

"What the hell is all that?"

The words popped out although I already knew the answer. Guns. There were guns. Not just the hunting rifle or two I'd expected him to have, but the kind of hardware I'd only seen in movies. Nasty-looking assault rifles with scopes and laser sights. Beyond them lay knives, a crossbow, and a whole stack of boxes. I didn't even want to think about what was in those.

And when Mitch faced me, he wore a new grin. Not the happy one, not the sexy one, but a malevolent, evil grin that made me sweat even more than I was already.

"This is my toy collection."

He loaded a magazine into his Colt and shoved the

gun into his waistband, then pulled me to the back of the room. I stood frozen as he dragged a heavy-looking workbench to the side and threw back the trapdoor that lay underneath it.

"Get in." He pointed at a dark flight of steps leading downwards.

"You're kidding? I'm not going down there."

"Yes, you are. Or so help me God, I'll have to make you."

I peered downwards, but I couldn't make anything out in the pitch black. "There might be spiders."

"Would you prefer a spider or a bullet to the head?"

"I don't know! Neither of them seems particularly appealing!"

"Stop shrieking and get in there." He pointed into the hole.

How could he stay so calm? "And what are you going to do?"

"I'm going to find Fritz, and I'm going to kill him. And while I do, I need to know you're safe, so get in the fucking cellar, Georgia."

"You can't! He's a professional assassin."

Mitch's wicked grin came back, and my blood froze.

"So am I, Georgia. So am I."

My heart missed a beat as I took him in, standing in front of a wall of weapons with hard muscles and harder eyes. He was actually serious, wasn't he? I didn't know him at all. Mitch, the artist I'd laughed and joked with, slept with, for fuck's sake, was just as evil as the man who'd been after me. *Congratulations, Georgia, you really are a terrible judge of character.*

He took the gun out of his waistband and motioned at the steps. I didn't have much choice in the matter, did I? One foot in front of the other, I climbed into my own personal hell.

As I reached the fourth step, he held out the gun to me. "Magazine's full and the safety's off. If anyone but me or Emmy comes for you, you shoot them, got it?"

I nodded. Anything to get away from this nightmare.

"I need to hear you say it."

"I'll shoot them." My voice came from miles away. This couldn't be happening.

"Good girl."

I'd nearly got to the bottom when Mitch knelt down and fisted his fingers in my hair, turning me to face him. He leaned in and pressed a chaste kiss to my lips.

"I love you, *perakh*. Never forget that. I love you."

Then the door slammed over my head and left me in darkness.

CHAPTER 29

XAV DRAGGED THE workbench back over the trapdoor and scuffed over dusty marks left on the floor. It wouldn't be impossible for Fritz to find Georgia down there, but it would take time, and Xav didn't intend to give him that.

He moved over to his toy collection to get ready. He'd spent years honing his craft, and these were the tools of his trade. Each weapon had been tested, customised where necessary, and now functioned as an extension of his own body. So, which should he choose to solve today's issue? He picked up an AR15 with a holographic sight then put it back down. No, not that one. Trouble was, today he couldn't be Xavier Roth, ex-Horseman and former member of Mossad's elite Kidon unit. He had to be Mitchell Gray, artist, stuck in an unexpected situation he couldn't control. That meant no fancy assault rifle and no grenades. Instead, he strapped a duplicate of his favourite Colt to his thigh and picked out a high-powered hunting rifle. It wouldn't be unreasonable for a mountain man to have those.

His indigo jeans offered reasonable camouflage, and he swapped out his checked shirt for a mottled green jacket. No shiny buttons, no silver zippers that might catch the sun. Yeah, he'd pass as a civilian, but avoid being a target when he got into the forest. Once he'd added a hat, he clipped a communications set onto his belt and slid in the earpiece. The batteries were fresh—he changed them religiously every month, just in case. Two seconds later, he'd linked into an encrypted channel.

"Smoke to Valkyrie, over."

"Yo, babe." Emmy's voice came back loud and clear.

"Hear you're still as professional as ever."

"I'm pro in the ways that matter. Don't worry."

Xav wasn't worried, not about Emmy anyway. No, the reason for the lump in his throat was the girl hiding in the bunker beneath the workbench, the one he loved and had now lost. Images of her flashed through his mind—of her beating pastry into submission when she got uptight, of her curled into him on the sofa, and finally, of her moaning beneath him as she came. He closed his eyes for a brief moment, wishing things could be different. That he really was just an artist living the simple life on a mountain. Of course, that could present difficulties in their current predicament.

"Xav?"

"I'm here."

"Put her out of your mind and get with it, will ya? Fritz rented a car at the airport yesterday evening, and the interesting thing is, when Mack hacked into the CCTV footage, he wasn't alone when he got into it."

Fuck. "A colleague? A hostage? Someone else?"

"From the way he carried himself and the way he was built, I'd say it's two against one."

"You got any good news?"

"Bradley's throwing a party to celebrate the French Open. Tennis and cakes. Actually, on second thoughts..."

Bradley, her assistant, was as crazy as she was. "About fucking Fritz."

"Shit out of luck there. Is Georgia secure?"

"She's in the cellar. Either I get her out or you do. I've told her to shoot anyone else."

"Understood."

Xav returned his attention to the weapons locker. A knife. He needed a knife. Killing a man up close and personal got messy, and he hoped to avoid it, but sometimes it was necessary, and he needed to be prepared. He considered his options then picked out the Emerson CQC 7-B, which Emmy had slipped into his pocket on an outing a few years ago, and clipped it onto the back of his belt. Spare magazines went next to it, and he pulled his jacket over them.

Deep breath.

Two years had passed since he'd last taken a life, and longer still since anybody had tried to kill him. For Georgia's sake, he hoped he hadn't lost his edge. Yes, he'd kept in shape, yes, he'd practised fight drills and yes, he still shot regularly, but that was no substitute for living the life he'd once led.

And Fritz was a bad enemy to have. Emmy had sent him dossiers covering everything from the man's training to his psychological evaluations—who knew where she'd dredged those up from—and he'd studied them thoroughly. Fritz was bloodthirsty but cold and rational, the worst combination. Xav preferred to think of himself as clinical. He liked to cut out the bad and leave the good intact.

Much like Emmy, in fact. Fuck, he wished she was there with him in person, not just on the radio.

At least one woman in his life was still speaking to him. He'd seen the disgust on Georgia's face when she realised who he was. What he was. And the fear. He'd scared her, and he couldn't undo that. He hated that his last memory of the girl he'd fallen for would be that one.

Because he wouldn't see her again. Whatever happened today, he was a dead man. The best thing he could do would be to leave her to a life of safety with her friend Pippa and that snivelling little husband of hers, if she still wanted him, although he hoped she'd see the light there sooner rather than later.

He closed up the wall in the garage, leaving only a dusty facade, then turned off the lights before slipping outside. The sun went behind a cloud as he moved silently up the mountain to the north, to watch and wait and plan.

Xavier knew every inch of his mountain, from the hidden hollow in the oak on the ridge to the red-tailed hawk's nest beside the deer track that wound towards the peak. He hunkered down in the soft earth, breathing in the smell of moss and last night's rain while he waited. Occasionally Emmy would check in from the plane, now over Colorado and about to land at Denver International.

Three hours had passed when a flock of hooded warblers rose into the air, signalling an intruder. Fritz? Or simply a passing deer? Xav focused in their direction, and it wasn't long before the faint movement of undergrowth caught his eye. A brief glimpse of a hand, followed by the outline of a head.

"They're here," he murmured to Emmy.

"Wheels down. We've got a car waiting."

Even with Emmy's driving, they'd arrive too late.

He watched, hidden, as a man dressed similarly to him crept along a gulley to the west. Not Fritz. This must be his new buddy. The crack of a twig suggested a lack of care, or possibly inexperience with this kind of operation. Either option was good news for Xav. He peered through the scope on his rifle and identified the newcomer's gun as an AK47. Sourced locally, most likely, seeing as he'd flown commercial and no professional would have wanted to draw attention to himself by carrying hardware on a plane.

And how long had he been in Colorado? A day at most. Xav bet the stranger wouldn't have taken the time to sight the weapon in properly, thereby sacrificing accuracy for speed. A rookie mistake. Xav smiled to himself, far more confident in his own Accuracy International, a birthday gift from Dime a number of years previously, and one that he practised with religiously every week.

A couple of minutes later, he spotted Fritz, who'd cut through the woods to the east. A quick scan revealed only a pistol. Tsk tsk. They'd come woefully underprepared. Lesson number one, boys—never underestimate your enemy. He was tempted to make it a turkey shoot and pick both of them off right that second. Emmy would arrive soon with extra muscle, and he had shovels in the garage. Nobody need ever know. But then he thought of Georgia and her future, and knew he had to go with an alternative plan. One that would set her free from her past. And him.

Smoothly, silently, he crept down the mountain, keeping an eye on the fuckers below him. Both were oblivious to his presence, focused solely on the cabin, in Fritz's case through the fancy pair of binoculars he'd brought along. Xav laid his rifle under a purple smokebush and made sure it was out of sight. He didn't need it anymore and carrying it would only slow him down. Emmy could retrieve it later.

For a second, he wished he could turn back the clock and run with Georgia. Somewhere far away, a place where he could be Mitch and she could be beautiful and they could hide until the end of time.

But he was Smoke, and he did not run.

He fought.

One deep breath and he mashed his heel onto a dry twig.

The sharp crack might not have sounded like much on a normal day, but under the circumstances, he might as well have shot off a cannon. Two heads swivelled in his direction as he bolted for the cabin, a stream of bullets kicking up the dirt behind him.

A flying kick made short work of the backdoor, and he took shelter behind the thick wood of the kitchen counter as bullets thudded into it. He'd sourced that timber from a local lumberjack and made the units himself, shaping and sanding until they were perfect. And always with an event like this at the back of his mind. Splinters of wood flew all around, but the hundred-year-old oak did its job.

Well, it was safe to say the first part of his plan worked. They knew he was inside, and there was no turning back now. A lull in the gunfire told him they were changing magazines, and he used those seconds to run up to his sleeping loft, where he hopped up onto the closet, half hidden in the shadows under the eaves, and waited.

"I'm gonna need a lift to Virginia," he whispered to Emmy. "And a place to stay."

"Why don't I like the sound of this?"

Ten minutes passed before the first of the visitors approached, both warier than they had been outside. Fritz came through the backdoor in a crouch, gun up as he scuttled behind the sofa. A faint crackle reached Xav's ears as he radioed through to his buddy, followed by a harsh whisper.

"He's hiding."

"Sure he didn't leave?"

"We were watching all the exits."

The front door opened a crack then more fully when the inside of the cabin stayed silent. Asshole number two's shadow slipping inside was Xav's cue to leave. He flipped open the hidden hatch in the roof, silent on well-oiled hinges, and threw out the rope securely attached to the ring on the ceiling. Seconds later, he closed the hole up and rappelled down the outside of the building then melted back into the woods. His woods. He'd miss them.

Not a single rustle sounded as he backed up the mountainside with practised ease, pausing only when he reached a sturdy boulder. Hidden safely behind it, he watched two heads pass in front of the windows of the great room and gazed sadly at his house, the only home he'd ever had. The design he'd put his heart into, not to mention hours of labour. That place held his paintings and his memories, especially ones of a lovely blonde-stroke-brunette who'd come into his life as a tiny bud and opened up into a beautiful rose.

Then he sighed and did what he had to do.

It was Red who'd built the app on his phone, designed to look like a simple calculator when in reality it was anything but.

Xav typed in a ten-digit number, ducked, and three seconds later his cabin blew sky-high.

CHAPTER 30

A GLANCE AT the glowing hands on my watch showed it was almost five in the afternoon. Three hours since Mitch put me in this hole, and now I was stuck here. When would he come back? I'd found a flashlight at the bottom of the steps and the stack of canned goods and bottled water in the corner meant I wouldn't starve right away—there was a can opener, thank goodness— but that wouldn't last forever. And the bucket in the corner was slightly alarming. Was I expected to pee in that? If so, death looked the more appealing prospect.

I turned off the flashlight to save the batteries, and also so I wouldn't have to look at the bucket any more. It was a good thing I wasn't claustrophobic because I'd surely have lost my mind by now. The cellar wasn't large, maybe twelve feet square, and the smell of my body odour, of my fear, smothered the mustiness that had pervaded when I first got there. Another hour ticked by. Why hadn't Mitch come back?

I was slumped in the corner of the dark cellar when the ground shook. After pacing the tiny space for the first hour, I'd finally given in and sunk to the rough wooden floor, but the low, rumbling boom reverberated through me and sent me scrambling to my feet. What had happened? Did they have earthquakes in Colorado? Even down there, buried in the ground, it felt like the world was ending.

Where was Mitch? Was he all right? I turned on the flashlight and tried again to open the hatch, but all I did was break my nails. Blood from my fingers smeared over the wood. After half an hour, I heard sounds—a car engine, shouts, a crunching noise. And was that a siren? But then it went quiet.

Back in my corner, I began to get cold. I couldn't find a blanket or any clothing, so I wrapped my hands around my knees and rubbed my legs, trying to get some warmth into them. Time moved slowly, far too slowly, but at eight o'clock I was still alone.

I jumped as a muffled crack sounded overhead, but no other sounds came. Was someone there, or had I imagined it? I called out, my throat dry and hoarse, but nobody came. Beads of sweat dripped down my forehead as I listened for any sign of life to show I hadn't been abandoned. Was Mitch coming back? Or Emmy?

I imagined Mitch was there with me, telling me what to do. Breathe, little flower. Breathe in and out. Why did he always call me flower? I'd never asked him, just accepted it like everything else he gave me, but now I longed to know. He made me feel like a rose—beautiful, delicate, something to be treasured. At least until today.

I'd had a lot of time to think about what he said, right before he shut the door on me. In fact, time was all I had.

His revelations shocked me to my core. How could Mitch be a killer? I tried to tell myself I'd misunderstood, or maybe he'd been playing a misplaced joke on me, but then I thought of his malicious smile, and I knew he hadn't been. Little things fell into place. His travels, the number of languages he spoke. The knife he kept handy in his bedroom. His friendship with Emmy, who seemed to inhabit a murky world herself. The ease with which he lied to me made sense as well. He probably did it all the time. Maybe I was just the latest in a long line of women he'd pretended to like.

But that look in his eyes, the very last time I saw him, how could he have faked that? Love tinged with sadness. I'd remember that moment forever.

It was after ten in the evening when I heard the workbench being dragged from over the trapdoor. I crouched in the corner, pointing the gun upwards.

A voice called out, muffled by the wood. "Georgia, it's Emmy. I know you've got a gun down there, so for fuck's sake don't shoot me."

I dropped the pistol, relief washing through me. She threw the trapdoor back, flooding the steps with light as I blinked in the glare at the bottom.

"You okay to climb out?"

"I think so."

I grasped the hand she offered but still landed on my knees at the top. Strong arms pulled me up, and I found myself plastered to a man's muscular chest. "Mitch?"

"No, babe. Nick."

I wept in relief at seeing a friendly face, but it wasn't the one I wanted.

"Where's Mitch?" I croaked.

Emmy yelled at somebody to bring a blanket, and they wrapped one of those silver foil sheets around my shoulders. A man in a green uniform began asking me questions. When did I last have something to drink? Had I eaten that day? Did I feel faint? Was I injured in any way?

I shook my head, both to answer no and make him go away. I didn't want to talk to a stranger.

"Did you hit your head?"

"Please, leave me alone."

"You might be hurt."

Emmy stepped in. "Take the hint, buddy."

"Mitch? Where's Mitch?"

Nick's arm tightened around my waist as Emmy answered. "I'm so sorry, Georgia."

Somehow I held it together. I'd cried in front of Mitch, but I wasn't going to cry for him in front of all these people. I didn't think he'd want me to. Not when he'd tried so hard to make me strong.

Emmy squeezed my hand, so cold in her warm one. "Do you want to go home now?"

"Is Fritz dead?"

"Yes."

"Was it Mitch?"

"Yes."

The last thing he'd done was die to save me. Assassin or not, I knew in that moment that I loved him, and my biggest regret would be not having told him so.

Nick kept his arm around me as we left the garage and walked down the track. I was grateful for his support when I saw the cabin, or rather when I didn't see the cabin, because there was nothing left but a mound of smoking rubble. My knees buckled, and he picked me up and carried me past the charred remains. Hoses snaked back and forth like giant worms as firemen damped down what was left. As I sobbed, two firemen climbed over a pile of splintered timbers carrying a body bag, one at each end.

"Is that him?" I whispered.

"I don't think they've worked out which is which yet." Emmy glanced to the side, and I saw an ambulance, a twin black bag resting atop a gurney outside its doors.

It was real. Mitch had gone. The man who brought me alive and made me feel was gone. I'd never see his smile, hear his laughter, or feel his arms again.

It was at that moment that my soul died. I felt it evaporate, fluttering away into nothing, and then the darkness claimed me.

I woke up in the back of an ambulance with wires sprouting from my arms and chest. The beep, beep, beep of someone's heart sounded in the background, but I knew it wasn't my heart because my heart was dead.

When I turned my head, I found Emmy and Nick sitting next to me in a silent vigil. A medic stood to the side, and when he saw me move he began fussing around, pushing buttons and asking questions. I closed my eyes again to block him out.

"Ma'am? Mrs. Beaumont?"

"What?"

"I need to ask you some questions."

"I don't want to answer them." And I didn't want to be there. I tried to sit up and pull the wires off, but the man pushed me down again.

"Please stay still, Mrs. Beaumont."

"No. Let me go. I just want to go."

"That's not a good idea. We still have tests to do and you're dehydrated."

I pushed his hands away as he tried to stick one of the ECG pads back on my chest. "Get off me."

Thankfully, Emmy helped me out. "Look, I think we can agree that apart from needing a drink and having a nasty shock, there's not a lot wrong with her, so we can just lose the cotton wool, and I'll take her someplace she can rest." She turned to me. "If that's what you want?"

"Yes, please."

She made the medic take all the monitoring equipment off then helped me outside. It was dark, the moon covered by clouds, but the place was lit up by so many floodlights it may as well have been a summer's day.

"You okay to stay if I take Georgia to Denver?" Emmy asked Nick.

"Of course."

"Just keep them away from the garage. There's all sorts of shit in there and none of it's relevant to this investigation."

She must have been talking about the guns. Somehow, I wasn't surprised she knew they were there. I hoped the police wouldn't find them—they'd start digging through Mitch's life, and I hated to think what they might turn up.

I looked the other way as Nick carried me past the cabin again, but I couldn't avoid the acrid smell of smoke that permeated the air. It made me gag, and I didn't think I'd ever get it out of my nostrils. Instead, I took one last look at the mountain where I'd laughed and talked with Mitch. The leaves would soon be weighing down the tree branches, providing shade and food until they burst into a riot of colour in fall. Deer would walk the tracks and the red-tailed hawks Mitch showed me would soar above the ridge. The mountain would live forever, a legacy of the man who'd once owned it.

Emmy's Ford Explorer was parked a way down the track, and Nick helped me into the passenger side. When I'd driven this same track with Emmy weeks before, I never imagined the twists and turns my life would take. I'd been through every emotion, but I was leaving with the worst of them all: devastation.

We rode in silence until we hit the highway, then I could take it no more. "You knew, didn't you?"

"Knew what?"

"What Mitch was." An assassin. I couldn't bring myself to say the word.

She nodded slowly. "I wouldn't have taken you there otherwise. I knew he'd keep you safe."

"He gave his life for me."

She nodded again. "Like I told you at the beginning, above everything, he was a good man."

CHAPTER 31

I SAT AT the white marble breakfast bar sipping a cup of strong, black coffee. Opposite me, Douglas smeared low-fat, low-sodium, low-taste spread across a piece of wholemeal toast, his own cup of decaf on a coaster next to him.

When he spoke, his condescending tone left me in no doubt I was being completely unreasonable. "You've been back for two weeks now. You can't keep sitting around doing nothing."

"I haven't been doing nothing."

"Baking and reading? That's hardly constructive. You can't possibly eat all those cakes—you'll get fatter. And were you actually trying to knit? Is that what that pile of wool in the lounge is? I'll buy you knitwear, for goodness' sakes, you don't have to waste your time trying to make it yourself."

"That's not all I've been doing."

Douglas took a bite of toast and wiped the crumbs from his mouth. "Oh, you mean those awful hounds? Most of them aren't even pedigree. Animal control should put them to sleep, then you wouldn't have to spend your days picking up who knows what. A lady in your position should most certainly not be stooping that low."

I balled my hands into fists. "How can you say that?

It's not their fault they're homeless. They deserve a chance."

He softened slightly at my tone. "Maybe I was a little harsh. Look, how about I write the shelter a cheque? Five thousand dollars? Then they can hire an immigrant to do the dirty work."

I wanted to throw something at him. Like my orange juice, and the jug it came in. If only his potential voters could hear his derogatory remarks—they'd desert him in droves.

"It's not just the animals. Pippa lost her son. She needs my support."

He held his hands wide, the voice of reason. "Surely it would be better if you took her on a spa break or something? You can get a manicure and a nice massage. I'll have my assistant book something for you both."

"Douglas, I'm not going on a freaking spa weekend. I'm helping at the animal sanctuary and that's final!"

He sighed in exasperation. "Fine. I'm sure the novelty of being there every day will wear off soon, anyway. And would you mind your language? You know how uncouth cussing sounds."

I ignored him. He'd always been like this, but I'd been conditioned to accept it before. To suck it up and get on with things. If he'd said that to me three months ago, I'd have been packing my bags for the spa and deciding what colour nail polish I wanted. Now I'd tasted freedom, every time Douglas opened his mouth I wanted to punch him.

He finished his toast and got up, leaving the plate for me to put in the dishwasher. Again.

"You haven't forgotten the Brookstein's soirée this

evening, have you?"

"No, and I also haven't forgotten that I said I'm not going."

He put his hands on his hips. "Look, Georgia, I told you how important it is for us to attend this evening. Several very important potential donors will be there, as will your parents, and don't forget the election's less than six months away."

How could I possibly forget? He reminded me every day, and his life revolved around getting elected as congressman for the Third District of Virginia. His plan was to serve two two-year terms in Congress then run for my father's place in the Senate. There was just the small matter of winning the seat in the first place.

"I'm still not going. I don't want to be out in public yet."

He patted me on the head, like one would to placate a small child. "Georgia, you're being ridiculous. We've got to get this sorted out. I'll make an appointment for you with Dr, Nielsen."

I didn't want to speak to Dr. Nielsen. He may have been my therapist, but he was also a golfing buddy of Douglas's, and I was fairly sure that after a glass or two of wine, the bounds of patient confidentiality slipped somewhat.

The thought of bowing to Douglas's wishes made me feel sick again. I'd had this argument, or at least a similar one, every day since I got back. It had got to the stage where it was making me physically ill. That wasn't surprising, as I'd always had a delicate stomach, but it left me drained. I went upstairs to the bathroom, leaving Douglas to do exactly as he wanted, as usual.

As I wiped my mouth, my phone rang. Mother. I

ignored it, because she spoke to Douglas more than I did, and she'd take his side and ship me off to therapy again. I just knew it. She'd made my first appointment with a psychiatrist three days after my fifteenth birthday when I'd refused to dress up and accompany her and Daddy on one of his campaign visits. The message was clear: Toe the line or life gets difficult.

And I was sick of it. Quite literally.

The front door slammed as Douglas left with Sy, his aide, a man who made my skin crawl every time he looked at me. He and Douglas got on perfectly. Sy had come over for dinner last night, and despite the fact I'd worn a kaftan, he'd stared at my breasts every time he spoke to me while Douglas forked in coq au vin and planned whatever bullshit he'd feed to the press this week.

But they'd gone now, and it was time to go and see Pippa. I thought the reporters camping outside would have gotten bored and given up by now, but flashbulbs still went off as I nosed my Mercedes past the gates with my security detail following. Daddy had insisted I have protection, at least for now, but thankfully he'd acquiesced to my request not to have them in the house. I couldn't take any more strangers.

For a moment, I was tempted to gun the engine, Emmy-style, but then I'd end up on the front page again. *Socialite attempts to run over paparazzi*. No, that would never do. So I attempted a half-smile and inwardly grimaced that more blurry photos of me in a ratty sweater and jeans would grace the gossip websites

by the time I got home. I hadn't even washed my hair—
I'd run out of energy for such trivialities.

The media had gone crazy right after the explosion.
I guess it wasn't every day a famous artist got blown up
while saving a senator's daughter. Mitch had always
been notoriously publicity shy, of course, and they
didn't even have a photo of him. That meant the bulk of
the coverage centred on me, and it had been relentless.
Re-lent-less. Every aspect of my life got pored over and
splashed across the tabloids. Childhood photos
appeared next to interviews with school friends. People
I didn't even remember lined up to spill details of my
life, most of which weren't true.

At Hope for Hounds, it had been worse. With Pippa
being a news story in her own right, the fact the two of
us were friends caused a storm. Thankfully, nobody
connected Jordi's death and my attempted murder—as
far as the public was concerned, they were two
separate, tragic incidents.

I'd agonised over whether to tell Pippa of
Blackwood's suspicions, but when I'd discussed it with
Emmy on the trip home, she'd advised against it.

"There's no evidence, and likely never will be now
Fritz is dead."

"But Pippa won't get closure."

"Closure's overrated. There's times when telling the
truth causes more pain and learning to recognise those
is important for everyone."

So I kept quiet and let the guilt eat away at me. I
didn't want to ruin my friendship with Pippa, and I
needed her more than ever now. It wasn't like I could
talk to Douglas—the man had the empathy of a wet
fish. I recalled the conversation we'd had the day I

arrived home.

"You mean to tell me you were staying with Mitchell Gray?" Douglas had asked, glancing at Mitch's painting, which took pride of place over the fireplace.

"Please don't be upset. He was connected to the security company."

"Upset? I'm not upset. That print I bought you should rocket in value now. We'll be able to sell it for ten times what I paid for it."

That was the moment I decided to get a divorce. And it got worse.

"And you know what they say—no publicity is bad publicity." Douglas looked positively happy now. "We can get you on the talk show circuit. I made some contacts while you were on your little break."

Little break? He made it sound like a vacation. "I'm not going on television."

"How about a photoshoot? You've ruined your hair, but I'm sure Sven can do something with it. Maybe extensions?"

"No, Douglas. I'm not doing a photoshoot either. Or any interviews, before you suggest it."

"Sometimes I don't understand you, Georgia. These are golden opportunities, and your moment in the spotlight won't last forever."

Thank goodness.

The media was strangely silent on the actual explosion, probably because the police wouldn't give them any details. The liaison officer told me they thought Fritz intended to detonate the bomb with me and Mitch inside, but when Mitch disturbed him, something went wrong, and they got blown up together instead. Apart from that, the cops were a little light on details. Either they knew less than I did or they simply weren't telling me anything.

I asked, and I kept asking, even though my eyes stung every time Mitch's name left my lips. They hadn't identified Fritz, and they were still trying to track down Mitch's dental records. Wherever he got his gleaming white teeth looked after, it wasn't in Wolf's Corner or even Denver. The liaison lady told me he didn't have any living relatives to give a DNA sample, and for some reason that made my chest ache even more. Nobody apart from me and maybe Emmy would mourn Mitch, and he deserved more than that. They'd only identified his body from Emmy's description of his height and weight, plus a phone triangulation signal that showed he'd been in the cabin right before it fell.

So far, the coroner refused to release him, and the liaison officer said it would be a few weeks yet. That twisted the knife in my heart just a little bit more. After all Mitch went through for me, he needed a proper burial.

But first I needed to get through Jordi's funeral, which would take place tomorrow. I'd intended to go with Pippa, but yesterday over dinner Douglas had announced he would accompany me. I almost told him to stay at home, because I knew he was only going for the photo opportunity, but in the end I acquiesced, as always. Otherwise I'd have sounded like a heartless shrew.

CHAPTER 32

PIPPA WAS HALFWAY through cleaning out the pens when I arrived at the kennels half an hour later, and she gave me a shaky smile.

"Where do you want me to start?" I asked.

"I really appreciate you doing this."

"I keep telling you, I'm happy to help. Shall I start emptying the beds from the other end?"

"Please."

I grabbed a pair of rubber gloves and began wadding up the old newspaper and stuffing it into a black garbage bag. After we'd taken the dirty paper out, we replaced it with clean. *The Richmond Times* donated their unsold copies so we were never short, and I couldn't deny seeing the dogs poop all over the stories about me for the last two weeks had made me smile. It was the most appropriate treatment for them.

I'd almost got halfway when the sounds of quiet crying drifted along the aisle. Pippa. It wasn't the first time she'd broken down like this, and I knew it wouldn't be the last. The day after I came back, I'd found her in the living room, staring into space as she clutched one of Jordi's shirts with tears streaming down her cheeks. She didn't move for hours, and all I could do was wrap her up in my arms and offer what little strength I had left. Now, she slumped in the corner of a kennel with a creased copy of *The Richmond Times* in her lap, and I saw right away what the problem was. Dammit, when I sanitised the newspapers yesterday afternoon I'd missed one, and a picture of Jordi stared up at us from above the fold.

"He's never coming back," she sobbed.

"I know, and I'm so sorry."

What else could I say? Jordi was gone, and so was Mitch. The pain I kept bottled up tore at my soul, and for a moment, I felt jealous of Pippa because she could express her heartache publicly. Inside, I wept with her.

After we'd both pulled ourselves together as best we could, it was time to walk the dogs. We took them out on the trails at the back of the sanctuary, and today I clipped leashes on a sweet little spaniel that had been used for breeding then thrown out with the trash when she was no longer profitable, and an elderly Labrador abandoned by his owners when they moved out of state. Usually the walks were my favourite part of the day, but lately we'd been followed by reporters. We made the best of a bad situation by getting them to walk dogs too. On the first day, we had six of them and twelve extra dogs following us through the trees, but today we were down to two.

"Still not going to talk to us, ladies?"

Pippa stayed polite. "Afraid not, but thank you for your help. Will you be back tomorrow?"

"I don't think so. The boss says this story's just about run its course."

I let out a long breath, while Pippa managed a lopsided smile. "Maybe you'd consider writing an article about the sanctuary? We have an appeal on to raise money for a new kennel block."

He scratched his head. "I'll see what we can do."

We walked the rest of the way in silence, apart from the occasional excited bark from the dogs. The woods here were pretty, but not a patch on Mitch's mountain. I blocked out the men walking next to me and pretended Mitch was at my side instead, strong and silent. I thought about him constantly, and I'd never forget him. Never.

As we put the dogs away, Pippa turned to watch our assistants drive off. "All this attention's brought in a lot of extra donations."

"That's good."

"I guess, but it feels like I'm profiting from what happened to..." She gave a sniff. "T-t-to Jordi."

"You're not profiting at all. It's a charity."

"But still... I suppose the project's giving me something to focus on. You know, to take my mind off things." A tear ran down her cheek. "I want to make something positive come out of this."

"You will, Pip. You will."

"I hope so. We're halfway to the target now. Only seventy thousand bucks to go, but a month ago we only had thirty."

I'd been thinking about the appeal for a while now. Pippa spent half her time looking after the hounds, and the rest organising table-top sales and online auctions. Her hours would be better spent if she could concentrate on what she loved, not fundraising.

"I'm going to donate the rest."

Her eyes went wide. "What? Are you crazy? That's a huge amount of money!"

"I know, but it's sitting in my trust fund doing nothing, and I'll probably never spend it otherwise. It could do so much good here. You know this place is the only thing that's kept me sane for the last few years, and I want to see the new kennels built as much as you do."

"You need to think about this."

"Believe me, I have. I've done a hell of a lot of thinking over the last couple of months and my decision's made."

I couldn't tell Pippa it was partly guilt that drove me. Her son's death was my fault, and like her, I wanted something good to come from the nightmare we'd both lived through. The Hope House project would give us both a reason to keep going. The plans were to build a block of thirty brand new kennels and a grooming facility on a plot of land Pippa owned at the side of the existing buildings. It would save hundreds of extra dogs each year.

She threw her arms around me. "If you're sure, then that's the best news I could have wished for."

"I'll ask Douglas to transfer the money. Do you think I could stay for dinner this evening?"

"Of course. Is everything okay?"

"Douglas wants me to go to a function with him, and I've told him I don't want to go. I know if I go home he'll try and make me."

"Oh honey, you can stay as long as you want. I can only offer the couch, but you're welcome to it."

"I'll have to face him eventually, but thanks. I might take you up on it in the near future." Up until now, I'd kept my feelings bottled up inside, but they kept bubbling to the surface, and I needed to talk to someone. "I'm planning to ask Douglas for a divorce."

She leaned back and stared. "You can't be serious?"

I was. Where did the real danger lie? In death? Or in a life not truly lived?

"I just can't deal with him any longer. Since I got back, things have been so uncomfortable."

"Maybe you need time to adjust. It can't be easy walking back into your life as if nothing happened."

I hadn't breathed a word about Mitch to anybody yet, but now it tumbled out. "It's not that. While I was away, I learned what it was like to have someone who understood me and valued me as a person, not just because I picked up his dry cleaning and had dinner on the table when he got home."

"Wait a minute, you've met someone else?"

"I sort of did." My breath hitched as I choked back a sob. "But he's not around anymore."

She took my hand and led me towards her tiny apartment, no more than a few rooms tacked onto the end of the main kennel block. "There's a bottle of wine in the fridge, and it's got our names on it."

Over first one bottle of red and then a second, I told her all about Mitch. Well, not *all* about him. I left out the part about him being a professional killer. When I confessed I'd slept with him, Pippa let out a low whistle.

"I didn't think you had that in you."

"Neither did I, but it happened. I still don't know what came over me."

I even told Pippa Mitch's final words. "He said he loved me. Right before he went back to the cabin."

"Honey, I'm so sorry. You've been grieving too, and I didn't even know it."

"Nobody does, and nobody can. I did a bad thing, Pip."

"People make mistakes when they're in love. If Mitch was alive, would you want to be with him?"

"Yes, if he'd have me." Even with everything he'd told me, I couldn't have stayed away.

"From the sounds of it, he'd have you. In every way possible."

"Pippa! You can't make dirty jokes at a time like this."

"It's laugh or cry, Gee. Laugh or cry." Her eyes were still red from the latter.

I did both, a strange, alcohol-induced combination, interrupted only by my ringing phone. Douglas. I turned the damn thing off and tossed it onto the couch. Yes, it wasn't very nice, but I felt liberated, a feeling I'd missed since I left the mountain. I'd deal with Douglas's anger tomorrow. Tonight, he couldn't touch me.

CHAPTER 33

XAV WATCHED, HANDS on hips, as the bulldozer bit into the first patch of vivid green turf, its yellow bulk looking out of place against the watching forest.

He turned to Emmy, standing next to him on the hill. "I know tradition dictates we should have some kind of ceremony, but I don't feel like there's much to celebrate, do you?"

"Seven good men and most likely one kid lost their lives over this, and Nick got shot. I'm with you there." She turned to face him. "Sure you want to live here? There's still time to change your mind."

"No, it's the right decision. I've had two years to think about things. I spent ten years saying I'd quit when I made $50 million, and when I hit that target, I didn't stop to think whether stopping was the right thing. I just shut down. I didn't realise how much I'd changed since I started out."

"We all change."

The bulldozer dug another chunk of earth out of the ground, expanding the hole into a trench. Clouds moved overhead, blocking the afternoon sun for a time before continuing their slow journey over the horizon.

"You ever think about quitting?" he asked.

"Thought about it. Would I do it? I don't think so."

"Why not?" He was genuinely curious.

"I believe in what I do, and I'm good at it." There was no arrogance in her tone. She was stating a simple fact, as if she'd said water was wet or the sun was hot.

"What about you, though? What about how you feel inside?"

"I cope."

The trench was getting long now, and deep, the excavated dirt piled up neatly on a tarpaulin to the side.

Xav stared into the distance, watching a hawk circle above the trees. Not a red-tailed hawk like on his mountain, but a paler Cooper's hawk.

"I'm going to start work again." When she didn't answer, he continued. "Since I quit I've been dead inside. It wasn't a quick death, more like a slow cancer eating away at me. I couldn't paint for shit. Hell, I couldn't even get up in the morning. When Georgia was with me, I felt alive again. Now she's gone, and I want that feeling back. The only other thing that gave it to me was work. I reckon I've got a few years left in me."

"You have to do what's right for you. I'll support you whatever, you know that."

"Yeah, I do. You've been a good friend over the years."

"Likewise."

He turned to face her. "I gave one of the middlemen a call. Let him know I'd be available soon."

"Which one?"

"Jax."

She nodded. "He'll be glad. He's been busy. He keeps calling me, but I've got too much shit on of my own. You know I can give you work if you want it?"

"I'll think about it. It'd be strange, having to fit in with other people. I've never been the corporate type.

The only people I've worked with since I left Mossad are the Horsemen."

Emmy shrugged. "I'll have stuff you can do alone. You can work as a contractor if you like."

"Let me know when you get something, and I'll let you know if it's a job I can do."

She nodded again. "Look on the bright side, if the need comes up in the next week or two, we've got a big hole ready and waiting for the bodies."

He laughed, a hearty chuckle. "You never change, do you?"

Just then, Bradley jogged out of the construction trailer set up for the workmen, clutching a canary-yellow hard hat to his head. His white pea-coat was somehow still spotless, despite him prancing around a building site all morning.

"Emmy, this is ridiculous. Do you know they only have these hats in yellow? What goes with yellow?"

"Nothing. I think that's the whole point."

He ignored her. "If I'm expected to spend weeks on this building site, I'm getting something custom made. Maybe a selection, then I could coordinate."

She covered up a smile. "Whatever you want, Bradley."

He turned to Xav and pointed. "And you! You're lucky I managed to delegate Mack's wedding planning to Lara and Tia, otherwise I wouldn't have time for all this." He looked at his watch. "Speaking of time, I have an appointment with the kitchen designer in an hour. She squeezed me in as a favour seeing as we've already bought one kitchen from her this year."

"I appreciate it."

Bradley huffed and marched off to the Lamborghini

he'd managed to coax along the rutted track that wound through the woods. Xav watched him go. "I'd forgotten just how obnoxious and efficient Bradley could be."

"You'd better believe it. Not many people would have the build started when three weeks ago nobody had even had the idea."

"I'm amazed it got through planning control that fast."

His pointed look went unnoticed as Emmy watched the pile of dirt grow taller. "Me too, but when I had lunch with the head of the planning board, he was happy for us to build whatever we wanted."

"Funny, that. What did you do?"

"Nothing at all. We had a nice chat, and he told me about his family. Did you know both his kids are huge soccer fans?" She shrugged, hands out, palms up—the picture of innocence. "The fact that their school reached its fundraising target to build a new all-weather pitch last week was merely a happy coincidence."

He slung an arm around her shoulders and squeezed her close. "Don't ever change."

Once Emmy had jogged off into the distance, Xav returned to the tiny cabin he currently called home. It lay on the edge of the clearing, fifty yards from where the foundation for his new house was being dug.

When his old place came to a dramatic end, he'd been in a bind. He couldn't simply rebuild and move back in because he was, after all, supposed to be dead. Emmy came up with the solution. Not being short of a few bucks, every time a piece of land joining onto hers or her husband's came up, they bought it. And when the old-timer who'd lived here passed on the year before, she'd snapped up his eleven acres. As they already had two large houses and a number of outbuildings, they'd done nothing more than snap a heavy duty padlock on the gate and leave it be.

"So why don't you have it?" she asked. "You could tear down the place that's there and build whatever you want."

"I thought you liked your privacy?" Did she feel guilty for her part in the problem?

"From strangers, you idiot. Not you. Having a friend who's also a trained killer next door can only be good for security."

"In that case, thank you."

"You realise Bradley will want to throw a housewarming party?"

"You realise I'll be out of state when that happens?"

She'd laughed, the throaty sound he'd missed for the past few years. "So, you want to stay at Riverley Hall while you build your shit? Or Little Riverley?"

Never ones to do things by halves, Emmy and her husband owned two houses next to each other and split their time between the two. Black's house was his old family place, a true stately home, all ornate stonework and period features. Emmy's modern home was metal and glass, bulletproof because Black had insisted on it. It had just been refurbished after an unfortunate incident involving some grenade launchers, a selection of guns, and a fourteen-man assault team.

"Tempting offer, but I like my own space."

He'd hated sharing, ever since he'd been squashed into a dorm in his days as an army conscript. The exception, of course, had been his time with Georgia, but that wasn't to be.

Georgia. He'd dreamed about her again last night, and when thoughts of her sweet smile and soft curves drove him too crazy to sleep, he'd flipped on the light and reached for his sketchbook. Oh, he knew he needed to stop dwelling on what he couldn't have, but she'd snared his heart and it showed no sign of breaking free.

The old cabin he'd adopted as his temporary accommodation had been built for practicality rather than style. Its walls were hewn out of rough logs and crooked beams spanned overhead inside, giving it a shabby vibe some might call rustic. Small—just one room—and basic, but he'd lived in worse places. Bradley had wanted to redecorate but Xav decided against it. It wasn't like he'd be there long.

On the left-hand wall, a wide plywood shelf served as a kitchen counter, kitty corner to an old-fashioned dresser that held plates and a few utensils. The elderly cooker had gone into the dumpster, together with the ratty couch and lumpy mattress, while Bradley sorted out a microwave, a refrigerator and a new bed. Plus a few potted plants, a furry throw, and a weird statue that looked like two dogs humping. Modern art, allegedly.

A squat wood-burning stove kept the place cosy, and the only disaster was the tiny bathroom. The water pressure from the underground spring proved intolerably low. Until they could fix it, he was stuck with the old iron tub and no shower.

So he made regular trips to Emmy's place to use her

pool and gym. By road, it was over four miles, but on his newly purchased dirt bike, that distance got quartered. He'd done the journey so many times—every morning, in fact—he'd begun to wear a track through the woods that separated their land.

Why so often? Because he'd started training with her and her team. Although he'd kept in better shape than your average Joe, beside Blackwood's team he felt like that kid who always got picked last at sports practice. In the years since he'd last worked out with her, he'd forgotten just how vicious she could be.

That morning, as he'd changed out of his sweat-drenched workout gear, he'd looked at himself in the cracked mirror next to the bed, the mottled spots it had developed over the years doing nothing to hide the bruises spread over his body. But his muscles were harder, more defined, and every day he got stronger.

This move represented a new start for him. A new beginning.

Although one with some familiar aspects. His new home would be similar to the old one, albeit without the spectacular view. Rather than staring off the side of a mountain, this time the balcony outside his studio would face the grassland that gently undulated into the woods beyond.

He gladly sacrificed that view, though, because this time he'd also be forgoing the sense of isolation he'd come to hate. Some space was good, but too much ate away at his sanity.

With Emmy around, he'd been able to bounce his ideas for the new cabin off her, and it was she who'd suggested the basement, although it didn't appear on any plans. He'd have a secure spot for his toys, which

Emmy had collected from Colorado once the heat at the old cabin died down. And now, in Virginia, he'd get the opportunity to play with them more often.

Sitting out in the chilly afternoon sun one day, he'd sketched out the garden he planned to plant, one which blended the pool and deck into its surroundings. A couple of shade trees with gently sweeping boughs, colourful plants that would attract wildlife for him to paint. Maybe in time, hawks would come to nest nearby. And he still had a couple of months to talk Bradley out of the mock-pagoda and fountain.

Yes, this place would be everything he wanted. Everything he needed. Xav only wished the circumstances that prompted the move had been so very different.

CHAPTER 34

I PACED UP and down Pippa's tiny living room, stepping around her coffee table and over discarded dog toys as I went.

"I can't believe it, Pip. I just can't. Who does Douglas think he is, refusing me access to my own money?" I paused to take a breath. "Georgia," I mimicked, "You're clearly of unsound mind at the moment. I insist you speak with Dr. Nielsen. Unsound mind? Who even says that? He sounded like some nineteenth-century upper-class English twit!"

Pippa watched from the couch as I wore a groove in her carpet. "Deep breaths, Gee, deep breaths."

"This is to get back at me because I refused to go to his stupid dinner last week, I know it is."

"He didn't look too happy at the funeral, either."

I paused my steps, closing my eyes with embarrassment. While Pippa sobbed her heart out on my shoulder, Douglas spent half an hour outside the chapel, smiling for the cameras and giving soundbites. I'd snapped when he tried to pull me into a photo and dragged him inside. We hadn't spoken for the whole car ride home.

"No, he wasn't."

"So, what exactly did he say about the donation?"

"Just that he wasn't allowing me to take money out

of my trust fund for the sanctuary because he thinks I've gone cuckoo." I made the universal sign with my fingers for emphasis. "I'm not crazy, am I?"

Douglas had a way of making me doubt myself. He'd made me so upset this morning I'd been sick twice, and now I felt really tired.

"Of course not. You're just doing what *you* want for once in your life, and he doesn't like it."

Thank goodness Pippa was calm. One of us had to be.

"What can I do, though? He won't listen to me."

"If you're set on making this donation, why not speak to the bank yourself?"

Oh, if only. "I thought of that. When he left for work, I looked for the documentation, but I couldn't find it. I went through all the files I could get to in his study. It must be in one of his desk drawers, and he's locked them."

"Do you know where he keeps the key?"

I shook my head. "I looked everywhere I could think of."

Pippa leaned back on the couch, looking thoughtful. "What kind of desk is it?"

"One of those oversized wooden ones." The type men used as a penis extension.

"But nothing fancy?"

"Just ugly."

"I'm sure I could get the drawers open. When I was a kid I used to break into my brother's desk all the time to steal his candy. All you need is a couple of bobby pins and a nail file."

"Really?"

Her brother worked as an orthodontist in California

now, and candy was like a swear word to him.

"Hard to believe, isn't it?"

"But you could get into Douglas's desk?"

"I can't promise, but I'll have a go."

The following afternoon, I skulked behind the drapes in the front room, acting as lookout while Pippa attacked Douglas's desk with hair accessories. He was supposed to be at the office all day, but it would be just our luck if he came home early for once. I'd been staring down the driveway for fifteen minutes when a loud whoop sounded from the back of the house.

"Did you do it?" I called.

"I did it."

I abandoned my vigil and ran into the study, anxious to see what Douglas had squirrelled away.

"You take the right side, I'll take the left," Pippa told me.

I yanked the top drawer open. "Paperclips? Why does he feel the need to lock up paperclips?"

Paperclips, pens, post-it notes. The most valuable thing in there was a Sharpie.

Beside me, Pippa wrinkled her nose. "What are all these tissues?"

"Tissues?"

"Yeah. They're all wadded up." She fished around in them. "They're sort of crispy." More fishing. "Ewwwwww! I'm going to be sick."

She danced around the room, frantically wiping her hand on the drapes.

"What? What's wrong? Have you gone quite mad?"

"No, have a look."

I peered into the drawer. Under the tissues, a woman with an impossibly large pair of breasts stared back at me and... "Oh my goodness! Who does that to themselves? It's surely got to hurt."

"What?"

"The piercing that woman's got. Isn't that what you're squealing over?"

"No! I touched one of the tissues. I bet they're his little trophy collection. Think about it... Porn magazines and tissues?"

I thought about it. When I'd finished being sick into the trash can, we closed that drawer, never to be opened by us again. I guess he wasn't checking his emails after he left our bed on date nights. That realisation had me running for the bathroom again.

When I came back, Pippa was still standing by the desk. "Are you sure you want to open the other drawers?"

"No, but we have to anyway."

The middle drawers were stuffed with boring papers. Contracts, brochures, sets of accounts. Pippa flicked through the wordy stuff while I looked at the accounts, both of us keeping an ear out for the door.

"I think this is all work stuff," I said.

"Nothing for your trust fund?"

"Not that I can see."

The bottom drawer on my side contained more of the same. I was halfway through my second pile, bored to tears, when Pippa rattled a small bottle of pills.

"What are these?"

"I don't know. Douglas didn't mention being on any medication."

"Zithromax," she read, "for the treatment of Chlamydia. O. M. G."

"Chlamydia? Isn't that, like, a sexually transmitted disease?"

"Exactly."

"Douglas has an STD?"

"The label's got his name on it."

"Bu... but... but where did he get it? We've been together for the last eight years."

"This prescription's dated three days ago. Oh, Georgia, as if you didn't have enough going on."

She put the bottle down and hugged me. I wanted to vomit again, but I didn't have anything left. All this time I'd been feeling guilty, and Douglas had done the dirty on me?

"What do I do now? I mean, do I confront him?"

I fell into Douglas's executive chair, my ass squeaking on the leather.

Pippa crouched down in front of me and took both my hands in hers. "I think for now, what we need to do is get you tested. Just in case."

Oh hell, I hadn't even thought of that. Pippa tidied up our mess and locked the desk back up while I stared into space. How could Douglas have done this to me? Was it because I'd been away?

As I thought of the bottle of pills in the drawer, my guilt over sleeping with Mitch eased, just a little. Two wrongs didn't make a right, but...chlamydia?

Last year I'd led a dull and boring life, revolving around clothes, parties, and being seen where Douglas thought it was important. The odd scandal always livened things up, like the time Felicity Marston got caught in the bathroom at a party with her panties down and a man who wasn't her husband. Now *I* was the scandal. So far I'd been shot at twice, once in the country club of all places, and then been present while two men got blown up. Everybody was talking about me already, and the future would only get worse. Monica and Mindy would be burning up the phone lines tomorrow.

Because after today's discoveries, I couldn't spend another night under the same roof as Douglas.

But before I could pick up the tatters of my life, I had to suffer the embarrassment of getting screened for STDs. Being shot in the head began to look like an attractive option. Oh, how I longed to disappear, to vanish quietly from the planet. Poof! Was NASA looking for volunteers for the manned mission to Mars?

"Do you want me to make the appointment?" Pippa asked.

"I'm s-s-so sorry about all of this."

Her top smelled comfortingly of dog as she pulled me into a hug. "We'll always be here for each other. And...at least this keeps my mind off...other things. Do you want me to call the doctor?"

"I-I-I...I don't even want to think about it."

"I'll make the appointment. There must be a clinic near here."

"Please, not near here. The other side of the city. No, Blacksburg. Or West Virginia. And could you avoid giving them my name?"

She gave my hand one last squeeze as she stood up. "I'll see what I can do."

Ten minutes, some googling, and a hushed conversation later, she gave me a wan smile. "I've found a place on the other side of Richmond that can fit you in. They needed a name, so I gave them mine, and you can pay cash. Nobody's going to be talking about me at the country club."

I'd expected the clinic to be a seedy place full of dubious characters, but it wasn't as awful as I thought. Pastel pink walls, a forest of plants, and a selection of magazines made it more like Dr. Nielsen's waiting room. Pippa sat with me as I fidgeted, bouncing my knees up and down and no doubt annoying everyone around me. We'd told the bodyguards she had a nasty bout of cystitis, and they were sitting in the parking lot, looking uncomfortable.

"Miss Sullivan?" A nurse gazed around the room.

"That's me." I tried to straighten out my skirt, so wrinkled from where I'd been clutching it.

"Follow me, please."

The nurse asked a whole bunch of questions I didn't want to answer, so I lied and told her I had a one-night stand, cringing inside as I did so. My one-night stand hadn't caused the problem.

"Best we test you for everything, just to be on the safe side."

"Do whatever you have to."

She spouted out a list of horrible-sounding diseases as I stripped my panties off so she could take swabs. When she stuck the needle in my arm for more samples, I cursed the day I'd ever sat next to Douglas freaking Beaumont in the cafeteria at Harvard.

"That's it, miss. As you've opted for the express service, you can come back tomorrow for the results."

Thanks, Pippa. I wasn't sure I wanted to know.

Pippa had driven me to the clinic in the ancient van she used as her daily transport as well as driving dogs here, there and everywhere, and we piled back in for the trip to her apartment. I'd packed a few essentials before I left home earlier, and between us we hauled both my suitcases up the steps and into the lounge. But I was too tired to open them. Instead, I curled up on the sofa, ignoring Douglas's six phone calls and the succession of text messages asking me what exactly was he supposed to eat for dinner if I wasn't there?

Cyanide? Arsenic? Those sounded like good choices to me.

I barely slept, and I felt so sick from apprehension I threw up my toast the next morning. Pippa hovered outside the bathroom, and I knew I was worrying her.

"I'm fine, Pip. It's just this whole Douglas thing on top of everything else. He's turned me into a wreck."

"Is there anything more I can do to help?"

Tears slipped down my cheeks. "You're already doing so much. I don't know how I'd cope without you."

I felt awful for piling all my woes on her, especially so soon after Jordi's death. She hurt too, I saw it in her eyes every time she took a quiet moment, and from the way she avoided going near Jordi's room. His toys were still piled up next to the couch, and neither of us dared to touch them.

But she gave me a sad smile. "What are friends for?"

At eleven, we climbed back in the van again for our

second trip to the clinic. I kept my head down and my hair fluffed around my face, just in case we happened to see anybody I knew.

"Look on the bright side. In an hour you'll know. If you have caught anything, they can start treating it."

"They tested me for HIV, Pip. HIV! They can't cure that, can they? If he's given me that, I'll cut his balls off myself."

"Do you want me to come in with you for the results?"

"Would you?" I wasn't sure I could walk in there by myself.

Today's nurse was older, and she gave me a motherly smile as she led us into a small office decorated in the same pale pink as the waiting room. I perched on the edge of an uncomfortable plastic chair while she opened the envelope with the flourish of a gameshow host.

A smile came over her face. "It's good news, Miss Sullivan."

Oh, thank goodness. "Everything's clear?"

"Everything's clear. That means you and your baby should be fine."

The nurse's words echoed in my ears. Did she just say baby? She couldn't have. I must have misheard. "I'm sorry, my what?"

Her smile slipped, replaced by concern. "You didn't know you were pregnant?"

My last thought, before everything went black, was of Mitch, telling me he loved me.

Chapter 35

I WOKE UP in a different room, eggshell blue this time, flat-out on a gurney while a drip pumped goodness-knows-what into my arm. A grey-haired doctor stared down at me.

"I gather you've had a bit of a surprise, Miss Sullivan."

A surprise? The only surprise was that my heart hadn't given out. "Something like that."

"Well, I'm here to help you. You're a little dehydrated, but when you feel better we can talk things through. We'll help you make the best decision for you and the baby."

Decision? What decision? Did he mean abortion?

Oh hell, he *did* mean abortion, didn't he? I tried to be sick again, and a nurse thrust a paper bowl at me, but there was nothing left inside to come out.

"It's okay, Gee. You're doing well."

Oh, thank goodness—Pippa was still with me. I turned my head and saw her standing by the door, paler than usual.

The doctor gave me a practised smile. "We'll let the fluids do their work, and I'll be back soon."

The second he and the nurse left, Pippa hurried over to the bed. "Pregnant? You really didn't know?"

"It's not like I had anything to compare it to."

"Sorry, I mean, I know you'd have told me. It's just... Wow. Is it Douglas's? Or your mystery man's?"

I looked down at my pooch, full of cakes and cookies, and now, it seemed, a baby. "I don't even know. I was on the pill with Douglas, but Mitch... Mitch pulled out."

Memories of that night flooded back, of the heat in his eyes as he came on my breasts, of the way he'd held me afterwards.

"You didn't take your pills with you?"

"They're still in the nightstand at...at Douglas's." I couldn't call it home. Not anymore. "But I haven't had a proper period since I went away. I thought it was stress."

"Whoa. So it could be either of them? This is big."

I glanced at my stomach again. Well, not yet, but it certainly had the potential to be. "What the hell am I supposed to do? How do I find out?"

"A scan. You need to have a scan." She looked at the door. "Give me a minute. I'll be back."

I stared at the wall while I waited, willing myself to breathe. How was I supposed to have a baby? Okay, I knew the theory, and that didn't bear thinking about, but how was I supposed to look after it? Alone? I'd never even had my own dog before.

"So, you'd like a scan?" The nurse was back, Pippa at her side.

"I think so. Is there any way of telling the age of the baby?"

"We can estimate to within a week or so."

"Can you do it now?"

"Do you feel up to it?"

Not at all. "Yes, absolutely."

"Then let me check with the doctor, and we'll get set up."

I clung to Pippa's hand as the sonographer stuck a probe somewhere I didn't want to think about. In just two days, I'd doubled the number of people who'd paid a visit down there, and the only saving grace was that I was becoming numb to the humiliation.

On the screen beside me, a tiny black dot appeared in a sea of grey, and the lady pointed at it.

"See, here's the gestational sac."

"The baby?"

"Yes, the baby."

"Do you know how old it is?"

"Oh, I'd say about five weeks."

I let out the breath I'd been holding in a whoosh. The baby belonged to Mitch. A little of the heaviness that had weighed me down for the last two days lifted, and I managed a smile. There was a tiny piece of Mitch still alive, and it was growing inside me. The road ahead would be hard, and Douglas would only make it harder, but I wanted this baby more than anything. I'd just have to give it enough love for two parents.

"In the circumstances, is that good or bad news?" Pippa asked, as we drove back to Hope for Hounds. I clutched a print-out of the sonogram in my hand, and I couldn't stop looking at it.

"Good, definitely. Douglas will be furious, and my parents too, but if Douglas was the father everything would be a million times more difficult."

"You're still going through with the divorce?"

"I can't be with someone who treats me like an accessory, screws around behind my back, and doesn't even mention he's caught an STD."

"It's just a big decision."

"I know. I also know it's the right one."

Pippa fell silent for a beat. "Yes, I think it is."

I didn't even have to ask Pippa if I could stay for a while. When we got back to her apartment, she made up my bed on the couch again and handed me a cup of ginger and lemon tea.

"This helped the sickness when I was pregnant. I'm sorry about the couch, but I can't... I can't clear out Jordi's room yet. I just can't."

"I wouldn't expect you to." I hugged her, and we clung to each other as we both fought tears. "I'm here if you ever need help like that, but until you're ready, it stays exactly as it is."

"I'll help you with the baby too. The building project can go on hold for a bit. You and the baby are more important."

"I'm so sorry, Pip."

"Don't be. This time next year, nothing'll stop us, you'll see."

"I hope so. But I still need to get to my trust money. I need it to live on."

"We can sort that out another week. First, you need to rest up and get your strength back. The doctor said you were dehydrated, so you need to drink more. At least now you know why you keep throwing up—it's not only your delicate constitution."

"How long does morning sickness go on for?"

"It should be gone in a couple of months."

I groaned. "A couple more months? I don't think I

can take this for a couple more days."

She laughed. "I'll get you some ginger cookies tomorrow. Those helped me too."

I wanted to ask her a thousand questions about childbirth and babies, but I saw the sadness that flashed through her eyes. Now wasn't the right time.

Instead, I helped her prepare lunch, or rather dinner, for us and the dogs. While we'd been at the hospital, they'd been cooped up in their kennels, and they all needed a run before we put them to bed. It promised to be a long day.

"Are you still okay to help with all this?" Pippa asked.

"I'm pregnant, not dying," I blurted, then clapped my hands over my mouth when I realised what I'd said.

Pippa started laughing—not because it was funny, but the kind of hysterical laughter that bubbles out rather than tears.

"Laugh or cry, Gee, remember?"

I did. And I remembered saying the same thing to Emmy long ago, back in another lifetime.

Douglas called twice while we ate dinner, and I ignored him both times. Then he started with the text messages, three of them, and I deleted each with a small smile of satisfaction. Then the phone rang again, except this time it was my mother.

"Georgia, darling, where are you?"

Not *how* are you. *Where* are you. "Did Douglas ask you to call?"

"Well, yes. He's worried about you. We all are. And he was wondering if you've seen his cuff links with the little golf balls on them? He has a dinner at the golf club tonight with a group of campaign donors. Is it really too much to ask for you to return home and attend it with him? I've even bought you a new dress, and if you don't wear it soon, it'll be out of season."

"I'm not worried about me. I feel wonderful. In fact, I've never been better. And no, I'm not having dinner at the golf club, the country club, or any other club. I'm eating spaghetti out of a can and loving it."

I caught a glimpse of myself in the mirror above the sideboard, hair sticking out in all directions. Well, I wouldn't pass the entry panel for the country club at the moment, that was for sure. I'm sure my mother would have frowned, if not for the Botox she had injected religiously every three months.

"Georgia, what's wrong with you? Have you been taking drugs?"

"No, mother. I'm finally working out what's important in life. It's not dinners and it's not new dresses. And it certainly isn't Douglas."

"Douglas is right. You've completely lost your marbles. Where are you? I'll have our driver pick you up, and we'll get you an emergency appointment with Dr. Nielsen. I'm sure he'll oblige. After all, Douglas is a very good friend of his."

"Forget it. No marbles, no driver and no Dr. Nielsen. I've got things to do, and they don't involve telling some idiot with a couch all about my feelings."

She spluttered on the other end of the phone, but before she could think of another argument, I hung up. That felt good. Okay, I felt guilty as well, but it felt mostly good.

CHAPTER 36

XAV PUFFED ALONG behind Emmy like a couch potato with a New Year's resolution. It was seven a.m. and she'd woken him up at four to go running. He'd picked her up and deposited her outside, locking the door behind her, but the little witch went around the back and climbed in through a window. So there he was, twenty-two miles into what Emmy termed a gentle morning jog. Why hadn't he brought a gun so he could shoot her and her perky attitude and go back to bed? He'd much preferred Georgia's wake-up call—coffee and a sweet treat for breakfast.

Two miles later, Emmy, who'd rubbed salt into his blisters by wearing a headset and chatting to people in the office most of the way around, took another call.

"Yeah...mmm hmm...interesting... Yuck... Okay, I'll tell him."

She clicked off, hopped over a log, and jogged backwards in front of him. "You'll never guess what?"

"Something urgent's come up, and you need to go into the office?" He lived in hope.

"Nope."

"I'm not guessing. We'll be here forever." That and he didn't have any spare breath.

"You're no fun."

He glared at her.

"Fine. Okay, when the Georgia thing was in full swing, Mack set up flags on the key players so we'd get notified if they had any contact with the police, hospitals, banks, etcetera. Well, guess who went to his doctor a few days ago complaining of yellow shit coming out of his cock?"

"Tell me."

"Take a wild stab in the dark. Which, ironically, is probably what he's been doing."

"I'm gonna go with Douglas."

She gave him a high five. "Chlamydia."

He stopped in his tracks, and Emmy ran on a few strides before turning back.

"The dirty little shit. He cheated on her."

Emmy nodded. "It certainly appears that way. Do you need to get checked out?"

He closed his eyes. "Fuck. Yeah, I should."

"I assumed as much."

Xav hadn't told Emmy precisely what happened between him and Georgia, but she knew anyway. That didn't surprise him.

"You haven't had gunk coming out your cock, though, right?"

"Emmy, shut up."

"Just asking."

"Well, don't." He sat down on a fallen log, thinking dark thoughts. Douglas had the sweetest woman Xav had ever met, and the little fuck still wasn't satisfied? Why? What could another woman give him that Georgia couldn't apart from an STD? What did he want? What was going on in his sick little mind?

"If Douglas is screwing around, depending on who the other woman is, it could give him a motive to get rid of Georgia."

"We didn't find any evidence of it before. Sure, he stays in hotels a lot, but he travels for his job."

"He didn't get chlamydia by jacking off to his porn collection."

"No, he didn't." She cut her eyes to Xav. "He's into the kinky shit, though. Mack found more freaky-freaky on his home hard drive as well as those magazines in his desk drawer. Can't imagine that's Georgia's scene." She raised an eyebrow at Xav.

"Piss off."

She kept staring at him.

"Okay, fine, it's not. But you know what? I didn't miss it. Not with her. She made me feel different. I used to be in a much darker place."

"I know. Remember, I was there with you. Anyway, what do you want to do about Douglas?"

"I want to put him through a meat grinder."

"No you don't. Getting rid of the evidence is horrific. There's DNA everywhere, blood, bits of bone... Unless you could make it look like an accident..."

"Let's settle for taking another look at him, shall we?"

Emmy took off again at a sprint. Xav sighed and followed, anxious now to get back to work.

One day, he'd pay her back for this.

Revenge came a little sooner than he anticipated when Jax called at quarter to three the next morning. A few years back, curious about the type of person who would broker murder for a living, he and Emmy had tracked

Jax down. Jax, or Keith, as he was actually called, turned out to be a three-hundred-pound computer game addict with a serious vitamin D deficiency, who used his cut of the spoils to fund his caffeine and Cheez Doodles habit. Given that he lived in his basement games room, and his body clock had no idea whether it was day or night, a call in the early hours wasn't that unusual.

What was unusual was the job offer.

"Got a great proposition for you."

All Jax's jobs were "great" or "fantastic." Even the ones that involved lurking in a swamp in Cambodia for three weeks, getting bitten to fuck while living on field rats.

"Details."

"Okay, so it's not your usual kind of gig, but I'm shorthanded. You'd be getting me out of a bind."

"Give me the damn details."

"A politician's daughter. Should be straightforward for a man such as yourself."

The sound of a clanging alarm bell made Xav sit straight up in bed. No way—could he be that lucky?

"That wouldn't happen to be the same politician's daughter who made the headlines a few weeks back, would it?"

"Okay, I gotta be honest with you—the first guy screwed the job up. I need to fix things or my reputation'll suffer. The client's a mil down and pissed."

"Then you're talking bullshit. It isn't a straightforward job at all."

"I got the price up to a million five, but the deal is it's gotta look like an accident."

"I'll consider it."

Xav knew he'd take the job, for the simple reason that if he did, nobody else could, and that would give them breathing room to track the client down.

Jax adopted a wheedling tone, which reminded Xav exactly why he hated the man. It was unfortunate that the Jaxes of this world were a necessary evil.

"I'm not even taking a cut of this one, seeing as the first attempt was a failure, but how about on the next job you do for me I'll drop my percentage to five instead of ten?"

"Fine, I'll do it, but you owe me a favour. Send me the file." Xav rattled off an anonymous, single-use email address.

"You got it, and thanks, buddy. You know the drill—send the payment details." He gave an email address of his own before hanging up.

It was just after three when Xav abandoned his dirt bike outside the stone facade of Riverley Hall and slipped inside. Given that walking unannounced into the bedroom Emmy shared with her husband would be tantamount to suicide, he settled for standing outside the door and calling the phone he knew would be next to her on the nightstand.

One ring, two.

"What the—?"

"I'm in the hallway. Get your ass out here, sweetheart."

She stepped out a minute later, wearing a camisole, a pair of sleep shorts, and a thigh holster. Always prepared.

And pissed

Hands on hips, she asked, "What?"

"I just got a job from Jax."

"Congratulations. What do you want me to do? Throw you a party?"

"Yeah, I want a cake, candles, streamers, the whole works."

"Well, at least you wouldn't have to blow out the candles, hot stuff, you could just smile at them and they'd pass out."

"Aren't you even going to ask who it is?"

Emmy sighed. "Okay, who?"

"Guess."

"Douglas?"

He was lucky, but not that lucky. "Guess again."

"Georgia."

"Got it in two." Xav flashed her a grin.

"Fuck me."

He glanced into the shadowy room beyond her and knew her husband was listening to every word. "Not any more, Ems."

Words rumbled out of the darkness. "Is the right answer."

Yeah, nothing wrong with Black's ears. "Payment's coming, and you need to get your computer fairies to track it."

Emmy already had her phone in her hand. "I'll wake them up."

Two days later, Mack, Emmy's computer guru; Mack's fiancé, Luke; Emmy, and Xav sat in Mack's office at

Blackwood, waiting.

Mack fiddled with a chunk of computer code while Luke threw wadded up bits of paper at the mini basketball hoop over the trash can, missing with four out of every five.

Mack glanced across at him. "I hope you're going to pick those up."

He shrugged.

Emmy balanced on the coffee table in the lotus position. "I'm bored. Couldn't you have offered a prompt payment discount or something?"

Xav picked up the gun he'd just field stripped for the third time and pointed it at her. "Boom."

Black walked in with a file of documents. Xav and Black hadn't always seen eye to eye in the past, but the man appeared remarkably tolerant of Emmy's exes. Probably because he was a manipulative bastard who could use the connections to his advantage. Black was followed by Sloane, the pretty assistant he shared with his wife, who flashed a wide smile when she saw Xav.

"Long while since I've seen you around, Mr. Roth," she said.

"It's been that." Once upon a time, he might have made a play for Sloane, but not anymore. His heart belonged to a natural blonde with a death sentence hanging over her head.

"Y'all want coffee?"

Five yeses.

Black slid his file onto the arm of the sofa. "Anything yet? Emmy, sit up straighter."

She rose an extra inch. "Nope, still waiting."

"I spoke to Senator Rutherford."

Xav's heart skipped. "And?"

"Georgia's holed up with Pippa Sullivan."

At least she wasn't with the prick. "How is she?"

"Coping. The senator couldn't understand why she didn't want to stay with her husband, but I respectfully suggested he let her make up her own mind in that regard."

"Thanks," Xav muttered.

"Her protection detail reports she's looking better too."

"Good."

But it wasn't. He'd hoped the agony of missing her would lessen with time, but so far, it showed no signs of easing.

A ping from one of the six computers on Mack's desk made all heads swivel. They'd had several false alarms already, but this time Mack grinned.

"Okay, here we go. It's $1.5million, on the nose. Payment reference says it's a donation for land mine victims. Nice touch."

Luke took a seat next to her, and Black picked the sofa and opened his file while Emmy began pacing. She always swore it helped her think. Xav stripped his gun for the fourth time, hoping he got to use it soon.

It was almost three hours later when Luke nudged Mack. "Do you see what I'm seeing?"

She peered at his screen, reading the lines of text. "Oh wow, that's cold."

"Do we have something?" Emmy asked.

Mack nodded. "We do indeed. The payment came from the trust fund of one Georgia Ann Rutherford."

Xav sat up straight. "You're shitting me."

"Wish I was."

Luke scrolled down the screen, "Look, there's

another payment almost six months ago, for a million bucks. I don't think we need to guess what that one was. No other transactions apart from investment income in the last twenty years."

"Why didn't we pick this up before?" Black asked.

"Georgia's is the only name on the account. Nobody expected her to pay for her own murder."

"And it's still an unlikely scenario. So who did?"

"Three guesses," Xav put in. "The senator, his wife or Douglas. Who else would know about the trust fund?"

Black closed his file. "A bank employee. An attorney."

"No motive. My money's on Douglas. He's the one screwing around on Georgia."

Mack shook her head. "Why kill her now? He's been messing around with kink for ages. I found seventeen thousand images on his hard drive. Seventeen *thousand*. And they went back years."

Emmy nodded in agreement. "He's got too much to lose if Georgia's not around." Still pacing, she ticked the points off on her fingers. "Even if he inherited the trust fund, a good chunk of it's been spent already. His social standing would take a dive. Senator Rutherford might withdraw his support for his election campaign, and Douglas wants to be the fucking president." She stopped mid-stride. "Fuck. Oh, fuck."

"What?"

"President. He wants to be president. Remember when I said he'd been practising his signature?"

"Yeah, so?"

"And the sheet of signatures was with articles about Obama's 2008 election campaign?"

Four blank looks, then Black slowly shook his head. "That's not cold. The fucker's liquid nitrogen"

Xav got to his feet. "Will someone kindly explain?"

Emmy did. "What happened on the eve of the 2008 election? Obama's grandma died. The papers were filled with pictures of Madelyn Dunham, her grieving grandson, and speculation he'd get the sympathy vote."

"You reckon he'd kill his own wife for votes?" Xav spat the words.

Mack called a tabloid website up on her screen. "It makes sense. He's barely been out of the news since this thing kicked off, and have you seen this morning's offering? Heartbroken Douglas Beaumont suspects his beloved wife's having a nervous breakdown."

Xav gripped his gun. "He's dead. Douglas is dead."

Black, the voice of reason, held up a hand. "We need to confirm first. Mack, can you see how the transfer from the trust fund was initiated? Was it electronic?"

"It was," Luke answered for her. "Let me find out the IP address. They should have recorded it somewhere."

At four that afternoon, Xav drove Luke's sister, Tia, through the streets of Richmond. Luke wasn't entirely happy about the plan, but Emmy and Tia had talked him into it.

"It's only a coffee shop. Nobody's going to kidnap Tia in a coffee shop." They'd traced the origin of the transfer to Java, an upmarket café in downtown Richmond.

Luke frowned at Emmy. "Why can't you do it? You love coffee."

"Because the barista's still in his teens, and I'm not that much of a cougar. Tia's perfect."

"I'm eighteen now," Tia chimed in. "I can do what I like."

"Over my dead body."

"That can be arranged," Emmy reminded him.

Luke sighed, and his expression softened as he glanced at Tia. "Look, I'm just worried, okay? I've only got one sister. What if something goes wrong?"

But nothing did go wrong. Emmy won the argument as usual, and Tia hustled off to buy an iced latte.

Xav went in first and sat sipping a double espresso while he listened to Tia explain to the freckle-faced barista about the problems she was facing.

"So there's this rumour going round school that my boyfriend came here with the assistant-vice-captain of the cheerleading squad, only he says he didn't, but three separate people told me he kissed her and there were tongues." She gave the boy a cute smile. "Did you happen to see anything?"

"What do they look like?"

"Uh, my boyfriend's kinda big, because, you know, he's on the football team. And you know, cheerleaders." She mimed a large chest.

"I don't remember anything."

"But it was only this morning."

"My shift didn't start until two."

Tia pouted, she smiled, and she flipped her hair. Then she pointed to the camera above Xav's head. "Do you think they might be on film?"

Half an hour later, Tia ran out to Xav's car, clutching the barista's phone number, a complimentary banana muffin, and DVD footage from all four cameras in the store.

"You owe me shopping vouchers. I like Bloomingdales."

"You've been spending too much time with Emmy."

Tia stuck her tongue out. "She taught me everything I know."

"Should I be worried about how good Tia's getting at this?" Luke asked Emmy as he cued up the DVD.

Xav and Tia had made it back to Riverley Hall in record time, and Xav decided he liked Emmy's Dodge Viper. Now he didn't have a driveway full of potholes to contend with, maybe he'd buy something sportier himself.

Emmy shrugged. "Hey, when I was her age, I was stealing cars and getting into bar brawls."

"You've still got all that to come," Black added.

Luke put his head in his hands.

Mack took over and fast-forwarded through the footage. Twenty minutes before the transfer was made, they watched Douglas walk in and order a coffee. He added three sugars and extra cream before settling onto a sofa directly under camera number three. Mack zoomed in, and those watching saw him open up the bank website and furtively look around everywhere but above him before he clicked the button to send the money.

"Gold star for Java and their high-resolution

cameras," Emmy said, before taking Xav and Black by the hands. "Come on, boys, we have planning to do."

CHAPTER 37

XAV SLAMMED EMMY hard against the wall of the hotel elevator as he devoured her mouth. Oh, he'd missed this. A swipe of the tongue, a nibble of her lip, and he began to feel the effect in his pants. In return, she raked her fingernails down his back and pulled his ass towards her. Just like old times.

Almost.

Xav caught the red light of the security camera blinking down at them and adjusted his hand in Emmy's brunette wig. He didn't want to dislodge it. The bell pinged for the fourth floor, and they stepped out, his arm around her waist as they hurried along the hallway. Emmy wheeled a small suitcase behind her, while he slung a rucksack over his shoulder. Just one more couple on an overnight break in Sin City. As they reached room 405 of the Black Diamond hotel, he pressed her against the door and kissed her once more, for luck. She already had half his buttons undone before they fell inside.

The door slammed behind them, and she stepped back, straightening her dress. "Always good to put on a show, isn't it?"

"Always. How long have we got?"

"I said eleven, which gives us two hours."

Xav opened the balcony doors and peered up at the

moonless night then down at the lights of the strip. "Sky's dark."

"Good. I like the dark." She smiled, but it didn't reach her brown-tinted eyes.

Part of him said to back out of this job. Emmy was the wrong person for it. He knew it, and she knew it, but she was doing it anyway. Because after the cabin fiasco, she owed him a favour, and she always paid up.

"You sure you're okay with this?"

"Fine."

Liar. He'd wanted Snow. Her primary weapon was poison, but sex ran a close second. The job would have suited her perfectly. But Snow was eating ice cream in sunnier climes, so tonight Emmy was doing the dirty work with Snow radioing in later to provide technical support.

They could have waited. They should have waited. But Emmy had seen the same opportunity he did, one that was too good to pass up, and for better or worse, they were going for it.

Three weeks ago, on the day Douglas wired the money to pay for his wife's murder, Mack hacked into his calendar and found he was attending an event called More Bang for Your Buck at the Black Diamond hotel. It turned out not to be the hooker's convention they'd first assumed, but rather a seminar on maximising publicity opportunities. As Xav dreamed of removing the little turd's testicles with a pair of pliers, Emmy had taken one look at his schedule and said, "We'll do it there."

"Aren't you worried about offing somebody in your own hotel?"

She'd grinned at him. "No publicity is bad

publicity."

Well, they'd certainly get plenty of publicity tonight if Xav had anything to do with it.

Douglas had cheaped on the room rates and booked a single at the Excalibur, and earlier in the evening, Emmy just happened to bump into him in the bar there. She'd channelled *Pulp Fiction* in a black bobbed wig and blood-red lipstick complete with cleavage he knew wasn't hers. Xav had gone with a suit. Did that make him John Travolta?

As Emmy slid onto the stool next to Douglas, Xav took a seat a few tables away—close enough to see what was going on, but not quite within punching distance. He adjusted the earpiece under his blonde wig as he waited for Emmy to work her magic.

Unsurprisingly, the bartender didn't make her wait. "Sex on the Beach, honey." Her voice came into Xav's ear, crisp and slightly trashy.

That got Douglas's attention. He sat up straighter, slipped off his wedding ring, and dropped it in his pants pocket. Asshole.

When Emmy's drink arrived, the ten-dollar bill she was about to hand to the bartender fluttered to the floor, and she hopped off the stool to pick it up. As she bent over, Douglas's eyes fixed firmly on her ass. So far, so good.

"Allow me." Douglas handed a note of his own to the man.

"Ooh, thank you, sweet thing."

"I'm Douglas."

"Brandy. It's nice to meet you."

Emmy shook his proffered hand and showed her pearly whites. It didn't escape Xav's notice that she wiped her own palm on her skirt afterwards. Sweaty. Nice.

"Brandy's an interesting name."

"My mom used to work in a bar. My sister's called Sherry."

Emmy shrugged out of her jacket and draped it over the empty stool next to her, revealing a sheer black blouse over a black bra that left little to the imagination. Douglas's gaze slid downwards and fixed on her tits.

"So, what brings you to Vegas?" he asked.

"I'm attending a marketing conference, but it doesn't start for a few days. I always like to come early for these things." She giggled. "You know, so I can meet new people. How about you?"

"The same. Well, not for the marketing conference. I'm at a different symposium, one for high-profile businessmen who want to make a difference. Being a positive influence is very important to me."

So important, in fact, that he'd spent the afternoon in Hooters with a bunch of like-minded twats. Xav had watched them from a couple of booths away as they'd dared each other to touch the waitress. One point for a leg, two for a breast.

"That's an admirable quality. Have you managed to influence anybody since you've been here?"

"Not yet, but I'm working on it."

The slimy little shit rested his hand on her leg, and Xav admired Emmy's restraint as she dropped her own on top of it. With her other hand, she fingered his tie.

"I like your tie. Is it real silk?"

"Of course, I only ever buy handmade. I'm a man who likes quality." He stroked her leg with his thumb, and Emmy shuffled across the stool towards him with half-closed eyes. "Mmm, don't stop."

"Oh, you like that then?"

"Yeah, it feels sooo good."

Fucking hell, did men really fall for this shit? Emmy sounded like a second-rate hooker, but after the chlamydia incident, they'd had a chat and decided that was the type Douglas most likely chose.

And now he puffed out his chest. "I can do other things that would make you feel good."

"Oh really? I'm listening." She intertwined her fingers with his.

"Thing is, we'd have to go somewhere a little more private so I could show you."

"I'd like that." She leaned into him and dropped her voice to a whisper. "Are you married, Douglas?"

He let go of her hand in a hurry. "What? Why?"

"Because I've found that frustrated husbands make the best lovers, and I want to know what I'm letting myself in for. It's the same with frustrated wives. My husband has no idea how to please me in the bedroom. If it wasn't for my little conference trips, I think I'd end up getting a divorce."

Douglas grabbed her hand again and bobbed his head in agreement. "I completely understand. My wife's terribly frigid, a real wet fish. She won't even go down on me."

"That fucking cunt." Xav hissed into his own microphone, and Emmy had to have heard. But she didn't miss a beat.

"So, Douglas, are you going to keep me up all night?"

"I certainly am."

She tousled Douglas's hair. "Oh you like that, do you?" She dropped his hand into his lap. "Yes, you do. I can feel it."

Douglas let out a groan, loud enough that Xav didn't need his earpiece to hear it, while Emmy continued with her smut. "You're in luck tonight, big boy. I just love the feel of a man's cock between my lips."

Douglas was practically panting, and now he adjusted himself in his underwear. "I've got a room upstairs if you'd like to join me?"

Emmy pouted, a look that didn't suit her. "Oh, Dougie. Can I call you Dougie? It sounds so hot."

He nodded.

"Dougie, I promised to meet my boss for dinner. I'll be available later, though. Very available." She fumbled in her purse. "I'm staying at the Black Diamond. Room 705. Take my key and meet me there at eleven. Just let yourself in. I'll be waiting."

"I'll be there. Bang on eleven."

CHAPTER 38

IN ROOM 405, Emmy got ready under Xav's gaze. She'd waxed every inch of herself, the hair on her head was firmly back under the black wig, and her eyebrows and eyelashes were sealed in place with clear mascara so she didn't drop any stray hairs. She gave a twirl in a black leather thong and matching demi-cup bra.

"How do I look?"

Xav shrugged. "I'd do you."

"Careful, don't be too enthusiastic."

She pulled on a black blouse and a pair of black pants then slipped her feet into a pair of thin rubber-soled plimsoles.

"Time?"

"Half ten."

Emmy picked up the lightweight rucksack, also black, from the chair next to the bed and studied the items laid out on the quilt. Paracord, new, in a sealed bag. A blue silk tie. A pair of handcuffs and a cheap folding knife. A handful of little blue pills. Condoms, unlubricated and with no added spermicide, and a new tube of KY jelly.

"That's quite a shopping list Snow gave you."

"One I hope I'll never have to buy again." She pulled on a pair of elbow-length kid leather gloves, black, of course.

"Ready?"

"As I'll ever be."

"Okay, comms check."

Courtesy of Red, the microphones were built into their new watches, and the earpieces weren't visible even on close examination. Snow had a matching set and should be dialling in right about now.

Emmy moved into the bathroom and closed the door. "Valkyrie to Smoke, over."

"Receiving, loud and clear."

A click told them a newcomer had joined the channel. "Snow to Valkyrie. Am I late to the party?"

Emmy's voice softened. "Right on time, honey."

"You sure you want to do this?"

"Unless you want to come and blow the asshole for me?"

Snow's throaty laugh echoed from who the fuck knew where. "Would if I could, but I'm sucking off a mafia boss in two hours, so I don't have a window."

The bathroom door cracked open, and Emmy walked out. No, she was not okay. Xav didn't know all of her history, but he knew she avoided the honeytrap jobs wherever possible. She hated the thought of being naked with a stranger, and she detested the prospect of unwanted men touching her body. Xav had done one such job with her a few years back, and she hadn't been the same for weeks.

Only Black could fix her afterwards, and he'd been summoned by Hades III to sort out the Ace problem once and for all. Right now, he was incommunicado in Europe, and although he knew what Emmy was doing, judging by the phone call Xav overheard a few days ago, he wasn't happy about it either.

Emmy stood stiffly while Xav went out to the balcony and looked around. "The guy in 406 is smoking a cigarette. Give it ten minutes."

There were frosted glass privacy panels between each balcony, but even so, there was no reason to deliberately tempt fate and risk somebody seeing them.

The second time he went out, he gave the all-clear. Emmy donned the rucksack, and he steadied her as she climbed up onto the balcony railing. She reached her arms overhead. The balcony to room 505 was directly above, but there was still a good two feet of air between the edge of it and her outstretched hands.

She bent her knees and sprang upwards, grabbing onto the railing above, just like she'd practised a hundred times on the mock-up version they'd built back at Riverley Hall. The only difference was this time she was four floors up. One slip, and the emergency services would be scraping her off the sidewalk sixty feet below. Then Emmy was five floors up, then six. Xav watched as she did the same thing one more time and finally hauled herself over the balcony of room 705. Now, all they had to do was wait.

Xav lay back on the bed, arms folded under his head. He pictured Emmy doing the same thing three floors up. Just waiting, breathing, making sure her head was in the right place. Snow was probably on a sun lounger with a cocktail.

As plans went, it was a simple one. The best ones usually were. When Emmy realised Douglas was staying near the Black Diamond, she knew it would make a good location for what she had in mind. Owning it meant she was familiar with the layout, the balconies, and the location of every camera. Hell, she'd probably picked those locations herself.

Mack had helped design the hotel computer system, and as always, she'd left herself a backdoor. Room 405 got booked out to Mr. and Mrs. Smith from Washington State, on a dirty weekend for their first anniversary. The complimentary bottle of champagne in the minibar had been a nice touch. The couple in 505 were never going to show, and 605 remained empty, giving Emmy a clear run up to 705.

Ah, room 705. Douglas had booked that via the hotel website, or at least, his credit card had. Just before shift changeover earlier in the evening, the cameras above the reception desk suffered from a minor malfunction as Mack checked Mr. Beaumont in remotely. The keycards were easy enough to clone, and the stage was set.

All they needed was their main player.

Xav closed his eyes as Snow talked softly to Emmy, keeping her on track. Pour the whiskey. Crush the pills. Turn up the heating, because she didn't want to get cold, did she?

At exactly eleven, a sharp rap on the door of room 705 made him sit up. If Douglas had one redeeming quality, it was that he'd turned up on time for his own death.

And Emmy's words as she opened the door were music to his ears. "Ooh, honey—you kept your tie on."

The rustle of clothing. The clink of glasses. Laboured breathing.

"No, honey, don't you worry about that. The whole eight-inches thing is a myth."

Then Snow's detached tones. "If he's got a dick the size of a peanut, use your tongue more 'cause it's not something you've had practice with."

Emmy's mouth had been around Xav's cock a number of times, but somehow, listening to her do another man seemed more personal. He tuned out the chatter, at least until it got to the good bit.

"Honey, let's play a game."

"A game?"

"Pass me your tie."

Snow stepped in again. "A half-Windsor knot will work, or a trinity. Only takes seven pounds of pressure to collapse the carotid artery, sweetie."

Then, almost an hour later, Emmy's strangled whisper. "It's done."

"Thank fuck," he muttered.

And some final words from Snow. "Look after her, you asshole."

Seconds later, Emmy dropped onto the balcony outside. Xav got up to meet her as she slipped through the door.

"Get out my way."

She pushed past him and ran into the bathroom. He followed and held the strands of black hair out of her way as she threw up once, twice, three times. Finally, when there was nothing else left, she sat back on the floor, leaning against the wall.

He brought her a washcloth and a glass of water. She drank some of it then threw that up as well.

"What can I do?" he asked.

"Get him off me," she whispered. "Just get him off me."

He turned the shower on then gently undressed her, picking her up and carrying her into the stall like a small child. Stepping in behind her, he lathered up the shower gel and washed her all over, but it wasn't enough. She grabbed the cloth and scrubbed herself until she went pink.

"Easy, Emmy."

Silence.

"What can I do?"

"Nothing. I just need Black." Her voice was tortured, her soul torn.

"He can't talk right now."

"I know."

Xav shut the water off and wrapped her in a towel, then carried her over to the bed and cradled her in his lap. "Are you going to be okay?"

No answer.

He sat up all night and held her as she stared into space. Her eyes kept trying to close, but she wouldn't let herself sleep. He understood why, but it didn't make it any easier to watch. Finally, the sun peeped over the horizon and rose slowly higher in the sky. At seven, he pulled Emmy up and set her on her feet.

"Got to go, Ems. Got to work. Can you manage to do this one last part?"

"Of course." She stood up straighter, the change dramatic.

Xav realised then why those close to her called her a robot, why they said she was a weapon, a tool. She pulled on the right clothes then sashayed out the hotel with him, waving at the guy on the desk in the lobby as she went. He loaded her into a waiting cab, and they set off for the airport. On the journey, she chatted with the cab driver, telling him about their visit to the Grand Canyon and what an awesome stay they'd had.

As soon as she got onto her husband's Learjet, she

shut down again.

Where the fuck was Black?

Nobody knew, according to the driver of the Porsche Cayenne that picked them up at Silver Springs Airfield.

"Hang in there, Ems."

Nothing.

Great. He had a catatonic ex-girlfriend to deal with, and the only cure was AWOL. Could things get any worse?

Oh, yes. Yes, they could.

The car stopped outside the front door at Riverley Hall, and Xav half-carried Emmy as she walked up the steps. Now what? Should he put her to bed? Handcuff her to it? What if she had one of her sleep episodes? The door opened automatically, and he helped her inside. Then groaned.

Riverley was styled on an old English stately home, complete with suits of armour flanking the front door. A magnificent chandelier illuminated the tiled floor, and blood-red couches sat against the walls on either side. And from those couches, eight besuited clones tracked him, all wearing matching sunglasses.

Fuck him. The circus had come to town.

No, not the circus.

James.

The man himself descended the stairs, stopped a foot away, and looked at his watch. A politician's watch —not too cheap, not too expensive, made by Niall in the good old US of A. "Took your time. How is she?"

"Not good. Does Black know you're here?"

"He asked me to come."

"Really?" Xav hadn't missed the way Black's eyes turned green whenever James was around.

"He knew what you'd do to her."

Xav didn't like that tone. "She offered."

"You didn't have to accept. Some things are more important than revenge. You need to stop thinking with your dick."

Xav reached for the pistol at his back, and eight hands mirrored his move. He dropped his arm to his side again. There were some battles a man didn't fight, and that was one of them.

"Because you don't? And that's made you happy, has it?"

That comment hit the nerve it was intended to. Sometimes, the right words could be as effective as a bullet. James glared at him, then picked Emmy up and climbed the stairs.

Xav slept for most of the day, and even when he woke up, he avoided the first floor until the row of armoured cars parked in the back courtyard disappeared. If he had to face James again so soon, he was in danger of losing his head, literally. At loose ends, he headed for the peaceful sanctuary of the second floor library and stood out on the balcony while he checked his phone. Douglas had made every gossip website there was, front and centre. Good job, Emmy. Now he owed her more favours than he could ever repay in one lifetime.

It was nine in the evening by the time he ventured downstairs and found his sheepish-looking ex sitting with Black at the kitchen table.

"You okay?"

She managed a smile. "Sorry. I fucked up a bit."

"You got the job done."

"I mean afterwards. James said I worried you."

"You did. But it's me who's sorry. James was right. I shouldn't have asked you to do it."

Black fixed him with a lazy gaze. "You couldn't have talked her out of it. Believe me, I tried. Emmy does what she wants to do."

"James doesn't think that way."

"He does. But where my wife is concerned, he has an unfortunate tendency to speak before he thinks."

"But—"

"It's been dealt with. As has Hades."

"Hades? I thought Ace was the problem?"

"Hades was the bigger problem. But it turned out the old bastard was quicker on the draw than we thought. Ace shot him in the stomach, he shot Ace, and all I needed to do was ensure they both bled out as they should. An easy day's work."

Suddenly, James's presence made more sense. He'd been cooking up a scheme with Black as well as playing not-so-happy families with the man's wife.

"So, no more Horsemen?"

"Not officially."

"But unofficially?"

"I'm still here. Emmy's here. You're back. Pale's available. We've got Red, Dime, and Snow. It's more like the old days, wouldn't you say?"

"Yeah. Just like the old days."

CHAPTER 39

DESPITE THE BEST efforts of my parents and Douglas, Pippa and I were still sharing an apartment. It may have been squashed, but Pippa's company made up for it.

"How's Titch?" she asked from the kitchen one evening.

"I swear he's grown since this morning."

Two weeks ago, a gorgeous German shepherd dog had arrived at the shelter, courtesy of animal control. Despite being plump, she ate like she was starving, and we soon found out why when she surprised us three days later with a litter of puppies. Titch was the smallest of six, but he wasn't getting enough milk, and after worrying all through the first forty-eight hours, Pippa and I made the decision to hand-rear him. He was so damn cute that I didn't care about getting up every two hours to give him a bottle of milk.

"Has he opened his eyes yet?" Pippa asked.

"No, but it's going to be soon. I know it."

I adored Titch, and in the evenings he'd snuggle up on my chest, looking for warmth. I'd named him too, and I couldn't help thinking of Mitch every time I whispered it—I knew Titch would grow up to be loyal and protective just like the man I'd loved. Oh, how I longed to keep him, but that tiny puppy would soon be a full-sized dog, and Pippa's apartment would burst at the seams.

"I'll find you the perfect home, little one. I promise."

I needed to find my own home too, because I wasn't going back to Douglas much to my parents' disappointment. Last week, they'd come to talk to me, or talk sense into me, as my mother put it.

She stayed for two hours, alternately trying to cajole and force me into going back to Douglas. Her arguments ranged from me hurting my back lifting sacks of dog food, to Douglas losing the election and it all being my fault, to the ladies she golfed with looking down on her because she had a daughter who scooped up doggy poop for a hobby.

My father didn't say much, but as he left, he slipped me a handful of bills and told me to buy something nice. I could have kissed him, but we weren't that sort of family.

Douglas turned up once, and only once.

The week before last, I'd watched through a crack in the drapes as he picked his way across the yard, hammered on the door, shouted out my name, then hammered on the door again.

"Georgia, I know you're in there."

Pippa, crouching behind the sofa, shook her head. I gave her a thumbs up. She didn't need to tell me not to go out there.

"Georgia, this is getting beyond a joke."

Yes. Yes, it was.

"If you don't come out here, I'm cancelling your car lease."

Who needed a Mercedes anyway? He stomped off

across the yard, and I couldn't help sniggering when he planted one of his Gucci loafers right in the middle of a pile of poop.

Tonight, a roll of thunder sounded as Pippa walked into the lounge, carrying two steaming portions of lasagne. I shuffled Titch into his box next to me and settled the plate onto my lap. We didn't stand on ceremony here, and I relished that.

"We're in for a storm tonight," she said.

"Sure looks that way."

"Are we still going to the bank tomorrow?"

"The appointment's at eleven thirty. Let's hope it dries up before then."

I'd finally decided to get my trust fund sorted, once and for all. Then I could stop sponging off Pippa, sort out accommodation and start preparing for a baby whose existence grew more real with every passing day. I'd lost some of my fat from working with the dogs, and when I turned sideways in front of the mirror, I saw the first hint of a tiny bump. Soon, I wouldn't be able to hide it, and I'd have to tell my parents. Coward that I was, I'd kept my predicament from everyone but Pippa so far.

I still couldn't bring myself to deal with Douglas, but when my mother called earlier, she informed me he'd just flown to Las Vegas for some sort of conference, so at least I didn't have to worry about seeing him for a few days.

I'd turned procrastination into an art form.

The downpour carried on as I fed Titch after dinner, cradling him in my arms as I stood in front of the window. The last time I'd seen a storm this fierce was the first night I'd spent with Emmy, in that dingy motel in who-knows-where. Would I ever be brave enough to dance in the rain like her?

Rivulets of water ran down the glass and splashed into the puddles underneath as I watched my reflection. I barely knew that girl, the one looking back at me. Her face was tired, her eyes haunted by a thousand bad decisions and the loss of half her soul. Maybe I couldn't dance, but I settled Titch back into his bed then opened Pippa's front door and walked into the rain, standing there until it washed through me and made me feel again.

Emmy was right. It stung, but it reminded me I was alive.

"Do I look smart?" I asked Pippa the next morning.

"Smarter than I ever have."

I might have packed in a hurry, but I'd managed to bring a navy pencil skirt, which thankfully still fitted but wouldn't for much longer. With a white blouse, I looked presentable enough for an appointment with Hugo Tranter, my relationship manager, a title which implied a closeness I didn't feel, seeing as I'd never met the man before.

I did one last check in my purse—yes, I had my passport and driver's licence for identification, plus tissues, ginger cookies, and lipstick. All set. I made one last check on Titch, safely ensconced with Matilda, who volunteered one day a week, and climbed into Pippa's van.

Hugo Tranter tried not to look down his nose at Pippa's jeans when we arrived at the bank, but didn't quite succeed. I suspected it was bred into him to do so. The man was the epitome of a city boy—chalk stripe suit, red braces, wing tips. He only needed to act like an asshole to win at banker bingo.

"Let me introduce myself. I'm Hugo Tranter. Call me Hugo."

I'd intended to. We shook hands, and he checked my identification documents.

"What can I help you with today, Mrs. Rutherford-Beaumont?"

"Firstly, you can change the name on my account to Ms. Rutherford. I'll be losing the Beaumont shortly."

He swallowed. "As you wish, Ms. Rutherford."

"Then I'd like to donate $75,000 to charity and use the remaining money in the trust to provide myself with a monthly income."

Hugo settled behind a desk that put Douglas's to shame and called up my account details. "I must say, you've been awfully generous with your charity donations this past year. Not many people give so much."

"What charity donations?"

"Oh, don't be modest. The million dollars you donated to help premature babies seven months ago, and the one point five million dollars you gave to land mine victims. Both worthy causes, if I may say so."

"You're joking, right? I didn't make those payments."

He read through the detail, and I clutched the arms of the chair to stop myself from falling off it. "They were authorised online with your pass code. To do that, you'd need your bank card and your PIN number, plus your mother's maiden name and date of birth."

"My mother's maiden name and date of birth are common knowledge. You can look them up on Wikipedia, for goodness' sake. And what card are you talking about? I've never received a card or a PIN number."

"They were sent to your house, Ms. Rutherford. Last April, a week apart. Are you telling me you didn't make these transactions?"

"That's exactly what I'm telling you."

Hugo lost a little of his colour. "You're suggesting someone took the money fraudulently?"

"Yes."

"That's a very serious allegation. If you want to make a formal complaint, I'll need to involve the police."

"Great—get them involved. Somebody's stolen $2.5 million from me."

CHAPTER 40

I THOUGHT I'D cry, but I was so angry I'd gone beyond tears. Half of my trust fund, gone. I wanted to hit something, preferably my soon-to-be-ex-husband. "How could he do this to me, Pip?"

She handed me a cup of tea. It should have been wine—no, gin—but the bump-to-be dictated otherwise. "You think it was Douglas?"

"Who else? The card and PIN number got delivered to the house last April, and Douglas always opens the mail."

"Don't you have a maid? Maybe it was her?"

"Manuela took last April off to visit her family."

I'd given her permission, and Douglas had been furious. After the argument, I'd ended up doing more cleaning than Manuela normally did for the whole time she was away.

"You know, I always thought Douglas was slimy, but this? I didn't think he had it in him."

"He lied about everything." Getting in practice for his time in politics, no doubt. "He's turned into a monster."

"What do you suppose he wanted the money for?"

I thought that through. He hadn't been spending extravagantly at home lately. No new cars, nothing for the house. But there was obviously another woman somewhere. Maybe he was using my money to build a life with her. I pictured the gifts he'd be buying her, flowers and jewellery, and felt even sicker than usual.

The only other possibility was his election campaign. He'd press-ganged all of our acquaintances into donating, but campaigns cost a lot of money. I knew that from my father's efforts and said as much to Pippa.

"It's the woman, I bet you. Somewhere out there is a skank driving around in your Mercedes."

A walk in the woods with the dogs did nothing to calm my temper, and when I got back, I knew what I needed to do. There comes a stage in every girl's life when she still needs her daddy.

Only he didn't pick up, his PA did. "Margot? It's Georgia."

"Georgia?"

"The senator's daughter."

"Oh, of course. That Georgia."

How many of us were there? "Is my father available?"

"He's in a meeting. Would you like to leave a message?"

"Could you ask him to call me?"

"I'll make a note."

Great—by the time he phoned me back, I'd probably have chickened out of what I planned to say. It didn't take a genius to work out what Douglas would tell him: That I'd given the money willingly. And who wouldn't believe Douglas's story? I was his wife, after all.

The one chink of light in another dark day came when I went to feed Titch. He bumbled around his box in all his floppy-eared cuteness then turned to look at me. And I meant, *look* at me.

"Pip! Titch's eyes are open."

She rushed over. "Aw, he looks so adorable."

"Doesn't he just?"

Dusk had fallen when we began to prepare dinner— spaghetti bolognese, simple and fast. Pippa took the easiest job, the garlic bread, while I chopped up the onions. Dammit, they always made me weep.

The knock at the door made us both jump.

"Are you expecting anyone?" she asked.

I shook my head. "It had better not be Douglas back early, not while I've got a knife in my hand."

Pippa beat me to the window and peered out. "It's the police. Looks like Hugo the toff was more efficient than you thought."

The two men dwarfed the tiny living room. They both looked to be in their forties, but the one on the left hadn't aged well. His paunch hung over his pants, and most of his hair had fallen through his head and come out his nose and ears. And the other one appeared more nervous than me.

The one with the moustache spoke first. "Georgia Rutherford-Beaumont?"

I was too tired to correct him on the Beaumont. "Yes."

"I'm afraid I have some bad news. You might want to take a seat."

They couldn't recover the money, could they? I knew it, I freaking knew it. Still, I obediently perched on the edge of the sofa as he continued. "The body of your husband was found in his hotel room in Las Vegas this morning."

What? What did he just say? "I don't understand."

"I'm very sorry for your loss. This can't be easy."

Hold on, Douglas was dead? As in gone, kaput, not breathing, dead? Men like Douglas didn't die. They just got elected into a higher office.

"He's dead?" I asked, just to make sure.

"Yes, ma'am, I'm afraid so."

I knew how I *should* feel: Upset. No, devastated. I should be bawling my eyes out and collapsing in grief. But as I sat there, back straight and hands folded neatly in my lap, all I felt was a sense of relief.

But I could hardly tell the police that, could I? It would sound terrible. Instead, grateful for the smell of onion still permeating the small room, I let a few tears leak out and sniffled for effect.

Pippa sat down next to me and put an arm around my shoulders. "I think she's in shock, officer."

He nodded. "That's to be expected, ma'am. Will you be staying with her tonight?"

"Of course. I wouldn't let her be alone after receiving news like this."

A million thoughts flew through my head. What happened? Douglas would never have committed suicide—he thought far too much of himself to do that. It must have been an accident or murder. What if it was murder? Who did it? Was another hitman on the loose? Should I be in hiding again? Or worse, would I be a suspect? After all, I had the perfect motive, didn't I? Revenge. He'd taken my money.

But hang on—the officer said this morning, and he

said Las Vegas. I'd had that meeting with Hugo, and even if Douglas was killed earlier, I'd been with Pippa. She'd back me up on that. But what if the cops suspected I'd paid someone else to do it? I gave a sickening jolt as I thought of the two large payments made from my bank account, seemingly by me. I could be in trouble here.

My mind ran wild as I began to tremble. Bringing up my baby in jail wasn't an appealing prospect. "How did he die?"

The moustached cop spoke again. "The investigation hasn't concluded yet, but I understand it looks as if he had an accident in his hotel room."

"Like he slipped in the shower?"

"Not exactly."

"Then what?"

"Better that the coroner finalises his report first."

Pippa planted herself in front of him. "If you know who Douglas is, you know this'll be all over the news first thing tomorrow. Better Georgia finds out what happens from you than a reporter."

He looked away, unable to meet my eyes. "My colleagues in the LVPD said it looked like a case of auto-erotic asphyxiation gone wrong."

"Auto-what? What on earth is that?" Pippa asked the question for me.

The nervous one surprised me by answering. "B-b-basically, it's a kind of sex game. Restricting the supply of oxygen to the brain gives a more intense orgasm. It's surprisingly common for men to do this to themselves. We see around a hundred deaths a year in the United States because of it."

Mr. Missionary-Position died in a sex game? Six

months ago I wouldn't have believed it, but now I'd seen those magazines in his desk drawer, it didn't seem so far-fetched.

"So he killed himself?"

"Not on purpose."

"Well, thank you for letting me know."

For the last time, I summoned fake Georgia and put on expression number nine. Grief.

"We'll be in touch when we've got more information. Again, we're very sorry for your loss."

Pippa showed them to the door, and then we were on our own again. She looked at me, and I looked at her.

"I guess that's one problem solved, then."

She let out a breath. "I was afraid you'd be more upset than that."

"I know I should be, Pip, but I'm just not. Yes, I was married to Douglas for a long time, but I just feel...well, nothing. That was pretty much what I felt through most of our marriage, too. There was no passion, only lies and more lies. He lied to me, and I lied to myself when I said I loved him."

It was true. Being with Mitch had made me see that. I'd had more passion, felt more emotion in a couple of weeks with him than I had in all my years with Douglas. It was still Mitch I grieved for.

"I hate to say it, but him being gone might make things easier for you."

"That's how I feel, too."

But I could never tell anyone but Pippa that. Another secret to keep.

My father appeared a couple of hours later with my mother in tow. He must have had a word with her because she stayed in the background, remarkably quiet, while he did the talking. Unsurprisingly, he'd already heard about Douglas.

"How are you doing, Twinkle?"

"I'm okay, Daddy. Pippa's helping me."

"Is there anything you need? Money?"

"I have money. I have my trust fund."

I decided against mentioning the payments to him for now. Drawing attention to them didn't seem sensible under the circumstances.

"If there's anything I can help with, you tell me."

"I promise. Do you have any more information on what happened? The police barely told me a thing."

"Best you don't know the details. It's not something you want to hear. Just keep your head down, and it'll all blow over in a few weeks when the next scandal happens. You know how it is."

I did, indeed I did.

But that didn't stop me from poring over the worst of the gossip websites the next morning. Daddy was right; I didn't want to know. A maid found Douglas naked in his hotel room, his dick in his hand and the end of his silk tie wound around the light fitting. He'd apparently been working towards a climax he never reached. By the time she arrived to clean his room, he'd been dead for hours.

The door was chained from the inside, and they'd had to break it down to get into the room. The only other way in was from the balcony, seven floors up, but the police didn't feel it was possible for someone to get to it without a serious risk of death. According to detectives, the people in the rooms above and to the side hadn't seen or heard anything, and the one below was empty. They'd watched the comings and goings on the security cameras in the hallways and found nothing suspect.

It really was just a terrible accident.

CHAPTER 41

IT TOOK ANOTHER two weeks for the last of the reporters to finally disappear. A Hollywood starlet got videoed in Richmond snorting something she shouldn't, and they all hightailed it after her. It was almost a shame. Pippa and I had just got used to the extra help with walking the dogs again.

The day after they left, I put Douglas's house on the market. The realtor, a friend of mother's, twittered on and on about landscaping, square footage, and soft furnishings until I wanted to stick a corkscrew in my ear.

"Please, just take whatever price you normally market it for and knock a hundred thousand off. Two, if it'll make it sell faster."

"There's really no need. Give it a few months, and a place like this will sell full price. You could buy yourself a new Mercedes with the difference."

"If it's about your commission, just adjust it. I want to move, and I want to move quickly."

Her eyes lit up at the mention of more commission for less work. "If you're sure?"

"I'm sure."

I could afford to take a hit on the price because after my meeting with Hugo yesterday, I had more money than I thought. He'd ushered me into his office with a grin and waved me into his uncomfortable visitor's chair.

"Look." He spun his screen around to show me. "The money's back. Being honest, we're not entirely sure how, but we suspect it was a computer glitch. Our information systems department is looking into it. I'm terribly sorry if we worried you, Ms. Rutherford. We'd like to offer you a complimentary spa break as an apology."

What was it with men and spa breaks? Did they think a massage and a complimentary glass of champagne cured everything?

"I don't want a spa break. I want to draw a monthly income and make a donation to charity."

"Well, I can certainly help you with that. Six figures per annum is perfectly achievable without eating into your capital."

A hundred thousand. I could live on that, quite happily in fact. I didn't need or want the expensive clothes and furnishings that came with my old life. Now that the paparazzi had stopped hounding me, I planned to buy myself a little house near Pippa and devote my time to raising my child and caring for the animals.

I no longer needed to fake expression number two, happiness.

Hugo's revelation meant Douglas hadn't stolen my money after all. When I realised that, I felt a few moments of guilt, but when I found the file marked *Statutory Accounts* at the back of his closet that didn't contain any financials, but instead held keepsake photographs of Douglas with no less than sixteen other women, those feelings quickly disappeared. I did wish he was still alive, but only so I could kill him myself.

Every day, another chink of light shone through the dark clouds above me. I grew stronger, freer, like the majestic hawk that soared above the ridge in Mitch's painting. It still hung above the fireplace, watching as I packed up the remnants of my old life. One day, when everything wasn't so raw, I planned to return to the mountain. I wanted to hike up to the clearing and show our child how beautiful it was.

Even my mother commented on how upbeat I was, although she couldn't comprehend why I'd taken all of my evening dresses to the charity shop.

A month after Douglas died, I stood in front of the mirror, looking at the changes in my body. I loved my little bump, now obvious when I turned sideways. And I finally had those bigger breasts Douglas had always wanted.

Soon, I wouldn't be able to hide my expanding waistline. No, I still hadn't told anyone but Pippa. Yes, I knew I should have. But I also knew my mother would try to pass the baby off as Douglas's to save face. Her standing at the country club had already taken a battering after his death. Ladies that lunch shouldn't have sons-in-law that masturbate, at least not so everybody finds out about it. The only thing worse would be a daughter pregnant through adultery.

But I refused to hide my baby's parentage. It would be Mitch's name on the birth certificate, and it would be Mitch I told him or her about while growing up. One huge regret was I didn't even have a picture of Mitch to show our baby. He'd taken hundreds of me, but all I had was my memories, and they'd fade with time. But I had my painting. I took a lingering glance at it before I went back to packing.

Well, I say packing, but it was more throwing things away. The house needed to be emptied, and I had no wish to keep a two-hundred-piece Wedgewood dinner service, even if it did come all the way from England. I'd just finished taping the lid shut on another box when the doorbell rang.

If this was another reporter, he was going to get a piece of my mind.

It wasn't.

The mailman held out a package—large, rectangular, and quite thin. "Sign here, please."

What was it? The only thing I was expecting was a pile of baby T-shirts I'd ordered from the internet, and those were being delivered to Pippa's apartment.

Hmmm, it wasn't heavy. I carried it inside, fetched a pair of scissors and carefully cut through the outer layer of paper, revealing several layers of bubble wrap and a note.

Ma'am,

You don't know me, but I work as a crime scene investigator in Denver. My team processed the scene of a cabin that burned down there a few months ago. During our search of the wreckage, we found a picture trapped under a chest of drawers, which meant it survived the fire and subsequent soaking relatively intact.

Now we no longer need it for evidence, I thought you might like to have it.

Yours, Geoff Crawley

I slowly unwrapped the layers of bubble wrap, scarcely able to breathe. My hands shook as I finally turned the painting over. Oil on canvas, stretched over a thin wooden frame.

Me.

Me, looking into a mirror at an angle. The left-hand side showed the back of my head, my brown bob gleaming. Painted Georgia reached out to touch her reflection, an enigmatic smile on her face. I propped it up against the living room wall and sank down to the floor in front of it. The portrait was unsigned, but I knew exactly who'd painted it. Was that how he saw me? He'd made me beautiful.

As I studied the brushstrokes through my tears, my heart ached for the man I'd lost, partly through my own stupidity in making a phone call and partly because a madman had wanted me dead.

What might have been?

If the assassin hadn't found me so soon, would Mitch and I have grown closer again? I liked to think so. Would he have wanted this baby as much as me? He'd have been an excellent father, of that I was sure. He had so much love in him, even if he didn't let it show much.

What would have happened long term? Could I have got past his occupation? I didn't know. But I knew Emmy was right. He was a good man above everything else.

Oh, how I wished I knew more about him. Who he really was. But if all the media with their connections and weaselly ways had dug up was a single blurred photograph taken at the market in Wolf's Corner by a passer-by, what hope did I have? I'd seen that picture, and it wasn't even Mitch.

Hold on—maybe there was a way? I knew of one person who had history with Mitch, and that was Emmy. I had to try, at least, or forever regret it.

According to their website, Blackwood Security had their corporate headquarters about an hour's drive from here. Before I could chicken out, I grabbed the keys to Douglas's over-specced BMW and programmed the navigation system. As I drove, my mind churned. What if Emmy wouldn't tell me anything? Or worse, what if she told me something I didn't want to hear? So many times I almost turned around and drove right back, but thoughts of the baby forced me to keep going.

An imposing set of metal gates complete with Blackwood's shield and halo logo blocked my way. Beside them, a small parking lot lay empty save for a sign warning off trespassers. Guess they didn't want visitors. Undeterred, I bleeped the car locked and scurried to the gatehouse. An unsmiling man peered out at me.

"Can I help?" He didn't look like he wanted to.

"I'm hoping to see Emmy Black."

He tapped away at the keyboard in front of him. "She's not here today."

"She did say she spent a lot of time away on jobs."

"Even if she was here, she doesn't see anybody without an appointment." He picked up a business card and handed it to me. "Here's the phone number for reception. Why don't you give them a call?"

He turned away, and his message was clear. I'd been dismissed.

"What about a man called Nick?" I asked in desperation.

"Nick's a common name."

I racked my brains, but I couldn't remember him ever telling me his surname. "He was big with brown hair. Muscular. Er, handsome."

"That fits half the men here." His glare said I was wasting my own time as well as his.

Well, that was that, then. I'd done my best. All I could do was go home and try my luck with the receptionist, although if she was as helpful as the ogre on the gate, it would be a pointless exercise. I trudged back to the BMW, defeated. I hated that car. It was too big and the seats were uncomfortable, and to make matters worse, I needed to pee. Bladder aching, I got behind the wheel and burst into tears. Hormones, that's what it was. I'd been so damn emotional lately.

A knock on the window startled me, and I looked up to see a blurry brunette. Even through my tears I could see how pretty she was, and her sparkly dress accentuated her curves. I swiped at my eyes and tried to wind down the window, but only managed to open the fuel cap and turn on the radio before I gave up and cracked the door open instead.

"Yes?"

"I just wanted to check you're okay. You look upset."

She stated the obvious, but I didn't want to talk about my problems. I wanted to go back to Pippa's and drink alcohol-free wine. I still felt guilty over the bottle of the good stuff I'd quaffed before I knew I was pregnant.

"I'll be fine."

She wrinkled her nose. "You don't look fine." She pulled the door open wider and sat on the sill. "Is there anything I can do to help?" Unlike the guard, she looked like she meant it.

At her kindness, the tears ran down my cheeks unchecked. "Not unless you know a woman called Emmy Black, who apparently never sees anybody without an appointment, or can identify one particular Nick out of a whole bunch of them."

I bent my head and blew my nose. Then looked up in surprise as she started laughing.

"You're Georgia, right?"

I nodded. How did she know?

"I thought I recognised you. I'm Lara. I'm almost certain I know which Nick you want, and I definitely know Emmy."

"Really?"

"Leave your car here, and I'll give you a lift up to the main building."

She waved at the brute as she drove through the gates, and he glowered back at her.

"Don't mind Eugene. His job is to keep people out. I think he was born without the ability to smile."

I didn't know who Lara was or what she did at Blackwood, but with her beside me, we got through security really quickly. Once I'd been issued a visitor's badge, she led me up to a glass-fronted office set on a mezzanine so it looked down on the open-plan space below.

"You might want to fix up your face. You're a bit smudgy."

"Uh..."

"There's a bathroom right here."

She opened a door in the back wall and ushered me inside.

I closed the door behind me and took the opportunity to use the facilities. If nothing else, I'd avoided the need to hunt for a gas station bathroom on the way home. When I came out, Lara was sitting on the edge of the desk, swinging her legs. She turned a photo in a frame around to face me.

"Is this the right Nick?"

The photo showed him standing behind Lara, his arms around her as they smiled for the camera.

"Yes, that's him. You're his girlfriend?"

"Since last winter." She giggled. "Sometimes I still have to pinch myself."

"I'm sorry about him getting shot."

"I won't deny I got a bit upset when he came home."

"It can't be easy, having him work as a bodyguard."

"This job is part of who he is, and I love him for it. There's always a risk, but everything he does is for a good reason, even if I don't understand it." She looked at her watch. "His PA says he's in a meeting, but he won't be long. Do you want a drink?"

"A glass of water would be lovely."

A cupboard at the back of the office hid a tiny refrigerator, and Lara fished out two bottles of water, plus a couple of glasses. The cool liquid soothed my throat, dry from the worry of coming here.

And a few minutes later, Nick walked in and did a double take.

"Georgia Rutherford—there's somebody I never thought I'd see again."

"I didn't think I'd see you either. You look different."

"It's the suit, isn't it? Apparently I need to dress up for dinner tonight. How are you?"

"Good, mostly. Sometimes I have bad days." I shrugged. "That's why I'm here, really. Today is one of them."

"What's up? Can we help?"

Before I could stop myself, the whole story came out. Nick's jaw dropped when I told him I was pregnant.

"So I was hoping, I guess, that Emmy would be able to tell me more about Mitch, and that maybe she'd have a photo. I just want our child to know something about its father when it gets older."

Nick rubbed his temples. "I need to make a phone call. Give me a minute."

He strode off, jogging down the stairs that led to his office, and Lara reached out and squeezed my hand.

"Congratulations. I know the circumstances can't be easy, but I can see you'll make a wonderful mom."

"I'm going to do my best. At the moment, I'm trying to focus on the positive things, but it's so difficult."

Rather than keep talking about my situation, Lara chattered on about the friends she and Nick were going out with that evening, and how he refused to wear a suit more than once a month, so she had to make the most of it. I welcomed her normality in a world that was anything but.

Then Nick came back and kissed her hair. "Baby, can you do me a favour? Run Georgia over to Little Riverley? They're expecting her at the gate."

"Sure."

Where? "What's Riverley?"

"Lara's taking you to see Emerson Black."

CHAPTER 42

OUTSIDE BLACKWOOD, WE got back into Lara's Porsche. She'd gone for metallic black paintwork with cotton candy-pink leather. I may not have known her long, but it suited her. Classy on the outside and cheerful on the inside.

Half an hour later, she pulled up outside a pair of art deco style iron gates, fancier than those at Blackwood but every bit as solid. The high wall either side of them stretched as far as I could see. Nobody came out of the guardhouse, but slowly the gates rolled back and Lara pointed upwards.

"They watch with cameras."

The driveway wound past lawns and through trees before we arrived in front of a house dropped in from outer space. The metal, the glass, the impossible angles all looked alien in the surrounding countryside. Lara parked outside and led me up to the front door.

The man who opened it sported hair that matched Lara's car seats. He'd paired it with a pair of blue dungarees, and when he turned to show us in, the word "STUD" twinkled in diamante from his ass.

"She's in the white lounge," he informed us. "I'm going to check on the building. The roofing material's arriving this afternoon, and if I'm not there they'll dump it in the wrong place."

Stud walked out of the door we'd come in while I followed Lara through a maze of passageways, hoping she wouldn't leave me there because I'd never find my way out alone. Even with a map, I'd still be meandering around when night fell.

Emmy glanced up from her seat on the couch as we walked into a room more like an art gallery than a lounge. The pieces on display put many museums to shame. I couldn't resist walking over to the far wall when I glimpsed two familiar canvases.

"He painted two sets." I turned to see her watching me. "The ones in the cabin were the trial run."

The angel and the devil. Which one showed Emerson's true face?

Her footsteps made no sound as she walked over to join me. "This is one of his as well." She pointed out a view over a rocky desert, a single green tree providing a focal point. "It's one of his early paintings. Of where he used to live."

It didn't look like the United States. "Where was that?"

"Israel. He was born under the Star of David. He fought under it too."

Finally, I was getting some of the answers I craved. "I thought he was American. He sounded American."

"By the time you met him, he'd been living here for over a decade. He always was good at accents and languages. That ability to blend in was one of the things that made him so good at his job."

"I still can't understand why he chose to do that."

"He didn't. It's not a job you choose. It chooses you."

"What do you mean?"

She stared out of the window. On the patio outside, a set of furniture and a barbecue were covered up until the weather improved. It all seemed so normal when Emerson was definitely not.

"You start off as a foot soldier, then you find you're good at stuff. Stuff you never expected to be good at. They train you, and things that you never believed possible suddenly are. You go places and see the worst parts of humanity, and you can't unsee it. Your eyes are opened to the world, and you learn justice isn't always achieved in a courtroom or government chamber. Sometimes it's dispensed by people who for all intents and purposes don't exist."

"People like Mitch."

"Yes. He killed people, don't get me wrong, but he wasn't unethical. His moral compass was just aligned in a slightly different direction to most other people's."

"I think I understand that." After all, he'd taken care of me right up until he gave his life to save mine. "I miss him so much. More than anything, I wish I could tell him that."

She returned to the sofa and beckoned me to join her. I perched at the other end, as if the distance could swallow any words I didn't want to hear before they reached me.

"Let me tell you a story," she started. "All hypothetical of course."

"Of course."

"Once upon a time, an evil lord married a beautiful maiden. They lived a life their countrymen envied, until one day, he decided he no longer wanted to be her husband. But rather than tell her that, he took a different approach and hired a dark wraith to remove her from the picture."

"You're talking about me, aren't you? I'm the maiden?"

She shook her head. "It's hypothetical, remember? Anyway, the forces of black and gray foiled the lord's dastardly plan, but not to be deterred, he tried again. But this time, he made a small mistake when the person he engaged to do his bidding turned out not to be a wraith but rather a knight in disguise. The knight didn't like the story the evil lord had written and decided to change the ending."

I should have been surprised by the tale, but I wasn't. Not the first bit, anyway.

"You mean it was Douglas? He tried to have me killed? I found two large payments made from one of my bank accounts. Do you think that was anything to do with it? The bank said it was a computer error, but it seemed strange to me."

She just smiled and looked out the window again.

"Who was the knight?"

"It's just a story." Her tone didn't invite more questions.

Instead, I went back to the reason why I came. "Can you tell me anything more about Mitch? It's just... I-I-I'm pregnant, and it's his."

She looked down at my belly. Out of habit, I'd worn a loose-fitting top to hide the evidence.

"The bump barely shows yet. I have to turn sideways to see it."

"How far along are you?"

"Twelve weeks. Sometimes it doesn't seem real, but then the morning sickness comes back and I know it is."

She laughed, a small sound I'd have missed if the room hadn't been completely silent. "What do you want to know about Mitch?"

"Anything you can tell me. We never discussed his past or the future, just the present. I know so little. What were his parents like? Are they still alive? Where did he grow up? Did he play sport? Did he like animals? And I was wondering whether you might have a photo of him?"

She sighed, a thin exhalation of breath as quiet as her laugh. "Did you love him?"

"Yes. Absolutely, and I always will." I may have been confused when I was with him, but now I'd had the time and space to think there was no doubt in my mind.

"Are you sure? You're not putting him on a pedestal now he's gone? He wasn't the easiest man to live with."

"I know that. He was moody, and he could be rude, but he got me. He just got me. And he was also kind and gentle and generous and sweet." And amazing in bed, something she no doubt already knew.

"What would you do if he was still alive? Would you still feel the same way? The way you were living wasn't normal. You didn't have the realities of life to deal with."

No, we may not have done "normal" things, like deciding where to go on vacation or when to replace the car, but we'd been stuck together 24/7 and survived the stress of somebody trying to kill me. If we coped with that, surely we could have agreed on the basics?

"Honestly? I don't know how things would have worked out. But I'd have given anything to find out."

"He thought he wasn't good enough for you."

"You talked about me?"

"A little."

"And that's what he thought? Why?"

"A senator's daughter and an assassin? It's not exactly your normal match. He didn't see how it could work."

"What's normal? I mean look at Anna Nicole Smith and J Howard Marshall—a stripper and a billionaire. How could that possibly work?"

She gave a wry smile. "How indeed?"

"And I wish people would stop defining me by my father. They've been doing it my whole life. I never asked to be his daughter, even though I wouldn't change him for the world. I'm a person, my own person, and I can make my own decisions. That means I can fall in love with whoever I choose."

She laughed, louder this time. "Come on, let's take a ride."

"A ride? What's that got to do with anything?"

"You'll see."

CHAPTER 43

EMMY USHERED ME into a jeep parked at the side of the house then hopped in behind the wheel.

"Can you drive more slowly this time?"

I hadn't forgotten the wild ride halfway across the country.

"We're not going far."

"Where *are* we going?"

"It's a surprise."

After the last few months, I hated surprises. Mind you, the last time she'd decided our destination it led me to Mitch, so I figured they weren't always a bad thing.

I'd expected to turn left out of the driveway, towards the main road, but she spun the wheel right instead, onto a narrow lane. She still drove far too fast, texting as she went. I adjusted the seatbelt over my stomach and poised to grab the wheel, just in case.

After four or five miles, she turned onto a potholed driveway through the woods, and we bumped along for a minute or two before emerging into a hive of activity. The pink-haired man I'd seen earlier stood in the middle of it all, hopping around and doing a lot of pointing. He'd accessorised his ass with a silver hard hat, "BOSS" written on the side in matching diamante.

Above our heads, a crane truck unloaded pallets of

roof tiles, and I saw a wood-framed building taking shape by the trees on the far side. It reminded me of Mitch's cabin with a balcony and porch at the front.

"What is all this?" I asked.

"We're building a house. A friend needs somewhere to live."

That was nice. "So why am I here?"

"The reason's in that little shack thing over there." She pointed at a small hut set back in the trees. "Out you get."

I slid out into the late afternoon sun then realised she hadn't moved. "Aren't you coming?"

"No. You'll do just fine on your own."

Would I? As I took my first tentative step towards the trees, she wound down her window.

"Xavier," she called.

"What?"

"His name's Xavier."

Confused, I began walking away. This was the first time I'd stepped into the unknown by myself, and my heart fluttered as I walked into the trees. Dark, a little foreboding. What would I find?

Behind me, Emmy started the jeep's engine and pulled away. She was abandoning me? Thank goodness I still had my phone in my pocket. I'd need to get a cab back to Douglas's hideous BMW.

The door to the hut lay an inch ajar, and I tapped gently. No answer. Maybe nobody was there? Looked like I'd need that cab sooner rather than later. I knocked a bit harder, and the door swung open.

A man hung in front of me, gripping one of the beams spanning the roof as he performed a set of chin-ups. Sweat dripped down his muscular back and onto the floor. I shouldn't have licked my lips, but I did.

A wire snaked from his waist to his ears, and the faint beat of music drifted through the air. What should I do? Go out and wait for a bit?

Then he spoke with a faint accent I couldn't place. "Did you bring the beer?"

"I'm sorry?"

He dropped down and turned.

I screamed, as if I'd just seen a ghost. Because I had.

He caught me before I fell, cradling me in his arms as he carried me to a plain leather couch then set me down.

"Mitch," I croaked, then tried again. "Xavier?"

He straightened, arms crossed, looking defensive. "I see you've been talking to my nearest and dearest."

"Do you mean Emmy?"

"Yes."

"Is Xavier your real name?"

"It's the one I was born with."

"Xavier Gray?"

"Xavier Roth."

I didn't know what to say next. Whatever I'd been expecting when I climbed out of Emerson's jeep, it hadn't been this.

"You're not dead," I blurted.

He laughed, a deep throaty chuckle. Oh, how I'd missed that. "No, it appears not."

"What happened? They found your body."

"No, they found a body."

"Whose was it?"

He shrugged. "No idea. Fritz brought a colleague with him. Emmy found out there were two of them before they got there and warned me. Then I lured them into the cabin and blew it up."

"Wait a minute, you blew it up? You blew up your own home?"

"It was just a house. A home is the people inside it."

"But why?"

"It was easier that way. Killing Mitchell Gray avoided a lot of awkward questions, and it meant your life was less complicated. You could just go back and get on with things the way they were."

I felt like throwing something at him. "You idiot! I didn't want to go back to the way things were. I wanted to stay with you."

It was his turn to look surprised. "You did?"

"Yes!"

"But after what I told you... The way you looked at me..."

"I'd had a shock, okay? Cut me a little slack. I mean, it's not every day the man you love informs you he's an assassin. I needed a few minutes to think."

He looked at me strangely. "What did you just say?"

"I needed a few minutes to think?"

"No, before that."

"You're actually an assassin?"

"No, before that too."

"Oh, the man I love?"

"Yeah, that bit. You love me?"

"I'll love you until the sun falls out of the sky."

He wrapped his arms around me, and for the first time in weeks, I felt whole again.

"I love you too, *perakh*.'

"What does that mean? *Perakh?*"

"It's Hebrew for flower."

"Why flower?"

"Why not? You're beautiful and delicate. A splash of colour in a dull landscape." He buried his face in my neck. "And you smell nice."

"Hey, don't sniff me!" I tried to push him away, laughing, but he squeezed harder. "Get off, please, not so tight."

He sprang back, shocked. "I promise I won't hurt you. I'll never hurt you."

"It's not me I'm worried about." Oh, hell, I had to tell him. "It's the baby."

His eyes went wide. "What baby?"

My eyes dropped to the floor, where the dusty floor took on a new fascination. "Um, our baby?" How mad was he going to be?

He gently put his palm on my belly. "There's a baby in there?"

"Yes, there is."

He hugged me again, gently this time. "You've been dealing with this by yourself?"

"Pippa's been helping me. We've been helping each other."

"Shit. I had no idea. If I'd known—"

"What? What would you have done?"

"Fuck. I don't know."

"Are you okay with me having a baby?"

"Not *a* baby. *Our* baby. How could I possibly not be okay with that? Scary as fuck, but it's gonna be a little piece of you and me. A fucking miracle." He kissed me then, deeply, his love pouring into me. "Flower, if the sun ever fell from the sky, I'd climb right up and put it back."

"Did I tell you that I love you?"

"I'll never get tired of hearing it."

Mitch—Xavier—took my hand and pulled me along beside him as he locked the door and closed the drapes. The dim bulb of an old-fashioned floor lamp cast a yellow glow across the tiny room as he picked me up and laid me gently on the bed.

"We can still do this, right? With the baby, I mean?"

"Yes. I've been reading all the books I can find on it."

"Why doesn't that surprise me?"

This time was different than our first. He took his time undressing me, this time using the buttons rather than a knife, and as he kissed his way from my lips down to my happy spot, he stopped and gently caressed the bump.

"It's so tiny."

"Just wait. In six months I'll be fat and ugly."

"No, you'll be carrying our baby, and you'll be all the more beautiful for it."

He gave me one sweet orgasm with his tongue before sliding up my body to kiss me again. By then, I'd felt what he was hiding in his shorts, and I didn't want to wait any longer to feel it inside me.

"You're still wearing clothes. Not fair."

I felt a sudden chill at the lack of contact when he sat up. But then he flung his shorts on the floor, and when he came back, there was nothing standing between us. Nothing at all. No fabric. No Fritz. No Douglas.

Well, apart from one awkward conversation. "Um, I should probably tell you, I found out Douglas was sleeping around, but I got checked for everything and I'm clean."

"I never want to hear that man's name in our bed again."

That made two of us. And I liked the way it was "our" bed.

He slid into me slowly, and when he started to move, it was sweet and gentle, not like the frantic fuck we'd had last time. Stretched to a delicious tightness, I moaned softly as he moved in and out, hitting exactly the right spot until my next orgasm washed over me like a wave. He soon joined me in paradise, biting my neck gently as he groaned his release.

"I love you," I whispered.

He held my eyes with his. "I love you too, *perakh*."

I snuggled into him as he held me to his chest, happy that I'd found my own little slice of heaven in a tiny hut in the woods. The location didn't matter. The man was all that mattered.

"Will you stay with me?" he asked.

"Tonight?"

"Tonight. Every night."

"Nothing would make me happier. Or Pippa for that matter. I've been sharing her apartment, and things have been a bit squashed."

"You're not living at home?"

"Like you said, home is the people in it, and I don't want to be anywhere with reminders of D...you know who. This place is home now."

"Only temporarily. The new house'll be finished in a few weeks. Bradley's on fire." He chuckled. "The workmen have been calling him Little Adolf behind his back. Or I can rent a place in the meantime if you want more space."

"This is fine. It's got everything we need." I only

needed one thing, in fact, and I was wrapped up in it. My beautiful man. I ran my fingers across his chest, along his cheek... "You cut your hair?"

He ran his own hand along what was left, barely half an inch long. "It was about due."

"And you're not wearing your glasses."

"I don't need glasses."

Our comfortable silence was interrupted by a hammering on the door. "Xav, I know you've got Georgia in there, but I need to speak to you."

"Now isn't a good time, Bradley."

"But it's important. It's about your new kitchen tiles."

"I don't give a fuck about the kitchen tiles. Just pick something."

"Fine. But don't complain to me if you don't like them. I take it I can tell Emmy that Georgia won't need a lift back?"

"Yes, you can tell her that. Now would you mind losing yourself?" He turned back to me. "Sorry about him."

"Is he always like that? Who is he anyway?"

"He's Emmy's assistant, and yes, he's always loud and obnoxious but also fearsomely efficient. He'll grow on you, don't worry."

Bradley disappeared, and we settled back onto the bed. Xav held me close and stroked my hair, now an inch longer and in desperate need of having the roots dyed. We didn't say anything. We didn't need to. Just being together was all we wanted at that moment. I could have quite happily stayed there forever, but my stomach picked that moment to remind me I hadn't eaten anything since breakfast.

"Are you hungry?" Xav asked.

"A little."

"The baby might be hungry too."

"I'm not sure they think like that."

"But you don't know for sure, do you?"

"Okay, I'll eat." Overprotective dad-to-be alert. "What is there?"

He unwound himself and went to the refrigerator. "There's chicken salad or a turkey wrap, and I've got fruit and eggs. I could make an omelette?"

"In Colorado you had TV dinners and cookies. What happened?"

"Emmy's nutritionist happened. He's on a crusade this month. If anyone buys anything that isn't wholefood, raw food or nutritionally balanced, he confiscates it. Emmy's resorted to keeping the cookies and chocolate in her weapons locker."

I giggled. "At least now I know where I need to go if I have a craving."

"You've been having those?"

"Oddly, yes. I can't get enough grapefruit."

It was his turn to laugh. "You'd better have the fruit then, at least for now. I'm taking you out to dinner this evening. A proper dinner. I've wanted to do that for a long time."

"Like a date?"

"Exactly like a date. Where do you want to go? Emmy can get us reservations anywhere."

"I don't want to go somewhere we need reservations." Not after Douglas and his obsession with being seen in those places. "Somewhere cheap. Will you take me somewhere cheap?"

The tiny table in the back corner of a hole-in-the-wall Italian restaurant was perfect. Faded murals decorated the single room, and soft music played from hidden speakers. I didn't feel out of place in my jeans and comfortable top, and Xav, as he'd told me to call him, moved his chair next to me so our legs were pressed together.

"What do you want?" he asked, face flickering in the candlelight.

Ah, the novelty of being allowed to choose my own meal for the first time in my life, and I found I no longer cared what I ate. "You. I only want you."

He leaned over, and I felt his smile as he pressed his lips to my cheek. "You can eat me later. I'll allow it."

I'd always hated that with Douglas, but Xav? I wanted to taste every inch of him, and he had plenty of those. "Can we skip dessert?"

"You *are* the dessert, *perakh*."

It promised to be a strange new life, this one, but as I walked into our home later that evening, hand in hand with the man I loved, I knew I'd savour every second of it.

Epilogue

SIX WEEKS LATER, I stood in front of the oven in our new kitchen, in our new house, in our new forest, waiting for my cake to rise. I'd taken the recipe for an orange cake and replaced all the orange parts with grapefruit. Would it be edible? I had no idea, but I figured it was worth a try.

Titch lay at my feet, my little shadow, even if he wasn't so small any more. I loved the way he stayed close to me even if it meant I tripped over him from time to time. When we'd moved in two weeks ago, he'd come with us, and now he had his paws firmly under the table. The hand-carved oak table imported from Scandinavia that arrived after Xav got distracted by my, ahem, assets and told Bradley to order whatever furniture he wanted. The matching chairs looked a little unusual with their cracked metallic leather, but Titch seemed to like the taste of their legs and Xav said the teeth marks added character.

"You want a sausage?" I asked my puppy. "Do you? Xav bought the expensive ones."

Titch tilted his head to one side, and his ears flopped over. They still hadn't straightened properly, and it made him even cuter. I'd worried about asking Xav if I could adopt Titch, but it turned out he loved him just as much as I did, even when he ate part of the new sofa within a day of arriving.

I thought back to the conversation that had taken place soon after our first date. "Uh, do you like dogs?"

Xav had looked up at me from the floor where he was halfway through a set of drool-worthy crunches. "Yeah. Never had one, though. Work always got in the way. Why? Do you want one?"

"I really do. He's called Titch, and I hand-reared him at Hope for Hounds."

"Titch? What kind of dog is he?"

"A German shepherd."

"Thank fuck for that. For a moment, I thought I'd have to walk a Chihuahua."

"So I can have him?"

"Flower, you can have whatever makes you happy."

I pounced on him, sweat and all. "I love you!"

One thing led to another, and another led to bed. Living in a home where everything was close together certainly had its advantages.

Xav kissed me softly afterwards. "If I buy you a dog every week, will I get more of that?"

No, but it did get him a pillow in the face, followed by laughter, then more of what he wanted anyway.

"We'll have to buy all that puppy crap," he told me as we got dressed. "Or you could get Bradley to do it, but you'd end up with a three-level gold-plated waterbed."

"No way. I bet they don't even make those."

"You'd think, but Emmy's Spanish horse lives in a centrally heated stable with his own television and the wall's all painted up to look like a Spanish village. I know this because Bradley made me paint the fucking thing."

So we went out, together, and bought Titch a regular bed. Such a normal thing to do, in a life that was anything but.

Xav got more open about his past, including a far from ideal childhood. Losing his mother at seventeen devastated him, and he'd never got on with his father. One night, as we drifted off to sleep with his hand on my stomach, where it always rested, he whispered, "I want to be everything he wasn't."

"You already are."

The one thing we didn't talk about was his work. He said he couldn't, and I didn't want to know in any case. But he did allow me one question.

"Did you kill Douglas?"

He didn't meet my eyes. "If I had, what would you say?"

I'd already thought about my answer. "I would say thank you."

"I didn't, but I'll convey your thanks to the person who did."

"I still can't believe this." Pippa wiped tears from her eyes as we watched the first bricks for the new kennel block being laid by the building crew now set up on site.

When I'd told Xav about my plans to donate money for the Hope Project, he'd matched me dollar for dollar. Then he'd got Emerson to do the same, and a whole bunch of other people I didn't even know. Now Hope for Hounds would have forty new kennels, an education centre, plus two full-time members of staff to help Pippa and me, and in a twist I still pinched myself over, the first lady herself would be coming to open the facility when it was finished. According to my father, she loved animals.

"Are you sure you don't want the movie theatre?" Bradley asked. He'd replaced his BOSS hat with one that said "TOP DOG." The diamantes stayed, though.

Pippa tried to keep a straight face, but didn't do a very good job of it. "I don't think the dogs would sit still through the whole movie."

"But they could watch *Beethoven. Huckleberry Hound. Reservoir Dogs.*"

Xav rested his chin on my shoulder. "*Reservoir Dogs* isn't about dogs, Bradley."

"Isn't it?"

Xav ignored him. "Flower, we're late."

I looked at my watch. "We've still got two hours until the appointment."

"There might be traffic." He tugged at my hand.

"Okay, okay."

I followed him to his new car, a gleaming cherry-red Dodge Challenger, and rolled my eyes as he helped me into the passenger seat. Honestly, you'd think I was an invalid, not pregnant. But secretly, I couldn't help being as excited about today's scan as he was. Would we be decorating the nursery blue or pink?

"It's gonna be a boy," Xav told me as we pulled into the hospital parking lot.

"You keep telling yourself that. It's a girl."

Turned out the sonographer agreed with me. We'd be calling her Libi after Xav's mother. It meant *my heart* in Hebrew, which we both thought was fitting.

"You know what this means?" he said to me in the

car on the way home.

"Ponies, Barbie dolls, and cute dresses?"

"Nope. We'll have to have another try."

After the revelation of our daughter came the part of the day I'd been dreading. Dinner with my parents. For such a tough guy, Xav looked awfully nervous.

"Are you sure this is a good idea?"

"You'll have to meet them sooner or later."

"How about later?"

I pointed at my stomach, and even though I wore an empire line top, when I sat down the bump stuck out and gave the secret away. "I can't hide this forever. I've already been making up excuses not to see them for weeks."

"We could go on an extended vacation. Italy's nice this time of year."

"We're not going to Italy. I know the whole Douglas situation is awkward, but if they put up with him for all those years, they're going to love you."

Well, I was half right.

The moment Xav ordered our meals from Claude's in fluent French, my mother practically swooned at his feet, and if she had, his polished black Ferragamo shoes would have met with her approval. By the main course, her flirting was getting a little awkward, but she was a card-carrying member of his fan club.

"Are you sure you don't want to partner me in the charity golf tournament next week? Robert can't make it." She glared at my father. "Again."

"Afraid I haven't picked up a set of golf clubs in

years, but I'd be happy to make a donation."

"Oh, Georgia. What a charming young man."

Douglas who?

My father, however, was a different story. The moment he saw Xav, his eyes narrowed, and when they shook hands I thought he'd cut off Xav's circulation. Xav's nervous expression didn't escape my notice either, and that touched my heart because it meant he cared enough for meeting my parents to matter.

"This is Xavier."

My father ignored me as he glared at my boyfriend —I finally felt confident enough to label our relationship.

"What are you doing with my daughter?"

Xav managed a tentative smile. "Dating her."

"Uh, Daddy, it's a little more than that." I tried to make my smile warm enough to melt the frosty atmosphere. "We're having a baby together."

The way my father clutched at his chest had me reaching for my phone, ready to call an ambulance. But then he gritted his teeth and straightened up, and I relaxed infinitesimally, at least until he glared at Xav as if he could castrate him with his eyes.

"You got Georgia pregnant?"

"Don't say that like it's all Xav's fault. I was involved too."

My father closed his eyes briefly. "I don't even want to think about that."

Okay, probably that was too much information. I squeezed Xav's hand, putting on a united front. "I love him, Daddy."

I'd never heard my father let out such a long sigh, but after a painful minute, he gave his head a little shake and relaxed his shoulders enough for my pulse rate to drop. Then he poked Xav in the chest. "Avi, if you hurt Georgia, I will make your life a living hell. Do you understand me?"

Avi? Nobody shortened his name to that. "His name's Xav, Daddy. And he's the sweetest man I've ever met."

My father ignored me as he stared Xav down. "Do you understand me?"

"Yes. I'd die for your daughter."

Wasn't that the truth?

"In that case, we'll get along fine."

Xav wrapped an arm around me, and I laid my head on his shoulder, happier than I could ever remember feeling. From Douglas and Xavier, I learned that even the blackest clouds can have silver linings. After all, if I hadn't been marked for death, I'd never have found life.

WHAT'S NEXT?

**The Blackwood Security series continues in
Neon, the story of Mack's bachelorette party as
told by Bradley and Emmy.**

Six girls.
Five stars.
Four kinds of organic yogurt.
Three days.
Two guns.
One case of mistaken identity.
Welcome to Bradley's world...

For more details: www.elise-noble.com/Neon

The next full Blackwood Security novel is *Out of the Blue*...

Chess Lane is getting married. The church is booked, the guests are invited, and in three short weeks her husband will give her a night she'll never forget. Only her wedding happens a little sooner than she planned when she meets Jed Harker, a CIA agent with a big ego and a bigger... No, she doesn't even want to think about it.

Chess has hit rock bottom when a simple favour for a colleague leads her to Washington, DC and an offer she can't refuse. As chaos spreads faster than the plague one thing's for sure – her life will never be the same again. But will anybody else's?

For more details: www.elise-noble.com/blue

GRAY

I've also written a short story, from Mr. Gray's point of view, which is free with the seventh book in the Blackwood series, Ultraviolet.

If you enjoyed Gray is my Heart, please consider leaving a review.

For an author, every review is incredibly important. Not only do they make us feel warm and fuzzy inside, readers consider them when making their decision whether or not to buy a book. Even a line saying you enjoyed the book or what your favourite part was helps a lot.

Want to stalk me?

For updates on my new releases, giveaways, and other random stuff, you can sign up for my newsletter on my website:
www.elise-noble.com

Facebook:
www.facebook.com/EliseNobleAuthor

Twitter: @EliseANoble

Instagram: @elise_noble

I also have a group on Facebook for my fans to hang out. They love the characters from my Blackwood and Trouble books almost as much as I do, and they're the first to find out about my new stories as well as throwing in their own ideas that sometimes make it into print!

And if you'd like to read my books for FREE, you can also find details of how to join my review team.

Would you like to join Team Blackwood?

www.elise-noble.com/team-blackwood

END OF BOOK STUFF

After my foray to the romantic side in Gold Rush, I was missing the explosions, and so a couple of years ago Mr. Gray was born. For some reason unknown even to me, I decided to base the title of each Blackwood Security book on a colour, and so his name was a no-brainer. Xavier inhabits that murky space between black and white, as do so many of my characters. Although their views rarely reflect my own, I much prefer to write about people whose morals are a little shaky.

One trait I do share, though, is Georgia's love of dogs. I have two beautiful mutts in my life—Bella and Tia—and I've seen through volunteer work just what a difference a bit of care can make to an animal. And no, Blackwood's Tia wasn't named after the dog—Portia Cain came first, and the Staffie I rescued from life in a chicken coop had the same name by coincidence. Or maybe fate.

And now the thank yous. Firstly, to Michelle Jo Quinn who read through the (rather messy) alpha version of this book let me know it was worth making the effort to publish - you finally got your Mr. Gray :) If you haven't read Michelle's books, why not? They're awesome!

A huge thanks to my beta readers for Gray -

Chandni, Ramona, Harka, Jeff, Renata, Erazm, Helen, Terri, and Hafsa. Your help is so important in shaping my books in the early stages and I'm forever grateful to you.

And as always, thanks to my wonderful editor Amanda who helped me to polish the book, including pointing out that there was really no point in Emmy using a pseudonym for the first half. Not sure what I was thinking there!

And thanks to my proofreaders - Emma, John, and Dominique - for your assistance right at the end.

OTHER BOOKS BY ELISE NOBLE

The Blackwood Security Series
Black is my Heart (prequel)
Pitch Black
Into the Black
Forever Black
Gold Rush
Gray is my Heart
Neon (novella)
Out of the Blue
Ultraviolet
Red Alert
White Hot
The Scarlet Affair
Quicksilver (2019)
For the Love of Animals (Nate & Carmen)

The Blackwood Elements Series
Oxygen
Lithium
Carbon
Rhodium
Platinum (2018)
Nickel (2019)

The Blackwood UK Series

Joker in the Pack
Cherry on Top (novella)
Roses are Dead
Shallow Graves
Indigo Rain (2019)

The Electi Series

Cursed (2018)
Spooked (TBA)
Possessed (TBA)

The Trouble Series

Trouble in Paradise
Nothing but Trouble
24 Hours of Trouble

Standalone

Life
Twisted (short stories)
A Very Happy Christmas (novella)

Printed in Poland
by Amazon Fulfillment
Poland Sp. z o.o., Wrocław